Wait Until Midnight

Wait Until Midnight

Amanda Quick

LARGE PRINT

Oxford

Copyright © Jayne Ann Krentz, 2004

First published in Great Britain 2004
by
Piatkus Books Ltd.

Published in Large Print 2006 by ISIS Publishing Ltd.,
7 Centremead, Osney Mead, Oxford OX2 0ES
by arrangement with
Piatkus Books Ltd.

British Library Cataloguing in Publication Data
Quick, Amanda
        Wait until midnight. – Large print ed.
        1. Extortion – Fiction
        2. Psychics – Fiction
        3. Romantic suspense novels
        4. Large type books
        I. Title
        813.5'4 [F]

ISBN 0–7531–7455–3 (hb)
ISBN 0–7531–7456–1 (pb)

Printed and bound in Great Britain by
T. J. International Ltd., Padstow, Cornwall

To Frank, with all my Love

Prologue

Late in the reign of Queen Victoria . . .

Astonishing Exhibition of Psychical Powers

By
Gilbert Otford
Correspondent
The Flying Intelligencer

Mrs. Fordyce, the noted author, recently gave a thrilling demonstration of psychical powers before a small, private audience composed entirely of ladies.

Those who attended described a compelling scene. The room was darkened in a most dramatic fashion. Mrs. Fordyce was seated alone at a table that was illuminated by a single lamp. From that position she proceeded to answer questions and make observations of a most personal nature about many of those present.

Following the exhibition, it was generally agreed that only the possession of the most extraordinary psychical gifts could account for Mrs. Fordyce's uncanny ability to respond correctly to the inquiries put to her. The startling accuracy of her remarks about those in the room with whom she had not been previously acquainted left a marked impression.

Mrs. Fordyce was afterward besieged by requests for séances and sittings. It was also suggested that she apply to Mr. Reed, the president of the Society for Psychical Investigations, for permission to be tested at Wintersett House, the headquarters of the Society. She refused all such invitations, making it plain that there will be no more demonstrations or exhibitions of her abilities.

It is commonly held among those who study such phenomena that the use of psychical talents places considerable stress on the nerves, which, as nature has ordained, are far more fragile in women than they are in men.

Mr. Reed told this correspondent that a concern for the health of her nerves is only one reason why a female practitioner would be hesitant to conduct demonstrations. He explained that the innate delicacy of feeling and desire for modesty that is the hallmark of a true lady ensures that any woman possessed of both genuine psychical abilities and a fine sense of the proprieties will be extremely resistant to the notion of exhibiting her powers in any public setting.

CHAPTER
ONE

The face of the dead medium was a ghostly blur beneath the bloodstained wedding veil.

In life she had been quite pretty. The long, heavy skirts of a dark blue gown were crumpled around shapely legs clad in white stockings. The iron poker that had been used to crush the back of her skull had been dropped nearby.

Adam Hardesty moved across the small, shadowy room, willing himself to push through the invisible barrier created by the peculiar scent and chill of death. He crouched beside the body and held the candle aloft.

Through the gossamer veil he saw the glitter of the blue beads that trimmed the necklace around Elizabeth Delmont's throat. A matching pair of earrings dangled from her ears. On the floor next to her pale, lifeless fingers was a broken pocket watch. The glass had been shattered, the hands forever locked at midnight.

Removing his own watch from the pocket of his trousers, he checked the time. Two-ten. If the timepiece on the carpet had, in fact, been smashed in the course of the violent struggle that appeared to have taken place in the chamber, Delmont had been murdered a little more than two hours earlier.

A mourning brooch decorated with black enamel rested on the tightly laced, stiffly shaped bodice of the blue gown. The brooch looked as if it had been deliberately positioned on Delmont's bosom in a grim parody of funereal respect.

He picked up the brooch and turned it over to look at the reverse side. The flickering candle illuminated a small photograph: a portrait of a fair-haired woman dressed in a wedding veil and a white gown. The lady appeared to be no more than eighteen or nineteen. Something about the sad, resigned expression on her beautiful, unsmiling face gave the impression that she was not looking forward to married life. Under the picture a lock of tightly coiled blond hair was secured beneath a beveled crystal.

He studied the woman in the photograph for a long moment, memorizing every detail visible in the tiny picture. When he was finished, he carefully repositioned the brooch on Delmont's bodice. The police might find it a useful clue.

Rising, he turned slowly on his heel to survey the room in which Elizabeth Delmont had been killed. The space looked as if a violent storm had blown through it, leaving a trail of wreckage to mark its path. The large table in the center was overturned, revealing an odd mechanism underneath. Delmont had no doubt employed the concealed apparatus to cause the heavy wooden object to float and tilt in midair. Gullible sitters took such activities as a sign that spirits were present.

Two drawers had been built into the side of the table, just beneath the top. Both stood open. He walked closer and experimentally closed each drawer. As he suspected, when shut, they were undetectable to the eye.

He ran his fingertips around the entire edge of the square table, searching for other cleverly concealed drawers. He found none.

Several chairs were scattered carelessly about. A variety of odd objects littered the carpet, including a flute, a voice trumpet, some bells and a set of musical chimes.

A telescoping rod, a slate and some padlocks were tumbled in a heap near an open closet. He scooped up one of the locks and examined it in the light of the candle. It took only a few seconds to find the hidden spring that could be used by the wearer to unlock the device.

Next to one chair lay a deathly white arm that appeared to have been neatly amputated at the elbow. The gracefully shaped hand was still attached. He nudged it with the toe of his shoe.

Wax, he concluded; carefully detailed, right down to the white fingernails and the lines on the palm.

He was a skeptic who had no patience with the current rage for psychical research. Nevertheless, he was well aware that when news of the medium's death got into the papers, there would be no shortage of people who would be more than ready to believe that Delmont had been dispatched by dangerous spirits that she had summoned from the Other Side.

When it came to scandals, he had a single, inviolable rule: Do not become involved in one. The last thing he wanted was for Delmont's death to become a sensation in the papers, but there was little likelihood that could be avoided now. The only thing he could do was endeavor to keep his own name out of the press's reports.

He searched the remainder of the séance room thoroughly on the assumption that it was the place in the house where the medium would most likely have concealed her secrets. He discovered three more hidden compartments, one in a wall and two in the floor, but there was no sign of the diary.

When he finished, he climbed the stairs to Elizabeth Delmont's bedchamber and methodically went through every drawer and the wardrobe.

It was a futile effort. The only item of interest was a small catalog bearing the title *The Secrets of the Mediums.* The array of items offered for sale included a number of artificial body parts designed to simulate ghostly manifestations, trick mirrors and an odd contraption composed of wires and pulleys capable of producing the appearance of levitation. The firm guaranteed potential clients that all transactions would be conducted in strict confidence and with complete discretion.

Downstairs, he walked along the darkened hall, intending to let himself out of the house through the kitchen door. He had done his best. It was impossible to search every square inch of the house in hopes of finding another secret compartment or cupboard.

When he passed the gloom-filled parlor, he glimpsed a desk amid the assortment of heavy furniture.

He went into the room, crossed the red and black patterned carpet and quickly opened the various drawers. None contained the diary but casually tucked into a cubbyhole was a sheet of paper with a list of names and addresses. Yesterday's date and the words *nine o'clock* had been noted at the top of the page.

He studied the list for a few seconds before it came to him that he was most likely looking at the names of the sitters who had attended Elizabeth Delmont's last séance.

One of the names was heavily underlined. There was something vaguely familiar about it but he could not quite place it. That in and of itself was disturbing. He possessed an excellent memory. Such a talent had been necessary in the old days when he had sold gossip and other peoples' secrets to earn a living.

He moved in far more elevated circles now, but some things had not changed. He never forgot a name or a face or a rumor. Information gave him power in the glittering, treacherous jungles of Society, just as it had helped him survive on the streets of London in his youth.

He concentrated on the underlined name, trying to summon up an image or an impression or even a trivial bit of gossip. A fleeting memory surfaced. He was almost certain that Julia or Wilson had mentioned the name in passing. Something to do with a piece in the newspaper. Not *The Times*; he was certain of that. He read it faithfully every day.

The reference must have come from one of the less respectable papers, he decided. The sort that relied on lurid accounts of sensations — violent crimes and illicit sexual scandals — to sell copies.

He had paid no attention at the time because the person mentioned did not inhabit the relatively small world of wealth and privilege that was his hunting ground.

A trickle of ghostly electricity stirred the hair on the back of his neck.

Mrs. Fordyce. 22 Corley Lane.

This time he would not forget the name.

CHAPTER
TWO

The mysterious gentleman wore an invisible cloak fashioned of intrigue and shadow. There was something quite thrilling, even a bit unnerving, about the sight of him looming there in the doorway of her small study, Caroline Fordyce thought. Anticipation, curiosity and a strange awareness sparkled through her.

It was barely nine o'clock in the morning and she had never met Adam Grove before in her life. A lady endowed with a proper respect for the proprieties would never have permitted him to be admitted into the house; certainly not at such an early hour, she thought. But a too-careful observance of the proprieties made for a very unexciting existence. She ought to know; she had been excruciatingly cautious about the proprieties for the past three years, and things had been wretchedly dull indeed here at Number 22 Corley Lane.

"Please sit down, Mr. Grove." Caroline rose from her desk and went to stand in front of the garden window, putting the warm light of the sunny morning behind her so that it illuminated her visitor more clearly. "My housekeeper informs me that you have called to discuss a matter that you seem to believe is of grave importance to both of us."

Indeed, it was the phrase *grave importance* that had quickened her interest and induced her to instruct Mrs. Plummer to show Grove into her study. Such deliciously ominous-sounding words, she thought happily. The phrase *grave importance* practically vibrated with the promise of a Startling Incident.

People never called here at 22 Corley Lane with news of *grave importance*, not unless one counted the fishmonger's young daughter, who had quietly advised Mrs. Plummer to take a good whiff of the salmon before purchasing it last week, as it had gone off. The girl had explained that her father had treated the fish with some substance designed to conceal the odor of decay. She had confided that she had not wanted to be responsible for poisoning the entire household. "As if I'd have been taken in by that sort of sharp practice," Mrs. Plummer had announced, disdain dripping from every word.

Such was the nature of gravely important news in this household.

In all probability, this morning's surprise visitor would soon discover that he had got the wrong address and would take his news of grave importance elsewhere, Caroline thought. But in the meantime, she intended to take full advantage of the diverting interruption to her routine.

"Thank you for seeing me on such short notice, Mrs. Fordyce," Adam Grove said from the doorway.

Oh, my goodness, she thought. His voice was wonderfully compelling, low and deep and charged with cool masculine assurance. Another whisper of awareness shot through her. But this time it induced a shiver of caution. She sensed that Grove was a man endowed with a formidable will; the sort who was accustomed to achieving his objectives, perhaps at any cost.

Inspiration struck with the force of summer lightning. Adam Grove was exactly what she had been searching for all morning. He was perfect.

She glanced at the paper and pen on her desk, wondering if she dared take notes. She did not want to alarm Grove or send him packing too quickly. He would discover his mistake soon enough and take himself off to the correct address. Meanwhile, this was a golden opportunity and she did not intend to waste it. Perhaps he would not notice if she merely jotted down a few observations now and again during their conversation.

"Naturally, I felt obliged to hear your news of grave importance, sir," she said, slipping as casually as possible back to the chair behind her desk.

"I would not have called at this hour had not the subject of my visit been of the utmost urgency," he assured her.

She sat down, reached for her pen and gave him an encouraging smile. "Won't you please be seated, sir?"

"Thank you."

She watched him cross the small room to take the chair she had indicated. When he moved into the light, she got a close look at his expensively cut coat and trousers. Her fingers clenched around the pen.

Be careful, she thought. This man was from the Other World; not the unseen realm that was the source of such interest among psychical researchers, but the far more dangerous sphere of Society. It was a place where the wealthy and the powerful made all the rules and rode roughshod over those they viewed as their social inferiors. Three years ago she had had a disastrous experience with a man who moved in privileged circles. It had taught her a lesson she did not plan to forget, regardless of how mysterious and intriguing Mr. Adam Grove proved to be.

She studied him, trying not to be obvious about it. Grove was lean and well-made in a manly fashion. His movements were economical and restrained, yet endowed with a supple grace. One got the impression that he could react swiftly to a threat of danger but that both his strength and will were under complete control. He charged the atmosphere of the room with energy and a masculine vitality that was impossible to ignore.

No doubt about it; he was a perfect model for the character of Edmund Drake.

She quickly wrote *Charges atmosphere with masc. vitality* in what she hoped was an offhand manner, as though she were merely making a shopping list.

She decided that she should also make some notes regarding his style of dress. It was at once elegant and distinguished and yet quite apart from the current masculine fashion, which favored such eye-dazzling combinations as polka-dot shirts and plaid trousers.

12

Grove was attired from head to foot in tones of deepest, darkest gray. His shirt was the singular exception. It was a pristine white. The collar was turned back in the new "gates ajar" mode that appeared to be infinitely more comfortable than the usual high-standing styles. His tie was knotted in a precise four-in-hand.

No wonder she had been having so much trouble trying to decide how to dress Edmund Drake. She had been attempting to put him into the sort of boldly striped pants and brightly patterned shirts that she had observed on any number of fashionable gentlemen lately. Such glaringly bright attire was entirely wrong for Edmund. He needed to project menace and an aura of resolute determination. Polka dots, stripes and plaids did not suit him at all.

She wrote *Dark gray jacket and trousers* without glancing down at the paper.

Grove sat in the wingback chair in front of the hearth. "I see I have interrupted your morning correspondence. Again, my apologies."

"Think nothing of it, sir." She gave him her most reassuring smile. "I am merely making a few notes to remind myself of some small details that must be attended to later."

"I see."

Grove's hair was just right for Edmund Drake, too, she thought. It was of a hue that was very nearly black with the merest smattering of silver at the temples. It was cut short and brushed close to his head. He had not succumbed to the current rage for mustaches and short beards, but she could see the hint of a dark shadow on the hard planes and angles of his face. She realized that he had not shaved that morning. How odd.

Edmund Drake's clothing and hairstyle were not the only things that would have to be changed in order to make the character more ominous. She saw at once that she had erred when she had decided to portray him as handsome. It was quite clear to her now that his features should have the same chillingly ascetic lines that marked Adam Grove's face. Indeed, Drake must become a man who had been shaped by the hot, refining fires of a harsh and murky past.

She jotted down the words *Fierce features.*

From where he sat Adam Grove could not possibly see across the ornately carved back of the rococo-style desktop to discern what she had written but she sensed that he was observing her. She paused and looked up with a bright smile.

And immediately froze when she saw that impatience and cold intelligence had made dark green mirrors of his eyes.

Very carefully and again without looking down she scrawled the words *Eyes like emeralds. Glow in dark?*

"More notes to yourself, Mrs. Fordyce?" The slight twist of his mouth lacked all traces of politesse.

"Yes. My apologies." Hastily she put down the pen.

Now that he was sitting in stronger light she could see the lines of a grim weariness that bracketed his mouth and etched the corners of his eyes. The day was still quite young. What could account for that subtle air of exhaustion?

"Would you care for a cup of tea?" she asked gently.

He looked somewhat surprised by the offer. "No, thank you. I do not intend to stay long."

"I see. Perhaps you should tell me precisely why you are here, sir."

"Very well." He paused, ensuring that he had her full attention. "I believe you were acquainted with a woman named Elizabeth Delmont?"

For an instant her mind went blank. Then the name registered.

"The medium in Hamsey Street?" she asked.

"Yes."

She sat back in her chair. Of all the subjects he might have raised, this was the last one she would have expected. Although it seemed that the entire country was caught up in a tremendous fascination with séances, mediums and the study of psychical powers, she simply could not imagine a gentleman of Adam Grove's temperament taking a serious interest in such matters.

"I have met her, yes," she said slowly. "As it happens, I attended a séance at Mrs. Delmont's house last night together with my aunts." She hesitated. "Why do you ask?"

"Elizabeth Delmont is dead."

Stunned, she merely stared at him for a few seconds. "I beg your pardon?"

"Murdered sometime after the séance ended last night," he added, much too calmly.

"*Murdered.*" She swallowed hard. "Are you quite certain?"

"I found the body myself shortly after two this morning."

"*You* found the body?" It took her an instant to recover from that unnerving announcement. "I don't understand."

"Someone used a poker to crush her skull."

Ice formed in her stomach. It occurred to her that the decision to entertain a mysterious gentleman who claimed to have discovered a murdered woman might not prove to be one of her sounder notions. She glanced at the bellpull that hung beside the desk. Perhaps she should summon Mrs. Plummer.

But even as she started to reach surreptitiously for the rope to alert the housekeeper, she found herself succumbing to her greatest vice, curiosity.

"May I ask why you went to Mrs. Delmont's house at such a late hour?" she said.

As soon as the words were out of her mouth, she realized that she had blundered badly. Heat rose in her cheeks. There was only one reason why a wealthy, obviously virile man such as Adam Grove might have called upon Elizabeth Delmont at two in the morning.

Mrs. Delmont had been a very beautiful woman possessed of an alluring figure and a sensual manner that had certainly captivated Mr. McDaniel, the elderly widower who had been one of the sitters at last night's séance. The medium had no doubt had a similar effect on a number of gentlemen.

16

"No, Mrs. Fordyce, Elizabeth Delmont was not my mistress," Adam said, as though he had read her mind. "In point of fact, I had never encountered her until last night. When I did find her it was much too late for an introduction."

"I see." She fought back the hot blush and tried to project a worldly air. She was supposed to be a widow, after all; a lady possessed of some experience of the world. "Forgive me, Mr. Grove. This entire conversation has taken an extremely odd turn. I had no idea that Mrs. Delmont had died."

"*Murdered* was the word I used." Adam studied her thoughtfully. "You said this conversation was not proceeding along the lines that you had anticipated. Tell, me, why did you believe that I had come here today?"

"To be quite truthful, I assumed that you had mistaken the address," she admitted.

"If that was the case, why did you not instruct your housekeeper to verify that I had the correct number?" he asked with a depressing sort of logic.

"I confess, I was curious to know the nature of your news." She spread her hands wide. "We rarely receive callers who come upon business of grave importance here, you see. In fact, I cannot recall any such visitors in the whole of the three years we have lived here."

"We?"

"My two aunts live with me. They are out at the moment, taking their morning exercise. Aunt Emma and Aunt Milly are great believers in the importance of brisk daily walks."

He frowned. "I did not see their names on the list of sitters. You say they accompanied you to the séance last night?"

She did not like the way this was going. It was beginning to feel as though he was interrogating her.

"Yes," she said, treading carefully now. "They did not want me to go out alone at night. Mrs. Delmont had no objection to their presence."

"Why did you attend the séance? Did you really believe that Elizabeth Delmont could communicate with spirits?" He did not bother to conceal his scathing opinion of such a notion.

His sarcasm annoyed her. She felt obliged to defend her actions.

"I would remind you, sir," she said very crisply, "that a great many eminent, educated, well-respected individuals take spiritualism and other psychical matters seriously."

"Fools, the lot of them."

"A number of societies and clubs have been formed to conduct research into psychical events and to investigate the claims of mediums. Several learned journals in the field are published regularly." She reached across her desk and snatched up the copy of *New Dawn* that had arrived yesterday. "This one, for instance. It is published by the Society for Psychical Investigations, and I assure you the articles are well documented."

"Documented nonsense." He moved one hand in a dismissive manner. "It is obvious to any logical person

18

that those who claim to possess psychical powers are all charlatans and frauds."

"I daresay you are entitled to your opinion," she retorted. "But forgive me for pointing out that it does not imply an open, inquiring mind."

He smiled humorlessly. "How open is your mind, Mrs. Fordyce? Do you really take the business of manifestations and spirit voices and table rappings seriously?"

She sat a little straighter in her chair. "As it happens, I have recently conducted some research of my own."

"And have you discovered any mediums you consider to be genuine? Mrs. Delmont, for instance?"

"No," she admitted, reluctant to concede him the ground. "As a matter of fact, I do not believe that it is possible to communicate with spirits."

"I am relieved to hear that. It renews my initial impression of your intelligence."

She glared at him. "May I remind you, sir, that the field of psychical research is expanding rapidly. Lately it has begun to encompass a wide variety of phenomena, not just the summoning of spirits. While I do not believe that mediums can communicate with ghosts and phantoms, I am not at all prepared to dismiss other types of psychical powers out of hand."

His green eyes tightened ever so slightly at the corners, sharpening his gaze in a dangerous manner. "If you do not believe that mediums can contact the spirit world, why did you attend the séance at Elizabeth Delmont's house last night?"

No doubt about it, he was most definitely conducting an interrogation. She glanced again at the bellpull.

"There is no need to call your housekeeper to rescue you," he said dryly. "I mean you no harm. But I do mean to get some answers."

She frowned. "You sound like a policeman, Mr. Grove."

"Calm yourself, Mrs. Fordyce. I promise you that I have no connection to the police."

"Then why in heaven's name are you here, sir? What do you want?"

"Information," he said simply. "Why did you attend the séance?"

He was quite relentless, she thought.

"I told you, I have been conducting research into psychical phenomena," she said. "Your opinions to the contrary, it is considered a legitimate field of inquiry."

He shook his head in disgust. "Parlor tricks and games. Nothing more."

It was past time to ask a few questions of her own, she decided. She clasped her hands together on top of her desk and assumed what she hoped was a firm, authoritative manner.

"I am very sorry to learn that Mrs. Delmont was murdered," she said evenly. "But I'm afraid that I fail to comprehend why you are interested in the circumstances of her death. Indeed, if you and Mrs. Delmont were not, ah, intimately acquainted, why did you go to her house at two o'clock in the morning?"

20

"Suffice it to say that I had my reasons for calling on Elizabeth Delmont at that hour and that those reasons were extremely urgent. Now that she is dead, I am left with no choice but to discover the identity of her killer."

She was stunned. "You intend to hunt him down yourself?"

"Yes."

"Surely that is a job for the police, sir."

He shrugged. "They will make their inquiries, naturally, but I very much doubt that they will find the villain."

She unlocked her hands and seized her pen again. "This is very interesting, Mr. Grove. Indeed, it is riveting." She wrote *Determined and relentless* on the sheet of paper. "Let me see if I have got the facts in the correct order. You are conducting an inquiry into Mrs. Delmont's death, and you came here to ask me if I had any information concerning her murder."

He watched her swiftly moving pen. "That certainly sums up the situation."

Talk about a Startling Incident, she thought. Incidents did not come much more startling than this one.

"I shall be delighted to tell you everything I can remember, sir, if you will first explain your interest in the affair."

He studied her as though she were an unusual biological specimen that had turned up unexpectedly and was proving difficult to identify. The tall clock ticked in the silence.

After a long moment, he appeared to come to a conclusion.

"Very well," he said, "I will answer some of your questions. But in return I must insist that you keep what I am about to tell you in strictest confidence."

"Yes, of course." She jotted the word *Secretive* down on the paper.

He was out of the chair before she realized he had even moved.

"What on earth?" Startled by the suddenness of his actions, she gasped and dropped her pen.

He crossed the space between them in two strides, reached out and plucked the sheet of paper off the desk.

So much for his apparent weariness, she thought. And to think she had been feeling rather sorry for him.

"Sir." She tried to snatch the paper out of his hand. "Kindly give me that at once. What do you think you are doing?"

"I am curious about your list of errands, madam." He scanned the page quickly, his expression turning colder by the second. "*Dark gray jacket and trousers? Fierce features?* What the devil is going on here?"

"I do not see that my notes are of any importance to you, sir."

"I just told you that I insist that this matter be held in confidence. There is a potential for scandal here. I have a strict rule about that sort of thing."

She frowned. "You have a rule regarding scandals? What is it?"

"I prefer to avoid them."

22

"Doesn't everyone?" Unable to get hold of the paper, she took refuge in an air of haughty aplomb. "Trust me, sir, I, too, have no wish to become embroiled in a scandal. I certainly have no intention of discussing your investigation outside this house."

"Then why did you find it necessary to write down these comments?"

Righteous indignation welled up inside her. "I was merely organizing my thoughts."

He surveyed what she had written. "Am I correct in assuming that some of these scribblings relate to my attire and the color of my eyes, Mrs. Fordyce?"

"Well —"

"I demand to know why you put your observations on paper. Damnation, woman, if you think to make me a subject of your private journal —"

"I assure you, I have no intention of putting you into my personal journal." She was able to make the statement with perfect sincerity because it was nothing less than the exact truth.

"Then I must conclude that you are indeed deeply involved in this affair of the murdered medium," he drawled in tones of silky menace.

She was horrified. "That is not true."

"There is no other logical reason for you to be taking such personal notes. If you are not making a record of our conversation for your journal, then I can only conclude that you are doing so in order to prepare a report for your accomplice."

"*Accomplice.*" She shot to her feet, disoriented and badly frightened now. "That is outrageous, sir. How dare you insinuate that I might be involved in a matter of murder?"

He snapped the paper in front of her face. "How else can you explain the need to record this interview?"

She fought to pull herself together and to think clearly. "I owe you no explanations, Mr. Grove. Quite the reverse. I would remind you that you are the one who barged into this house today."

That accusation clearly irritated him. "You make it sound as though I forced my way inside. That was not the case. You instructed your housekeeper to admit me."

"Only because you told her that you had come upon business that was of grave importance to both of us." She drew herself up. "But the truth is that Mrs. Delmont's untimely death appears to be gravely important only to you, Mr. Grove."

"You are wrong on that account, Mrs. Fordyce."

"Nonsense," she declared in ringing accents, confident of her position. "I have no interest whatsoever in the circumstances surrounding the murder of Elizabeth Delmont."

Adam raised his brows. He said nothing.

Two or three seconds of tense silence gripped the room.

"Other than a perfectly natural curiosity and the quite normal concern that are only to be expected from a person who has just learned of a ghastly crime, of course," she amended smoothly.

"On the contrary, Mrs. Fordyce, I am convinced that your interest in this affair goes a good deal deeper than mere curiosity and casual concern."

"How is that possible?" she demanded. "I met the woman only last night. I had no intention of ever seeing her again. I would also remind you that I and my aunts were not the only people who attended Delmont's last séance. There were two other sitters present. I believe their names were Mrs. Howell and Mr. McDaniel."

He went to stand by the window, looking out into the garden. In spite of the veil of fatigue that drifted about him, his strong, sleek shoulders were set in stern, unrelenting lines.

"Both of whom are quite elderly and frail," he said flatly. "I do not believe that either of them possesses the strength or determination necessary to crush the skull of a younger, stronger person with a poker, let alone overturn a heavy table and a number of chairs."

She hesitated. "You spoke with them?"

"There was no need to interview them personally. I made some discreet observations and inquiries in the streets where they live. I am convinced that neither of them is involved in this business."

"Well, I suppose it is rather unlikely," she admitted.

"Tell me what occurred in the course of the séance," he said quietly.

"There is not much to tell." She widened her hands. "Just the usual sort of rappings and tappings. One or two manifestations. Some financial advice from the spirit world."

"Financial advice?" he asked with unexpected sharpness.

"Yes. Mr. McDaniel was told that he would soon be offered an excellent investment opportunity. It was

25

nothing out of the ordinary. Sitters are often informed by the spirits that they may be in line for an unexpected inheritance or that they will receive money from some unanticipated source."

"I see." He turned around slowly and looked at her with an expression that would not have been out of place on the face of the devil himself. "So the subject of money arose, did it?"

She clenched the chair back so tightly that the blood was squeezed out of her knuckles. She could scarcely breathe. Was he going to go to the police to lodge a charge of murder against her and her aunts?

She knew now that the three of them were in grave danger. They were all innocent, but she did not doubt for a moment that if a gentleman of Adam Grove's obvious power and position accused them of murder, they would be in desperate straits.

They had no choice but to flee London immediately, she decided, thinking quickly. Their only hope was to disappear again, just as they had three years ago. She tried to recall how much money was on hand in the house. As soon as Adam Grove departed, she would send Mrs. Plummer out to obtain a train schedule. How quickly could they pack?

Adam's black brows came together in a heavy line. "Are you all right, Mrs. Fordyce? You look as if you are going to faint."

Rage spiked through her, briefly suppressing her panic.

"You have threatened my life, sir, and the lives of my aunts. How did you expect me to react?"

26

He frowned. "What are you talking about? I have made no threats, madam."

"You have as much as accused one or all of us of murder. If you take your suspicions to the police, we will be arrested and thrown into prison. We will *hang*."

"Mrs. Fordyce, you are allowing your imagination to run away with your powers of reason and logic. I may harbor some suspicions but there remains the little matter of evidence."

"Bah. None of the three of us can prove that she did not return after the séance to murder the medium. It would be our word against yours, sir, and we are both well aware that three ladies in our modest circumstances who lack social connections would not stand a chance if a man of your rank and wealth chose to point the finger of blame at us."

"Get a hold of yourself, woman. I am in no mood to deal with a case of hysteria."

Her fury gave her strength. "How dare you tell me not to succumb to hysteria? My aunts and I are facing the gallows because of you, sir."

"Not quite," he growled.

"Yes, quite."

"Hell and damnation. I have had enough of these theatrics." He took a step toward her.

"Stop." She gripped the back of the chair with both hands and swung it around so that it formed a barrier between them. "Do not come any closer. I will scream bloody murder if you take one more step. Mrs. Plummer and the neighbors will hear me, I promise you."

He halted, exhaling heavily. "Kindly calm yourself, Mrs. Fordyce. This is all very wearying, not to mention a waste of everyone's time."

"It is impossible for me to be calm in the face of such dire threats."

He gave her a considering look. "Did you, by any chance, ever pursue a career on the stage, Mrs. Fordyce? You seem to have a distinct flair for melodrama."

"Oddly enough, I find a dramatic reaction entirely appropriate in this situation," she said through her teeth.

He studied her for a long moment. She got the impression that he was recalculating some secret scheme.

"Breathe deeply, madam, and compose yourself," he said finally. "I have no intention of having you or your aunts taken up on a charge of murder."

"Why should I believe you?"

He rubbed his temples. "You must trust me when I tell you that justice is not my chief concern here. I am content to leave that problem for the police, although I doubt that they will be successful. They are reasonably efficient when it comes to catching ordinary murderers, but this was not an ordinary killing."

She sensed that he was telling the truth. Nevertheless, she did not release her grip on the chair. "If you did not come here seeking justice for Elizabeth Delmont, what do you want, Mr. Grove?"

He watched her with cool speculation. "My only goal in this affair is to recover the diary."

She did not try to hide her confusion. "What diary?"

"The one that was stolen from Elizabeth Delmont's house last night."

She puzzled that out as best she could. "You seek Mrs. Delmont's diary? Well, I assure you, I know nothing of it and neither do my aunts. Furthermore, I can tell you with absolute certainty that I did not notice any diary in the room at the séance last night."

He contemplated her for another moment and then shook his head, as though he had reluctantly accepted defeat.

"Do you know, I believe you may be telling me the truth, Mrs. Fordyce. Indeed, it appears that I was wrong about you."

She allowed herself to relax ever so slightly. "Wrong, sir?"

"I came here this morning in hopes of surprising you into admitting that you had taken the damned diary. At the very least I thought you might be able to give me some notion of what had happened to it."

"Why is this particular diary so important to you?"

His smile was as sharp and deadly as a knife. "Suffice it to say that Mrs. Delmont presumed to think that she could use it to blackmail me."

Mrs. Delmont had evidently allowed greed to overwhelm caution and good sense, Caroline thought. No sane, sensible person would take the risk of trying to extort money from this man.

"What made you think that I might know something concerning its whereabouts?" she demanded.

He widened his stance and clasped his hands behind his back. "You and the other sitters at the séance were the last people to see Elizabeth Delmont alive, aside from the killer, of course. I learned from one of Delmont's neighbors that the housekeeper was given the night off."

"Yes, that's true. Mrs. Delmont herself opened the door to us. She said she always gave her housekeeper the night off on séance evenings because she could not go into a proper trance if there was anyone other than the sitters present. Indeed, the comment made me wonder if perhaps —"

"Yes?" he prompted. "What did it cause you to wonder about, Mrs. Fordyce?"

"Well, if you must know, it occurred to me that perhaps Mrs. Delmont did not like to have her housekeeper present while she conducted a séance because she was afraid that the woman would become wise to her tricks and perhaps expose her in exchange for a bribe. Psychical investigators have been known to pay the servants who work for mediums to spy on their employers, you see."

"A clever notion, Mrs. Fordyce." Adam looked approving of her logic. "I suspect that you are right. Mediums are notoriously secretive."

"How did you learn my name and address?"

"When I discovered the body, I also found a list of the sitters who had attended the final séance. The addresses had been put down alongside the names."

"I see."

Her imagination conjured up a disturbing image of Adam Grove methodically searching Mrs. Delmont's parlor while the body of the murdered woman lay crumpled on the floor. It was a chilling vision, one that said a great deal about Grove's nerve. She swallowed hard.

"I spent the remainder of the night and the early hours of this morning talking to servants, carriage drivers and . . ." He hesitated, as though choosing his words carefully. ". . . others who make their living on the streets near Delmont's house. Among other things I was able to verify Mrs. Delmont's housekeeper was busy attending her daughter, who was in the process of giving birth last night. Her alibi is unshakable. That left me with your name, Mrs. Fordyce."

"No wonder you look so weary," she said quietly. "You have been up all night."

He absently rubbed his stubbled jaw and grimaced. "My apologies for my appearance."

"It is hardly a matter of importance, given the circumstances." She hesitated. "So you came here today with the intention of confronting me in this alarming manner. Your goal was to frighten me and thereby trick me into revealing some dreadful conspiracy, wasn't it?"

He shoved a hand through his short, dark hair, showing no sign of remorse. "That was more or less my plan, yes."

Uneasily aware that he might not have abandoned the notion entirely, she searched her brain for other possible suspects.

"Perhaps Mrs. Delmont was the victim of a burglar who attacked her after he broke into the house," she suggested.

"I searched the place from top to bottom. There was no evidence that the doors or windows had been forced. It appeared that she had let the killer in."

The offhand manner in which he delivered that information deepened her sense of unease. "You certainly made a number of close observations last night, Mr. Grove. One would have thought that the proximity of a savagely murdered woman would have made it difficult to think and act so methodically and logically."

"Unfortunately, it appears that I did not make any especially useful observations," he said. He went toward the door with a purposeful stride. "I have wasted your time and my own. I would take it as a great favor if you would refrain from discussing this conversation with anyone else."

She did not respond to that.

He stopped, one hand on the doorknob, and looked at her. "Well, Mrs. Fordyce? Can I depend upon you to keep our discussion confidential?"

She braced herself. "That depends, sir."

He was cynically amused. "Of course. You no doubt wish to be compensated for your silence. Name your price, Mrs. Fordyce."

Another flash of anger crackled through her. "You cannot buy my silence, Mr. Grove. I do not want your money. What concerns me is the safety and security of my aunts and myself. If any one of us is placed in danger of arrest because of your actions, I shall not hesitate to give the police your name and tell them every detail of this discussion."

"I doubt very much that the police will give you any trouble. As you suggested, they will likely conclude that Mrs. Delmont was murdered by a burglar and that will be the end of it."

"How can you be sure of that?"

"Because that is the simplest answer, and the officers of the law are known to prefer that sort of explanation."

"What if they find the list of sitters and proceed to make them all suspects, as you did, sir?"

He reached into his pocket and pulled out a folded sheet of paper. "They won't find the list."

She stared at the paper. "You took it?"

"I am quite certain that none of the names on this list would be of any practical use to the police."

"I see." She did not know what to say.

"Speaking of names," he said rather casually. "I should tell you that it would not do you any good to give mine to the police."

"Why?" she asked coldly. "Because a gentleman of your obvious wealth and position does not need to worry overmuch about answering questions from the police?"

"No one is above the law. But that is not the reason why I advised you not to give them my name." His mouth curved in a cryptic smile. "The problem is that Mr. Grove does not exist. I invented him for this interview. When I walk out your front door today, he will vanish just like one of those ghostly manifestations that are so popular at séances."

She sat down quite suddenly, head whirling. "Good heavens. You gave me a false name?"

"Yes. Will you be so good as to indulge me with an answer to one last question?"

She blinked, still struggling to collect herself and her scattered thoughts. "What is it?"

He held up the paper that he had taken from her desk. "Why the devil were you making all these notes?"

"Oh, those." Glumly she surveyed the page he held. "I am an author, sir. My novels are serialized in the *Flying Intelligencer*." She paused. "Perhaps you read that paper?"

"No, I do not. As I recall, it is one of those extremely irritating newspapers that thrives on sensation."

"Well —"

"The sort of paper that resorts to printing news of illicit scandals and lurid crimes in order to attract readers."

She sighed. "I expect you prefer *The Times*."

"Yes."

"No surprise there, I suppose," she muttered. "Tell me, don't you find it rather dull reading?"

"I find it accurate and reliable reading, Mrs. Fordyce. Just the sort of newspaper reading that I prefer."

"Of course it is. As I was saying, the *Flying Intelligencer* prints my novels. I am required by the terms of my contract to supply my publisher, Mr. Spraggett, with a new chapter every week. I have been having some trouble with one of the characters, Edmund Drake. He is very important to the story but I have been having difficulty getting him down properly on paper. There has been something rather vague about him, I'm afraid. He requires sharpening up."

He looked reluctantly fascinated and, perhaps, bemused. "You took notes about my appearance and attire so that you could apply them to the hero of your story?"

"Heavens, no," she assured him with an airy wave of her hand. "Whatever gave you that idea? Edmund Drake is not the hero of my tale. He is the villain of the piece."

CHAPTER
THREE

For some wholly irrational reason, it annoyed him that she had cast him in the role of the villain.

Adam Hardesty brooded on the disastrous encounter that he had just concluded with the very unexpected, very intriguing Mrs. Caroline Fordyce while he made his way home to the mansion in Laxton Square. He was well aware that the lady's opinion of him should have been at the bottom of his long list of problems, especially given the rapidly rising tide of disasters that he was attempting to hold at bay.

Nevertheless, knowing that Caroline Fordyce considered him an excellent model for a villain rankled. His intuition told him that it was not his *fierce features* alone that had given her such a low opinion of him. He had the distinct impression that Mrs. Fordyce did not hold men from his world in high esteem.

She, on the other hand, had commanded his immediate and cautious respect. One look into her intelligent, curious, exceedingly lovely hazel eyes had told him that he was dealing with a potentially formidable adversary. He had warned himself to take great care in his dealings with the lady.

Unfortunately, respect was not the only reaction Caroline Fordyce had elicited in him. She had aroused all of his senses at first sight. Exhausted as he had been after the long night of fruitless inquiries, he had nevertheless responded to her in a very physical, extremely disturbing way.

Damn. He did not need this sort of complication. What the devil was the matter with him? Even as a youth he had rarely allowed himself to be controlled by his passions. He had learned long ago that self-discipline was the key to survival and success both on the streets and in the equally perilous world of Society. He had established a set of rules for himself and he lived by them. They governed his intimate liaisons just as they did everything else in his life.

His rules had served him well. He had no intention of abandoning them now.

Nevertheless, he could not stop thinking about that first glimpse of Caroline Fordyce and wondering at the compelling sensations that had gripped him. The image of her sitting at her dainty little desk, illuminated by the bright glow of the morning sunlight, seemed to have become fixed in his brain.

She had worn a simple, unadorned housedress of a warm, coppery color. The gown had been designed for ladies to wear in the home and therefore lacked the ruffled petticoats and elaborately tied-back skirts of more formal feminine attire. The lines of the prim, snug-fitting bodice had emphasized the feminine curves of her high breasts and slender waist.

Caroline's glossy golden-brown hair had been drawn up and back into a neat coil that accented the graceful line of the nape of her neck and the quiet pride with which she carried herself. He calculated her age to be somewhere in the mid-twenties.

Her voice had touched him with the impact of an inviting caress. From another woman it would have seemed deliberately provocative, but he sensed that the effect was not premeditated in this case. He was quite certain that Caroline's manner of speaking was an innate part of who she was. It hinted at deep passions.

What had become of the late Mr. Fordyce? he wondered. Dead of old age? Carried off by a fever? An accident? Whatever the case, he was relieved that the widow did not feel compelled to follow what, in his opinion, was the extremely unfortunate style for elaborate mourning that had been set by the queen after the loss of her beloved Albert. Sometimes it seemed to him that half the ladies in England were attired in crepe and weeping veils. It never ceased to amaze him that the fair sex had managed to elevate the somber attire and accessories indicative of deep sorrow to the very pinnacle of fashion.

Regardless, he had not noticed so much as a single item of jet or black enameled jewelry on Caroline's person. Perhaps the mysterious Mrs. Fordyce did not deeply regret the loss of Mr. Fordyce. Perhaps she was, in fact, in the market for a new attachment of an intimate nature.

This is no time to be drawn into those deep waters, he thought. There was far too much at stake here. He could not take the risk of allowing himself to be distracted by the lady, no matter how attractive or intriguing.

He crossed a street, pausing briefly to allow a crowded omnibus to lumber past, the horses straining to pull the heavy vehicle. The driver of a quick-moving hansom cab spotted him and offered his services. Adam waved him off. He could make better time on foot.

When he reached the pavement on the far side, he turned down a narrow stone walk and cut through a small, neglected park. His old life on the streets had left him with a knowledge of the city's maze of hidden lanes and uncharted alleys that few coachmen could equal.

When he emerged from the brick walk he saw a newsboy hawking the latest edition of the *Flying Intelligencer*.

Some idiotic impulse made him stop in front of the scruffy-looking vendor.

"I'll have a copy, if you please." He took a coin out of his pocket.

"Aye, sir." The lad grinned and reached into his sack to remove a paper. "You're in luck. I've got one left. Expect you're eager to read the next episode of Mrs. Fordyce's story, like all the rest of my customers."

"I will admit I am somewhat curious about it."

"You'll be pleased enough with this installment of *The Mysterious Gentleman*, sir," the boy assured him. "It begins with a very startling incident and ends with a fine cliff-hanger."

"Indeed?" Adam glanced at the front page of the cheap paper and saw that *The Mysterious Gentleman* by Mrs. C. J. Fordyce occupied three full columns. "What of the character of Edmund Drake? Does he come to a bad end?"

"Not yet, sir. Much too soon for that. Drake's still acting very mysterious, though, and it's obvious he's up to no good." The newsboy's eyes gleamed with anticipation. "He's hatching a nasty plot against the heroine, Miss Lydia Hope."

"I see. Well, that is what villains do, is it not? Hatch nasty plots against innocent ladies?"

"Aye, and that's a fact, but there's no need to worry," the boy said cheerfully. "Edmund Drake will meet a right dreadful fate. All of Mrs. Fordyce's villains come to terrible ends in the final episodes."

Adam folded the paper and tucked it under his arm. "Something to look forward to, no doubt."

A short time later he went up the steps of the big house in Laxton Square. Morton, bald head gleaming in the morning sun, had the door open before Adam could retrieve his key.

"Welcome home, sir," Morton said.

If he had not been so weary, Adam thought, he would have been amused by Morton's studied lack of curiosity. It was, after all, half past ten. He had left the house shortly before nine last night to go to his club and had not returned until this moment. One would assume that the butler must have a few questions. But Morton was far too well schooled or, more likely, too well inured to the eccentric ways of the household to remark upon the hour.

"Mr. Grendon has just sat down to a late breakfast, sir." Morton took Adam's coat and hat. "Perhaps you would care to join him?"

"An excellent notion, Morton. I believe I will do that."

He needed food as much as he needed sleep, Adam thought. And sooner or later, he would have to face Wilson and convey the bad news. Might as well get the business behind him.

When he walked into the paneled and polished breakfast room a short time later, Wilson Grendon looked up from the depths of his morning paper. He studied Adam for a few brief seconds and then removed his gold-rimmed spectacles and set them aside.

"You had no luck, I take it?" he asked without preamble.

"The medium was dead when I found her. Murdered."

"Damnation." Wilson's thick gray brows bunched over his formidable nose. "Delmont is dead? Are you certain?"

"Hard to be mistaken about that sort of thing." Adam tossed the folded newspaper onto the table and crossed to the sideboard to survey the array of dishes. "There was no sign of the diary, so I am forced to conclude that the killer stole it. I spent half the night and most of the morning making inquiries into the affair."

Wilson absorbed that information with a troubled expression. "The murder is certainly a strange twist."

"Not necessarily. The average villain would likely see a great potential for extortion in this matter." Adam picked up a silver serving fork and helped himself to a large heap of scrambled eggs and smoked salmon. "The prospect of money can make any number of people contemplate murder."

Wilson turned thoughtful. "Are you certain that the medium was murdered for the diary?"

"No." Adam carried his plate back to the table and sat down. "But it would appear to be the most logical explanation, given the timing and circumstances."

"Well, then, if you are right, whoever now possesses the diary will no doubt soon be in touch."

"I prefer not to sit and wait for the killer to send a message inviting me to pay blackmail." Adam dug into his eggs. "I intend to find him first."

Wilson drank some coffee and lowered the cup. "Did you learn anything useful in the course of your inquiries last night and this morning?"

"No. The only halfway promising suspect proved to be an exceedingly difficult and unpredictable female who thinks that I am an ideal model for a villain in a sensation novel."

"How odd." Wilson's pale gray eyes lit with interest. "Tell me about her."

Trust Wilson to seize upon the one aspect of the business that he least wished to discuss, Adam thought. He buttered some toast while he considered his response.

"There isn't much to tell," he said. "I am convinced that the lady in question is not involved in this affair."

42

Wilson leaned back in his chair. "This is not the first time that you and I have had occasion to discuss murder and potentially dangerous documents at breakfast."

"What we have done in the past along those lines were matters of business," Adam said shortly.

"Nevertheless, this is the first time in the long history of our association that you have mentioned a conversation with an exceedingly difficult and unpredictable female who found you to be a perfect model for a villain in a novel. Forgive me, but I find that quite intriguing."

Adam munched on his toast. "I told you, I do not think that the lady has any connection to this affair of the diary."

"She obviously made an impression on you."

"She would make an impression on anyone."

"You know what the French say: *cherchez la femme.*"

"This is England, not France." Adam put down the corner of toast and went back to the eggs. "Things are different here."

"Not always. I cannot help but notice that the lady appears to have had a very striking effect upon your mood, most notably your temper."

Wilson knew him far too well, Adam reflected.

"I would remind you that I have not slept in the past twenty-four hours," he said evenly. "It is little wonder that I am not in the best of tempers."

"On the contrary," Wilson said. "In my experience, the more there is at risk, the more cold-blooded and unemotional you become. Quite chilling, actually."

Adam gave him a look.

Wilson ignored him. "In fact, if one did not know you well, one might assume that you did not possess any of the warmer passions."

A tingle of alarm went through Adam. The fork in his hand paused in midair. "With all due respect sir, the very last subject I wish to discuss this morning is what you are pleased to call the *warmer passions*."

"Now, Adam, I am well aware that you do possess those sorts of passions. All the more reason why you should get married and employ them to produce heirs for the Grendon-Hardesty fortunes."

"You have no shortage of heirs, sir. Julia has already married and provided you with two of them. Jessica will be making her debut into Society next spring. She will no doubt attract dozens of offers within a fortnight. When she marries, she will supply you with still more heirs. And do not forget Nathan. Sooner or later he will lose interest in his philosophy and mathematics long enough to fall in love, marry and produce even more heirs."

"That still leaves you unaccounted for," Wilson pointed out. "You are the eldest of the lot. You should have been the first one to marry."

"It is absurd to sit here and discuss yet again my failure to find a wife when we should be occupied with a far more pressing problem," Adam said, hanging on to his temper with an effort. "I suggest we return to the matter of the diary."

Wilson grimaced. "Very well, but I must tell you that I am not nearly as concerned about it as you are."

"Yes, I can see that. Would you mind explaining why in blazes you are not worried about it?"

"The diary's sole value lies in the fact that it can be used as an instrument of blackmail. Sooner or later, whoever stole it from Elizabeth Delmont will make contact and attempt to extort money from you, just as Delmont did. When that occurs, you will track down the new blackmailer, just as you did Delmont." Wilson raised one narrow shoulder in a dismissive shrug. "It is simply a matter of time."

Wilson's logic was impeccable, as always, Adam thought. But he was unable to take a similarly sanguine approach to the problem.

"It is not in my nature to wait upon the convenience of a blackmailer who is also very likely a killer," he said quietly.

Wilson sighed. "No, of course not. Very well, find your blackmailer and deal with him. Then you can get back to more important matters."

There was only one really important matter in Wilson's opinion these days. He was determined to see Adam wed. Having made his decision, he had become relentless.

Adam felt the sort of affection, respect and loyalty for his mentor that he imagined other men felt toward their fathers. Nevertheless, he had no intention of marrying merely to satisfy Wilson Grendon's demands.

Wilson Grendon was in the latter half of his sixtieth decade. He was the last direct descendent of a once-powerful aristocratic family whose properties and finances had been sadly depleted by a long line of

45

wastrels and rakehells. Endowed with a steely will and a great talent for business, Wilson had devoted himself to rebuilding the family fortunes. He had succeeded beyond anyone's wildest expectations only to lose the very reasons that had inspired him: his beloved wife and two children.

Brokenhearted, Wilson had devoted himself to building an even larger empire. He had lost himself in the arcane machinations of his far-flung enterprises in England and on the Continent. On several occasions over the years, the long-reaching tentacles of the Grendon empire had proved useful to Her Majesty's government.

Wilson's agents and employees abroad often picked up rumors and information concerning clandestine intrigues and foreign plots. That sort of thing was passed along to the Crown, which, in turn, sometimes took advantage of the Grendon connections to send secret diplomatic messages.

The informal arrangement had continued after Adam had become involved in Wilson's business affairs, hence the occasional breakfast conversation concerning murder and mischief. For Adam, it all came under the heading of business; a natural extension of the career he had pursued while making his living on the streets. Information was a commodity, just like everything else. It could be bought, stolen, traded or sold.

Much in his world had changed fourteen years ago when he and Julia and Jessica and Nathan had moved into Wilson's big, lonely mansion in Laxton Square, but the way he made his living was not one of them, he reflected.

Society was under the impression that he and the other three were long-lost relatives of Wilson's. According to the story Grendon had put about, the family connection had been fortuitously discovered by his solicitor while going through some old papers. Wilson had immediately located the four young people, taken them into his household and made them his heirs.

Some portions of the tale were certainly true, Adam mused. He and Julia and Jessica and Nathan were, indeed, Wilson's heirs. But the relationship between the five of them was a good deal more murky and convoluted than anyone in the Polite World imagined.

While he had turned over much of the day-to-day operations of his financial empire to Adam in the past few years, Wilson was still as astute and cunning as he had always been. Because he was no longer required to apply his considerable abilities to his business affairs, he had a great deal of free time to work on other projects, such as maneuvering Adam into marriage.

"I can see that you are determined to press on with your search for the diary," Wilson said. "How do you intend to proceed?"

Adam reached for the silver coffeepot. "On my way home this morning I recalled that one of your old friends, Prittlewell, was fascinated by psychical research for a time recently."

Wilson snorted. "Prittlewell and everyone else in Society. I tell you, it is nothing less than astounding to see so many seemingly reasonable, educated people toss aside all common sense and natural skepticism when a medium levitates a table. I blame it on the Americans, of course. Whole thing started on the Other Side."

"The Other Side?"

"Of the Atlantic." Wilson snorted. "The Fox sisters with their rappings and tappings, the Davenports with their cabinet séances, D. D. Home —"

Adam frowned. "I thought Home was born in Scotland."

"He may have been born there but he was raised in America."

"I see," Adam said dryly. "I suppose that explains it."

"Indeed. As I was saying, this isn't the first nonsense imported from America and it likely won't be the last."

"Yes, sir. But my point is that your friend Prittlewell no doubt picked up some gossip and rumors concerning the community of mediums while he was attending séances and lectures on psychical research."

"Very likely. What of it?"

"I wondered if you might make some casual inquiries in that direction. Find out what he knows about Elizabeth Delmont and those who moved in her circle."

Enthusiasm lit Wilson's face. There was nothing he liked more than a bit of intrigue. "Very well. That might prove interesting."

And with any luck, it will keep you too distracted to concentrate on your schemes to marry me off, Adam thought.

He was about to continue with his attempt at distraction when he heard the distant, muffled sound of the front door opening and closing. There was only one person who was likely to call at this unfashionable hour.

"Julia is here," Adam said. "Remember, not a word of this to her. I do not want her to be concerned with this matter. There is no need for her to worry about it."

"I agree. Trust me, I will say nothing."

Light, brisk footsteps echoed in the hall. A moment later Julia appeared in the doorway. Both men rose to their feet.

"Good day to you both." She swept into the room with a glowing smile. "I hope you are prepared to endure another invasion of workmen and decorators this afternoon."

"Of course," Wilson said. "We are proud to do our small part in connection with what will be the social event of the Season. Is that not so, Adam?"

"So long as you keep your horde of laborers and decorators out of the library," Adam agreed, pulling out a chair.

She made a face at him as she sat down. "Never fear, everyone understands that your library is sacrosanct. But I fear that it will be very busy around here for the next few days. I'm having fountains and mirrors installed in the ballroom. I think the effect will be quite riveting."

"I'm sure it will be." Adam lowered himself back into his chair and reached for another slice of toast. "Your plans are going well, I assume?"

"Yes but I was forced to confess to Robert this morning that I may have overreached myself with the Roman villa theme this year."

"Nonsense, my dear." Wilson sat down, beaming with fatherly reassurance. "If anyone can turn that old ballroom into a Roman villa, it is you. I have no doubt but that you'll be successful. You will amaze and astonish Society once again, just as you did last year."

"I appreciate your confidence." Julia helped herself to some tea. "But if the affair does come off as planned, it is you, Uncle Wilson, who must take most of the credit. I could not possibly orchestrate such a major event without the use of the old ballroom. There simply is not enough space in the town house to stage anything more elaborate than a dinner party or a small soirée."

"Your husband is very wise not to invest his money in a large house here in town," Wilson said. "It would be a complete waste of money. He's got enough properties to maintain as it is, and your family is never in London long enough to justify the expense."

Julia nodded and set down the teapot. "I cannot argue with that. By the way, Robert said to tell you that he plans to take the children to the fair in the park tomorrow. He wondered if you would like to accompany them."

Wilson looked vastly pleased. "I shall check my appointment calendar to see if I am free."

His appointment calendar would no doubt grant him ample time to accompany the children and their father, the Earl of Southwood, on the outing, Adam thought. Wilson would have cheerfully rescheduled an audience with the queen to make room for an afternoon with the two youngsters.

Julia gave Wilson a knowing look. "Going to the fair will also provide you with an excuse to leave the house again while the decorators and the workmen swarm about the place. I must warn you that I can promise nothing but noise and commotion for the remainder of the week."

"A Roman villa is not constructed in a day," Wilson observed.

Julia drank some tea. "By the way, I had a letter from Jessica this morning. She is having a glorious time in Dorset. I gather that life on her friend's family estate is one grand round of picnics and games."

"We had a note from Nathan telling us that he will be coming down to see all of us on the occasion of my birthday next month," Wilson said.

"He is well?" Julia asked, a bit anxious. "I do worry about him devoting so much time to his books."

"Do not concern yourself," Wilson said easily. "He is perfectly content. I think he may have been born for the scholarly life."

Julia smiled. "Who would have believed it?"

The breakfast table chatter ebbed and flowed around Adam but he made little effort to contribute to the conversation. Not only were his thoughts focused on darker subjects, the long night was beginning to catch up with him. He wanted his bed.

"Is something wrong, Adam?" Julia asked abruptly. "You appear to be a million miles away. Am I boring you with my plans for the ball?"

"No. I was just thinking about some business that must be attended to this morning." He tossed his napkin on the table. "If you will excuse me —"

But it was too late. Julia was giving him a close, sisterly scrutiny. "What's this? Your shirt is rather crumpled and I do believe you have failed to shave this morning. That is quite unlike you."

"Julia, if you don't mind, I must be off." He got to his feet. "Enjoy your breakfast. I will see you all later."

Wilson inclined his head, eyes narrowing slightly. "Get some rest."

Julia's eyes widened. "Why do you need rest? Are you ill?"

"I am feeling quite fit, thank you." Adam grabbed the folded copy of the *Flying Intelligencer* and made his escape from the breakfast room.

He heard crisp footsteps in the hall behind him and stifled a groan. He should have known it wasn't going to be that easy.

"Adam," Julia called firmly. "A word, if you please."

"What is it?" He walked into the library and sat down behind his desk. "As I said, I'm rather busy."

"You did not happen to dress carelessly this morning." Julia sailed into the library behind him and crossed the oriental carpet to stand in front of the desk. "I do believe that you have just returned after having been out all night."

52

"Julia, there are some things that a gentleman does not discuss, not even with his sister."

"Hah! I knew it. You *were* gone all night." Curiosity sparked in her eyes. "Is it serious this time or merely another one of your boring little affairs?"

"I had not realized that you considered my personal life boring. Not that your opinion matters, given that it is my personal life, not your own."

She frowned in surprise at his tone. "I meant no offense."

Guilt sank its claws into him. He had not meant to snap at her like that. "I know. I apologize for my short temper. Wilson is right. I need some sleep."

"I suppose I find your affairs dull for the most part because you seem to find them dull," she said, thoughtful now.

"Forgive me, Julia, but I believe I have lost the thread of the conversation. Nor do I wish to rediscover it."

She nodded, as though confirming a private opinion. "That is it, of course. I should have reasoned it out sooner. I have always found your liaisons singularly uninspiring primarily because you never appear to be particularly inspired by them."

"I do not look to that sort of thing as a source of inspiration."

"Obviously. You treat your romantic associations with ladies the same way you do your business affairs. They are always well-planned and deftly handled according to your rules. You never exhibit any degree of strong sentiment or emotion. When a connection ends you seem almost relieved, as though some routine task had been completed, allowing you to move on to another project."

"I cannot fathom what you are talking about."

"I am talking about the fact that you never allow yourself to fall in love, Adam." She paused for emphasis. "Uncle Wilson and I believe that it is past time that you did."

He set his teeth. "Julia, I will give you fair warning. I have just endured one lecture from Wilson on the subject of finding a wife. I am not in the mood for another."

She ignored that, whisked her skirts aside and sat down in one of the leather chairs. "So, you have established a new liaison. Who is she, Adam? I cannot wait to learn her name."

It occurred to him that the simplest way to deflect Julia's attention while he continued his search for the diary was to encourage her in the belief that he was involved in a new love affair. If she thought that to be true, she would be less likely to question any unusual or secretive behavior on his part during the next few days.

He shuffled the papers while he mentally assembled his plan.

"You cannot expect me to divulge her name," he said.

"I am aware that you have a rule against that sort of thing, but it does not apply in this case."

"The rules apply in all cases."

"Rubbish. You have always taken your own rules far too seriously. Now then, were you with Lillian Tait last

54

night, by any chance? I knew that she had her eye on you. Did you finally succumb to her wiles?"

"What makes you think that I would waste an entire night and a good portion of the morning on Lillian Tait?" He stacked the papers he had just finished shuffling. "I can barely tolerate the lady's conversation for the length of a dance."

"I can imagine a number of reasons why you might find her quite entertaining in other circumstances. Mrs. Tait is a very attractive, very rich widow, and she makes no secret of the fact that she has no plans to marry again. She quite enjoys her freedom. All in all, she would appear to meet most of your basic requirements in a paramour."

"Do you think so?" He kept his tone deliberately uninterested.

"I know you better than anyone else in the entire world, with the possible exception of Uncle Wilson. I have been aware for some time now that you have very specific rules when it comes to your intimate liaisons." She paused meaningfully. "Do you know, I believe that is your chief problem, Adam."

He went quite blank. "What?"

"Your insistence upon living your entire life by *rules*. For heaven's sake, you've got them for everything, even your romantic connections."

He cocked a brow. "You stun me, madam. I was under the impression that properly behaved ladies did not discuss a gentleman's romantic connections."

She smiled serenely. "I assure you, every lady I know finds the topic of who is dallying with whom fascinating. Indeed, it is usually the first subject discussed at any tea or social gathering."

"Another illusion of feminine behavior shattered." He reached for a pen. "And here I thought that the only subjects you discussed with your friends were fashions and the latest sensation novels."

She clicked her tongue. "It is a mystery to me how so many seemingly intelligent gentlemen manage to convince themselves that women are shockingly ignorant of the realities of life."

The comment made him go very still. "We both know that the one thing you are not is shockingly ignorant of the realities of life, Julia," he said quietly. "I only wish that I had been able to do a better job of sheltering you and the others."

"Nonsense." The teasing light vanished from her face in a heartbeat. "Do not say such things, Adam. You protected us very well indeed when we were young. I suspect Jessica, Nathan and I would not have survived without you. But surely you did not think that I believed that you lived the life of a monk?"

He winced. "I had not realized that you gave so much thought to my private life."

"I'm your sister in every way but blood," she reminded him gently. "Of course I give the matter of your private affairs my closest personal attention." Her delicate brows rose. "As I recall, you gave mine even more intense scrutiny when I told you that I was madly in love with Robert."

"You were an heiress. It was my duty to make certain that you were not married for your fortune."

56

"Yes, I know, and you did not rest until you had assured yourself that Robert and I had indeed contracted a love match. Robert still shudders whenever he mentions the various inquisitions that he was obliged to endure in order to gain your trust and respect."

"I did not consider those meetings to be inquisitions. I preferred to think of them as opportunities for Southwood and I to get to know each other and establish a bond of friendship."

She laughed. "He told me that he came close to trying to drown you during that fishing trip to Scotland. He said the only thing that stopped him from pushing you into the loch was the knowledge that you were an expert swimmer."

"We caught some very fine fish on that trip."

"And then there was the time that you invited him aboard Wilson's yacht for a three-day sail along the coast. He dared not refuse for fear you would think him a weakling."

"The weather was excellent for sailing."

"He was violently ill throughout the entire trip. He says he still does not understand how you discovered before the journey that he is prone to *mal de mer*."

He nodded sagely. "I have my sources."

"My point is that you have always paid very close attention to my personal affairs, and I feel it is only fair to return the favor. Unfortunately, you have never given me much of interest to observe."

"I regret that you find me so exquisitely dull but there is little that I can do about the situation. Now then, I hate to interrupt this fascinating conversation but I have plans for this afternoon. I would like to get some rest before I go out."

She made a face. "You are not going to tell me her name, are you?"

"No."

"Why so secretive? Sooner or later I am bound to learn her identity. You know how gossip flows in Society." She paused, tilting her head slightly to one side in a quizzical fashion. "Unless, of course, your new friend does not move in Society."

He stood, reaching for the newspaper. "If you will excuse me, I am going to go upstairs and rest for a while."

"Very well, I give up, at least for now." She rose. "It is clear that you are not going to indulge my curiosity. But sooner or later —" She broke off, glancing at the paper in his hand. "I did not know that you read the *Flying Intelligencer*, Adam. It is not your sort of paper at all. It thrives on the most exciting sort of sensation and gossip."

"I assure you, this is the first and only copy I have ever purchased."

"You were lucky to get it." She started toward the door. "Mrs. Fordyce's latest novel is being serialized in it. She is very popular. I expect the copies will be sold out quickly. In fact, I made certain to send Willoughby off to find a newsboy first thing this morning. I couldn't bear to risk missing the next chapter of *The Mysterious Gentleman*."

A sense of impending doom struck him. "I did not realize that you read Mrs. Fordyce's work."

"Yes, indeed. Her new story is the best one to date, as far as I am concerned. The villain is a man named Edmund Drake. We do not know what he is about yet, but it is obvious that he has wicked intentions toward the heroine, Lydia Hope."

He felt his jaw tighten. "So I have been told."

She paused at the door. "Rest assured, he will meet a dreadful end. Mrs. Fordyce's last villain was taken off to spend his remaining days confined in an insane asylum. I expect she has something equally dire planned for Edmund Drake."

A short time later in the privacy of his bedchamber, he freed himself of his tie, waistcoat and shirt and settled down on the bed to get some badly needed rest. He tried to focus his thoughts on the next step in his plans to locate the diary, but for some bizarre reason he kept returning to the matter of Caroline Fordyce.

She was certainly not his usual type. But in other ways she fit what Julia was pleased to call his rules quite well. She was not an innocent young lady like Jessica, who had to be guarded as closely as a chest of gold until she was married off to a suitable husband. Nor was she the wife of a friend or a business associate, another category of female he was careful to avoid.

She was a widow and likely a rather worldly one at that. Surely only a woman of considerable experience could write the sort of lurid, melodramatic plots that made sensation novels all the rage.

Judging by her house and gown, Caroline certainly did not control a fortune but she did appear to be making a comfortable living with her writing. True, she did not move in elevated social circles, but that was an excellent thing, he decided. There would be less likelihood of gossip.

He groaned and covered his eyes with his forearm. He had enough problems at the moment. The last thing he should be considering was the possibility of having an affair with Caroline Fordyce.

Unfortunately, he seemed to be able to think of very little else.

CHAPTER
FOUR

When Caroline walked into the study later that afternoon, she found her aunts waiting for her. They were seated in front of the hearth, drinking tea. They looked at her expectantly.

"Well?" Milly demanded with her usual enthusiasm.

"There is no question about it. The mysterious gentleman who called on me early this morning did, indeed, tell the truth." Caroline sat down behind her desk. "Elizabeth Delmont was murdered last night after the séance. So much for the possibility that Mr. Grove, or whatever his name may be, is either mad or a mischief-making trickster."

It had been a weak hope but she had clung to it.

"What did you see when you went to Delmont's address?" Emma asked, looking, as usual, as though she was braced for the worst possible news.

Caroline propped her elbows on the desk and rested her chin on the heels of her hands. "There was a constable standing at the door and a crowd of curious neighbors and some gentlemen of the press gathered in the street."

"You were careful not to be seen, I trust?" Emma said anxiously.

"Of course." Caroline wrinkled her nose. "Not that anyone would have recognized me, in any event."

"Nevertheless, one cannot be too cautious in a matter such as this," Emma reminded her. "The murder will be a great sensation in the papers soon. It would not do to have your name linked to it in any way, especially in light of that unfortunate article concerning your demonstration of psychical powers at Harriet Hughes's tea."

"Don't remind me," Caroline muttered. "What a mistake that was. I don't know why I let you and Aunt Emma talk me into it."

"Now, now, it was very entertaining," Milly said lightly. "Harriet and her friends were all quite thrilled."

Emma frowned. "But who knows what the press might make of such a connection if Caroline were seen at the house where a medium was murdered? It could prove disastrous. We can only pray that it does not get out that she was among the sitters at Delmont's last séance."

"Mr. Grove led me to believe that he has no intention of giving the list of sitters to the police," Caroline said. But what if he changed his mind?

Emma echoed her thoughts. "Who knows what the man will do? He sounds quite eccentric, to say the least. Imagine setting out to find a killer on his own."

"It is certainly not the sort of behavior one expects from a gentleman who moves in elevated circles," Milly agreed. "I wonder what is in that missing diary that concerns him. And then there's that business of a false name." She made a tut-tutting sound.

So many questions, Caroline thought. She had not been able to write a single line after the man who had called himself Adam Grove had departed. He was gone but he had left his shadow behind. It hovered over the entire household.

She looked at the two people she loved most in the world. Anxiety gripped her. It was her fault that their lives had been turned upside down three years ago. She could not allow such a thing to happen again. She had a responsibility to protect them from another great scandal — or worse.

Emma and Milly had raised her from the age of two. They had taken her into their home after her mother had expired from an overdose of laudanum. She had called each woman aunt since she had learned to talk, but in truth Emma, her mother's sister, was the only one of the pair who was related to her by blood.

They were both women of a certain age. They had been something more than very good friends for years, sharing not only a home and the responsibility of raising a child, but a seemingly endless variety of enthusiasms and interests.

The pair made a striking contrast in both looks and temperament. Emma was tall, handsome in a severe manner and inclined to a dour view of the world. She was not entirely devoid of a sense of humor but laughter did not come easily to her.

Milly, on the other hand, was short, plump and so light of heart that those who did not know her well often concluded that she was a bit frivolous. Nothing could have been farther from the truth. Milly was as intelligent and well-educated as Emma but there was a strong streak of the romantic in her.

Caroline had long ago concluded that her aunts's tastes in gowns paralleled their temperaments. Emma favored dark, subdued dresses with a minimum of ribbons and flounces. She went about looking as though she were in perpetual mourning, a style that happened to be very much in fashion.

But there was another, equally popular direction in fashion these days. It emphasized a riotous jumble of colors, patterns, trims and designs, and it suited Milly perfectly. The dress she wore this afternoon was an excellent case in point. It was a mix of red and gold stripes and black and white checks. Fringe swayed from the madras plaid sleeves and neckline. A ruffled red petticoat peeked out from beneath the hem.

Emma poured tea for Caroline. "The entire affair is extremely disturbing. Do you suppose the killer was watching from the shadows last night when we left Mrs. Delmont's house? Waiting for his opportunity, as it were?"

"What a chilling thought." Milly sounded more thrilled than chilled. "I must admit, I thought the séance last night was quite exciting. I particularly liked the business of the ghostly hand rising up beside the table. Very effective. I feared that Mr. McDaniel would faint dead away when the fingers reached out to touch his sleeve."

"Elizabeth Delmont was a complete fraud, of course," Caroline said thoughtfully, "but I cannot help but admire her for pursuing such an interesting career. There are so few profitable professions open to ladies."

"Very true," Emma agreed. "Did you learn anything else of note this afternoon?"

"I noticed a young maid standing by herself, watching the commotion around Mrs. Delmont's house," Caroline said. "I requested the driver to stop the carriage so that I could talk to her. I thought it quite safe because I knew that she could not possibly have the faintest notion of my identity. She was delighted to tell me about the rumors that were going through the crowd."

"What did she say?" Milly asked.

"She told me that everyone was talking about how all of the furniture in the séance room had been overturned by supernatural forces."

Emma sighed. "I suppose that sort of gossip was inevitable, given that it was a medium who was murdered."

"Yes." Caroline picked up her teacup. "She said that there was also a great deal of talk about a broken pocket watch."

Milly looked curious. "What was remarkable about the watch?"

"Evidently it was found next to the body. The police think that it was smashed in the course of the murder." She took a sip of tea and lowered the cup. "The hands on the face of the watch were stopped at midnight."

Milly shuddered. "How very melodramatic."

Emma's lips thinned. "The watch will no doubt feature heavily in the newspaper accounts of the murder."

"I suppose it's possible that a disgruntled sitter decided to take revenge against Mrs. Delmont," Milly said. "Communicating with the Other Side can be an extremely emotional business for people who take that sort of nonsense seriously."

"Perhaps," Caroline said slowly. "But I have been giving the matter a great deal of thought and I have come up with another possibility."

"What is that?" Emma asked.

"The gentleman who called here this morning is convinced that whoever murdered Mrs. Delmont did so in order to obtain a certain diary. But as you know, I have spent a great deal of time lately at the headquarters of the Society for Psychical Investigations, and it is no secret there that Mrs. Delmont did have one very jealous rival, a medium named Irene Toller."

"You did say that there is a considerable amount of professional jealousy among mediums," Milly remarked.

Emma stirred her tea. "We can only hope that the police will arrest the villain quickly and put an end to the matter."

But what if the police did not find the killer? Caroline thought. Would they eventually turn up on her doorstep just as Adam Grove had? And what of the mysterious Mr. Grove himself? If he did not locate the diary, would he return to plague her with more questions and not-so-veiled accusations? Would he eventually decide to give the police the list of sitters at Delmont's last séance?

She knew better than most that men from his world could not be trusted.

Emma looked grim. "If only you had not taken a notion to use a medium as a character in your next novel, Caroline. You would never have gone to Wintersett House to study psychical research and we would never have attended Elizabeth Delmont's last séance."

But she had made those choices, Caroline thought glumly. And now she and her aunts faced the possibility of being dragged through the muck of another dreadful scandal, one that could well destroy her new career upon which they all depended financially.

She could not just sit here, waiting for disaster to crash down upon them like an avalanche. She must take action. There was too much at stake.

CHAPTER
FIVE

She dreamed the old nightmare again that night.

She clutched her heavy skirts and ran for her life along the rutted dirt path. Behind her the terrible thud-thud-thud of her pursuer's footsteps drew closer. Her heart pounded. She was tiring, sucking oxygen into her lungs in great, rasping gasps.

Fear and panic had provided an unnatural surge of energy at the start of the ordeal, but the weight of her gown had become a terrifying burden, slowing her desperate rush. The parasol attached to the pretty chatelaine that Milly and Emma had given her for her birthday bounced against her side, threatening her balance.

She did not know how much longer she could go on but she knew that if she stopped, she would die.

"You have to go away," her pursuer said, speaking in that eerie, unnaturally reasonable manner. "Don't you see? He will come back to me if you go away."

She did not turn her head to look back over her shoulder. She could not take the risk. If she stumbled or fell she was lost.

There was no point looking back, in any event. She knew all she needed to know. Her pursuer gripped a large, gleaming carving knife and was bent on murder.

"You have to go away."

Thud-thud-thud. The footsteps drew closer. The woman who was chasing her was not weighted down with a cumbersome dress. The would-be killer wore only a light linen nightgown and a pair of sturdy shoes.

"He will come back to me if you go away."

The woolen skirts of her gown felt like leaden weights in her hands. She was losing ground . . .

Caroline awoke in a cold sweat, the way she always did after the dream. It was no doubt the affair of the murdered medium that had inspired the return of her nightmare, she thought.

She had endured the dream off and on for three years now. Sometimes she would be free of it for a fortnight or even a month; just long enough to begin to hope that she had seen the last of it. Then it would come back without warning, shattering her slumber. Sometimes it would stick around for several nights in a row before disappearing again.

She swung her legs over the side of the bed and reached for her robe and slippers. There was no point in trying to go back to sleep. She knew the pattern all too well. There was only one thing to be done — the same thing she did every other night when the dream and the frightening memories returned to haunt her.

69

She made her way quietly downstairs to the chilly study. There she lit a lamp, poured herself a small glass of sherry and paced the floor for a time.

When her nerves had steadied and her pulse was no longer racing, she sat down at her desk, took out paper and pen and began to write.

Nightmares, murder and the enigmatic Mr. Grove aside, she had work to do. Mr. Spraggett, the publisher of the *Flying Intelligencer*, would be expecting the next episode of *The Mysterious Gentleman* at the end of the week.

The successful writer of serialized sensation novels survived by adhering to an inflexible schedule: A new chapter had to be written every week for some twenty-six weeks in a row. Each chapter consisted of approximately five thousand words. To maintain readers' interest, each chapter had to begin and end with a Startling Incident.

The time constraints placed on Caroline were such that she was usually obliged to begin research and make notes on her next novel while finishing off the last few episodes of the current one.

A few hundred words later she put down her pen and studied what she had written.

No doubt about it, the character of Edmund Drake was at last starting to take shape. Just in the nick of time, too, she thought. Drake had been a shadowy figure until now but he was due to take center stage in the remaining chapters.

CHAPTER
SIX

Two days later Caroline sat in the last row of the lecture hall and watched the stage as the gas lights were lowered in a dramatic fashion.

The room was plunged into deep gloom. The only area that remained well lit was the empty stage. There a single lamp glowed with a ghostly light, illuminating a table and chair. The sparse crowd hushed in anticipation.

Caroline noted that she had almost the entire row of chairs to herself. It seemed that Irene Toller had been overshadowed one last time by her dead rival. Here at Wintersett House, the news of Elizabeth Delmont's murder had captured the interest of everyone involved in psychical research. The halls and corridors of the aging mansion hummed with speculation and gossip. With so much excitement going on, very few people had elected to attend Irene Toller's demonstration of spirit writing.

The abrupt, theatrical darkening of the room had a disturbing effect on Caroline's senses. It was as though invisible fingers had brushed the nape of her neck. An unnerving awareness feathered her nerves. She could literally feel an unseen presence closing in upon her.

"Good afternoon, Mrs. Fordyce," the man who had called himself Adam Grove said very softly from a point just behind her right shoulder. "This is certainly a coincidence of amazing, one might even say metaphysical, proportions. Would you mind if I took the seat next to yours?"

She started so violently it was all she could do not to leap out of the chair. Indeed, she was barely able to stifle a small shriek.

"Mr. Grove." Breathless from the shock he had just given her and thoroughly annoyed by her own reaction, she gave him a repressing glare. The effect was no doubt lost on him due to the shadows here at the back of the room. "What on earth are you doing here?"

"The same thing you are, I suspect." He moved in front of her, obviously aiming for the neighboring seat although she had not invited him to take it. "Thought it might prove instructive to observe Irene Toller's demonstration of spirit writing."

"You followed me," she accused, whisking her skirts out of his path.

"No, as a matter of fact, I did not." He lowered himself into the chair beside her. "But somehow I am not unduly surprised to discover that our paths have crossed again."

"I do not converse with strange gentlemen to whom I have not been properly introduced," she said in her iciest tones.

"Right, I forgot." He settled comfortably into the seat. "I did not give you my real name when I called on you the other morning, did I?"

72

"In point of fact, you deceived me, sir."

"Yes, well, all I can say is that I thought it was for your own good at the time. But since fate has taken a hand in this affair, I may as well introduce myself properly. Adam Hardesty, at your service."

"Why should I assume that you are telling me the truth this time?"

"I shall be happy to offer proof of my identity, if you require it."

She ignored that. "You came here today because you found out that Mrs. Toller may have had a motive for murdering Mrs. Delmont, didn't you?"

"You evidently heard the same rumors."

"The rivalry between the two is common knowledge here at Wintersett House."

"I expect that it was curiosity that led you to pursue the matter." He shook his head. "Has no one ever warned you of the dangers of that particular vice?"

"I admit that I am by nature a curious person, Mr. Hardesty, but as it happens, it was not curiosity that brought me here today."

"No? Then may I ask what cork-brained notion made you decide to investigate a case of murder on your own? This affair is no longer any concern of yours."

"Unfortunately, I cannot be certain of that," she said coolly. "I thought it only prudent to look into the matter personally."

"The devil you say." He folded his arms. "How can you label such an action prudent? It is reckless, foolish and potentially dangerous."

73

"I had little choice. The situation is already extremely dangerous, in my opinion. It is obvious that you are a very relentless and determined man. After you left my house it occurred to me that if you do not turn up a satisfactory villain, you may decide to revert to your original theory, the one that points the finger of suspicion at my aunts and me."

There was a short, tense pause while he absorbed that. She could tell that he was not pleased with her logic.

"I admit I tried to rattle you a bit," he conceded, "but I thought I made it clear that I am reasonably well satisfied that you and your aunts had nothing to do with the affair."

"Reasonably well satisfied does not sound all that certain to me. Now kindly cease carping. The demonstration is about to begin."

Adam went silent but she knew that he would have a great deal to say later. She made a note to escape the room as quickly as possible after Irene Toller concluded her exhibition.

A small man dressed in a dapper suit accented with a fashionable polka-dot shirt and a striped waistcoat walked out onto the stage. He cleared his throat.

"Mrs. Irene Toller will now give a demonstration of automatic writing," he announced.

There was some scattered, unenthusiastic applause.

A woman emerged from behind a curtain at the side of the stage. Caroline had seen Irene Toller from time to time in the halls of Wintersett House. The medium appeared to be in her early thirties. She was tall and striking in a sharp-featured way. Her dark hair was styled in a profusion of complicated braids coiled around her head.

Irene made her way to the table with a stately tread. In her hand she carried a device composed of a heart-shaped wooden platform supported by two casters and a vertical pencil. Caroline recognized the instrument as a planchette. It had been invented several years earlier and was designed to allow the medium to write messages from the Other Side while in a trance.

"This would be mildly entertaining if it were not for the fact that murder has been done," Adam said in a low voice.

Irene Toller took her seat and placed the planchette on the table in front of her. She looked out at the small audience for the first time. Caroline was surprised by the forcefulness of the woman's grim gaze.

"Good afternoon," Irene said in a strong, resonant voice. "For the benefit of those of you who have never witnessed a demonstration of the planchette, I shall explain how the device operates. First, you must understand that there is a veil that separates this world from the realm where the spirits of the departed reside. Certain individuals such as myself are endowed with the ability to provide a conduit through that barrier. I am, in effect, only a channel — the medium — through which those who have gone before us can reach back into our mundane sphere."

An attentive stillness settled on the audience. Irene finally had the full attention of everyone present. She positioned the planchette above a sheet of paper and placed her fingertips upon the small wooden platform.

"I must first ready myself so that the spirits can make use of my hands for the purpose of writing out their messages," Irene continued. "When I have gone into the required trance, I will take questions from the audience. If the spirits choose to respond, they will make use of the planchette."

There was a murmur of anticipation. In spite of her own skepticism, Caroline found herself sitting forward slightly.

"Be warned, however, that the spirits do not always answer the questions that are asked in these public sessions," Irene said. "They often insist that certain inquiries be made in a more private setting."

Adam leaned over to speak quietly into Caroline's ear. "It sounds as if she is drumming up business for the more expensive séances that she holds in her own home in the evenings."

"Please be quiet. I am trying to listen to Mrs. Toller."

On stage, Irene was giving every sign that she was entering a trance. Eyes closed, she swayed slightly in her chair.

"Hark, you ethereal beings who exist beyond the veil that shrouds this mortal world," Irene intoned. "We would learn from you. We seek your guidance and knowledge."

Expectation vibrated across the audience. Caroline could tell that most of those present were only too happy to suspend logic here in this room. They wanted to believe that Irene Toller could communicate with the spirit world.

"A willing audience is always easy to convince," Adam observed softly.

Irene began to make a low, keening sound that sent a shiver through Caroline. The medium jerked several times, shoulders twisting.

The audience was riveted.

Irene's moaning halted suddenly. She stiffened, head snapping back, and then she straightened, somehow appearing taller and more imposing in the chair.

She opened her eyes and stared at the audience with an unnerving gaze.

"The spirits are here," she announced in a hoarse, fearsome voice that was different from the one she had used earlier. "They drift all around us in this room, invisible to the ordinary senses. They await your questions. Speak."

Caroline heard several gasps and low-voiced exclamations.

A man rose a trifle uncertainly from the first row of seats. "Beg your pardon, Mrs. Toller. But I wanted to ask the spirits what it's like over there on the Other Side."

There was a moment of utter stillness. And then, seemingly of its own accord, the planchette began to move beneath Irene's fingers.

Caroline sensed that everyone, with the glaring exception of Adam Hardesty, was holding his or her breath. The audience watched, fascinated, as the pencil fitted into the planchette glided across the paper.

After a moment the automatic writing device ceased moving. Irene looked somewhat haggard from the effort. She rolled the planchette aside, picked up the sheet of paper and displayed it to the audience. The glare of the lamp revealed a scrawled message.

"This is a realm filled with light and harmony," Irene read aloud. "It cannot be fully envisioned by those who are still trapped in the mortal plane."

Murmurs of appreciation and wonder rippled across the room.

"I have no talent for the writing of fiction," Adam whispered to Caroline, "but I vow that even I could craft such a script."

"If you cannot refrain from making comments on the demonstration, perhaps you would be so good as to sit in another section of the room, sir," Caroline snapped softly. "I am trying to observe Mrs. Toller. I do not appreciate the distraction."

"Surely you are not taking any of this seriously."

She pretended she had not heard that.

Another person rose to ask a question, a middle-aged woman this time. She wore deep mourning. A black net weeping veil concealed her features.

"Is the spirit of my husband, George, here?" she inquired, voice quavering. "If so, I want to ask him where he hid the stock shares. He'll know the ones I mean. I've searched everywhere and I cannot find them. I must sell them. I am desperate. Indeed, I am in danger of losing the house."

Everyone looked toward the stage.

Irene placed her fingertips on the planchette. There was another moment of stillness. Caroline expected the medium to announce that the departed George was not present. But to her astonishment, the planchette began to move beneath Irene's fingertips, slowly at first and then with increasing speed.

The planchette stopped abruptly. With an air of exhaustion, Irene picked up the paper.

"Behind the mirror above the fireplace," she read aloud.

"I am saved," the middle-aged woman cried out. "How can I thank you, Mrs. Toller? You have my most sincere gratitude."

"You must thank the spirit of your husband, madam," Irene said. "I am merely the medium through which he communicated the information."

"Thank you, George, wherever you are." The woman bustled out of the row of chairs and hurried toward the exit. "Please excuse me. I must find those shares immediately."

She dashed straight past Caroline, leaving a trace of lavender scent in the air, and disappeared around the curtain that blocked the light from the door.

"Now that was interesting," Adam said.

Excitement bubbled in the darkened lecture room. Another man shot to his feet.

"If you please, Mrs. Toller, I have a question," he called loudly. "If the spirit of Elizabeth Delmont is nearby, ask her to tell us who murdered her."

There was a startled silence.

At the front of the room Irene flinched violently. Her mouth opened and then closed very quickly.

For the first time, Adam gave his full and undivided attention to the stage. He leaned forward, resting his forearms on his thighs, and watched Mrs. Toller closely.

"I expect that she will claim that Mrs. Delmont's spirit isn't present," Caroline murmured to Adam.

"I'm not so certain of that," Adam replied. "Look. The planchette is moving."

Caroline stared, astonished. Beneath Mrs. Toller's fingers, the device drifted this way and that, drawing the tip of the pencil across a fresh sheet of paper.

Irene groaned. A visible shudder passed across her shoulders. She gave every appearance of struggling valiantly to keep herself erect in her chair.

When the planchette finally halted, no one moved.

Irene eased the device aside and picked up the paper. She gazed at the scrawled writing for a long time. Tension gripped the room.

Irene read the message in her new, raspy voice. "Elizabeth Delmont was a fraud. She angered the spirits with her false claims and tricks. The invisible hand of retribution reached out from beyond the grave to silence her."

As if the final effort had been too much for her, Irene collapsed facedown on the table. Before anyone could move, the single lamp flared violently and then went out. The lecture hall was enveloped in thick darkness.

Someone shrieked. A hubbub ensued.

"Please remain calm. All is well. This often happens when Mrs. Toller finishes her demonstration. Séances exact a great toll on the medium's nerves. I will have the lamp on in a minute."

Caroline recognized the voice of the small man who had introduced Irene Toller.

The lights came up slowly, illuminating the stage. Irene Toller and her planchette had disappeared.

CHAPTER
SEVEN

"Enough of these theatrics." Adam took a firm grip on Caroline's arm and urged her to her feet. "Browning had the right of it in his piece *Mr. Sludge, the Medium.* Anyone who claims to be able to summon spirits is a fraud."

"I would remind you, sir, that Mr. Browning's wife was very impressed by a séance conducted by the famous Mr. D. D. Home. Rumor has it that she was convinced that Home not only contacted the spirit world but that he actually caused manifestations to appear."

"With all due respect to the incomparable Elizabeth Barrett Browning, I am certain that she was tricked by Home." Adam steered her toward the door. "But I will admit that she was in excellent company. In his prime, Home managed to make fools of any number of people."

To his great satisfaction, Caroline did not resist his effort to get her out of the lecture hall. But he had miscalculated badly in one regard, he discovered. The gently rounded shape and the enticing, resilient feel of her arm through the fabric of her sleeve proved unexpectedly distracting. He had to struggle against a sudden urge to tighten his hold and pull her closer. This was the first time he had actually touched her. He could not suppress the flicker of excitement that crackled through him.

She was warm and vivid in a tightly laced green gown trimmed with white at the neck and sleeves. The short train of the dress was gracefully hooked up to enable her to walk without sweeping the floor with the hem. The design exposed the toes of dainty shoes the same color as the gown. A large, delightfully frivolous green and gold velvet bow decorated the rear of the dress where the skirts had been drawn up and back into a small pouf. Her hair was twisted into an elegant coil. A tiny flower-trimmed hat was perched at a rakish angle over one eye.

She looked good enough to eat, he thought, and he was ravenously hungry.

He guided her along the corridor, intensely, almost painfully conscious of her femininity. The faint, enticing scent of her body mingled with the flowers and herbs of the soap she had used in her bath. The fragrance thrilled his senses. He reminded himself that he was too old, was too experienced and had seen too much of the dark, raw side of life to be so easily overwhelmed by a woman. But there it was. All indications were that he had been struck by lightning.

They made their way down the main hall of Wintersett House, past an office, a large reception room, more lecture halls and a library.

As far as Adam could determine, only the ground floor had been opened to the members of the Society of

Psychical Investigations. The floors above were closed to the public.

The mansion was vast, bleak and quite ugly, in his opinion. It had been designed in the Gothic style with walls of heavy stone. The rooms were vaulted in the medieval manner. Very little sunlight penetrated the interior of the big house.

Just the sort of atmosphere the members of the Society no doubt thrived on, he thought.

When they reached the front hall, he saw two gentlemen engaged in serious conversation. The shorter of the two was a man of some forty or forty-five years of age. Although he was of less than average height, he was fashioned along solid, heavy lines, not unlike the mansion. He projected an intense, scholarly air with spectacles, whiskers, a receding hairline and a rumpled coat.

The short, bespectacled man was brandishing a photograph beneath the aristocratic nose of an elegant, well-dressed, rather bored-looking gentleman. The taller man was endowed with the sort of statue-perfect features that never failed to attract the eyes of the ladies. His jet-black hair was highlighted by a startling streak of silver.

"The tall, distinguished gentleman is Mr. Julian Elsworth," Caroline whispered. "He is the most fashionable practitioner of psychical powers in London at the moment. He gives occasional public demonstrations here at Wintersett House, but most of his sittings are conducted in private homes in the most exclusive circles."

She sounded far too enthusiastic about Elsworth, Adam decided.

"I've heard of him," he allowed. "We've never been introduced."

"A formal reception in his honor will be held here later this week," she said. "It will be followed by a demonstration of his abilities. There is certain to be a very large crowd."

"And the short gentleman?"

"That is Mr. Reed. He is the president of the Society for Psychical Investigations and the publisher of *New Dawn*."

At that moment Elsworth glanced up from the photograph that Reed was holding in front of him. He gave Adam a brief, considering look. Then, evidently dismissing him as unimportant, he turned to Caroline with a dazzlingly bright smile.

"Mrs. Fordyce," Elsworth said. "A pleasure to see you again."

"Mr. Elsworth." She gave him her gloved hand and then politely switched her attention to the shorter man. "Mr. Reed."

She glanced speculatively at Adam. "Allow me to present Mr. —"

"Grove," he said before she could decide what name to use. "Adam Grove."

The two men nodded politely but it was clear that Caroline was the one who interested them.

Reed's pale eyes were intense and serious behind the lenses of his eyeglasses. "Welcome back to Wintersett House. Have you returned to continue your literary research or have you finally decided to honor the Society with a demonstration of your own psychical powers?"

Adam tightened his grip on Caroline's arm. Psychical powers? What the deuce was this about?

Unobtrusively, she tried to free herself. He realized he was holding on to her as if she were in danger of being swept away by some invisible force. He quickly loosened his hand, but he did not release her. For some reason, everything in him was screaming at him to keep her as close as possible.

Caroline smiled politely at Reed. "As I told you the other day, sir, the item in the press was incorrect regarding several of the particulars of my demonstration at the tea party."

"But I spoke with Mrs. Hughes myself," Reed insisted. "She was very impressed by what she witnessed that day."

"Please believe me when I tell you that I do not possess any gifts that would be of interest to the researchers of the Society," Caroline said.

Reed's smile held a mix of understanding and approval. "Your natural delicacy of feeling becomes you, Mrs. Fordyce, but there is no need for alarm. I would not dream of putting you on a public stage. Rest assured that the tests would be conducted in private according to the strictest standards of science."

"I must decline," Caroline said firmly.

Elsworth raised his winged brows. "I fear you are being far too modest, madam. According to the piece in the paper you were evidently able to read the minds of

86

several of the ladies who were fortunate enough to be present at Mrs. Hughes's tea."

"Unfortunately, I have nothing to demonstrate to the Society," she said, more forcefully this time.

Reed nodded several times. "As you wish. I would not dream of trying to press you into doing something that would cause you discomfort." He paused and lowered his voice. "I expect you heard the tragic news of Elizabeth Delmont's death?"

"Shocking," Caroline said.

"We here at the Society are all quite stunned." Reed shook his head. "She was a medium of great talent."

Elsworth glanced back toward the lecture hall where Irene Toller had given her demonstration. "Not everyone held that opinion."

Adam's interest in the conversation went up a notch. "Yes, we did gain that impression from Mrs. Toller a few minutes ago."

Reed grimaced. "I'm afraid there was some professional rivalry between Mrs. Toller and Mrs. Delmont. Powerful mediums are often quite jealous of each other's gifts."

"She implied that dark forces from the Other Side were responsible for Mrs. Delmont's death," Caroline said neutrally.

Elsworth looked pained. "According to the sensation press there were some peculiar elements about the murder that will no doubt sell a great many copies of the papers."

"What sort of elements?" Adam asked with what he was fairly certain sounded like idle curiosity.

Reed heaved a troubled sigh and lowered his voice. "There were reports that Delmont's séance room was turned entirely upside down as though by some powerful supernatural force. Furniture scattered about like so much kindling." He paused for effect. "They also noted that a mysterious pocket watch was found next to the body."

"What is odd about a pocket watch?" Adam asked.

"According to the correspondent, the watch was broken," Elsworth explained, "most likely at the time of the murder. The hands were stopped at twelve o'clock." He smiled humorlessly. "Midnight is often viewed as a particularly significant hour in the world of psychical research, you know."

"Some feel that it is the time of the night when the veil between this world and the Other Side is most easily breached," Reed added with a somber, knowledgeable bob of his head. "It is all extremely disturbing."

Caroline glanced at the picture in his hand. "I see you have a photograph."

"Yes, indeed." Reed brightened and held it up for her to view. "I was just showing it to Elsworth here."

Caroline leaned closer for a better look. "It is very intriguing."

Adam studied the picture over her shoulder. The subject was an attractive young lady seated on a straight-backed chair. An amorphous, ghostly image of another woman appeared to hover in the air behind the head of the sitter.

"It was taken by a member of the Society," Reed explained enthusiastically. "The medium is apparently able to cause manifestations to appear."

"The problem is that no one trusts spirit photographs any more." Elsworth was clearly bored. "Too easily faked, I'm afraid."

"Like so many things," Adam said.

Caroline shot him a reproving glance. He pretended not to notice.

"Shall we go, my dear?" he asked. "It is getting late."

"I am in no rush," she said.

"You have evidently forgotten our appointment," he added, maneuvering her toward the door.

For a moment he feared she would dig in her pretty heels but instead she made her goodbyes to Reed and Elsworth.

Outside on the front steps of Wintersett House, Caroline paused to remove her dainty green parasol from the chatelaine that secured it to her waist and opened it with a snap.

"Really, Mr. Hardesty, there was no need to be rude. Mr. Reed is not only the president of the Society, he has done a great deal to promote serious, scientific psychical research."

"Scientific psychical research? Now there's a contradiction in terms if ever there was one."

"And as for Mr. Elsworth, you should know that in some quarters he is considered to be the heir to the crown of D. D. Home. They say that like Home, he can actually levitate his body."

"If you believe that, Mrs. Fordyce, may I suggest an interesting investment opportunity that has recently come to my attention? It involves a diamond mine in Wales. The stones are just lying about on the ground there, waiting to be scooped up by anyone with a bucket. You are bound to make a fortune."

"That is not amusing, sir. For your information, Mr. Elsworth has been examined several times by psychical researchers and pronounced genuine. One investigator claims that both Mr. Home and Mr. Elsworth may have descended from werewolves and that is why they have such extraordinary powers."

He looked at her, brows raised, and said not one word.

She had the grace to blush.

"Very well," she said gruffly, "I'll admit that particular thesis is rather unlikely. But I would remind you that Mr. Elsworth has something else in common with D. D. Home. His sitters have included the most exclusive people in London."

"I have news for you, madam. It has been my experience that the exclusive sort are just as gullible as everyone else."

"They say the queen herself requested a séance after Prince Albert died."

"Yes, I have heard that gossip." He guided her down the steps. "Unfortunately, grief-stricken people, no matter their rank, are notoriously easy victims for those who would take advantage of them."

"I do not know why I even bother to try to hold a logical discussion on psychical research with you. It is obvious that your skeptical opinion has been set in granite."

"That is not true." He angled her across the street toward his carriage, a dark, unadorned vehicle that could easily be mistaken for an anonymous cab. Because the vehicle did not draw attention on the street, he preferred to use it on the occasions when he elected not to walk to his destination. "As it happens I am very eager to discuss the psychical talents of one particular individual."

"And who might that person be?" she asked, looking quite wary.

"Why, you, of course, Mrs. Fordyce. I cannot wait to hear all of the details concerning the demonstration of psychical powers that you gave at Mrs. Hughes's tea."

Durward Reed waited until the pair had disappeared through the front doors of Wintersett House before he turned back to his companion.

He did not care for Julian Elsworth. With his aristocratic airs, cold intelligence and strange psychical talents, the man made him nervous. There were times when he was convinced that Elsworth privately held him in contempt. But there was no denying that, with his entrée into Society, Elsworth had brought a great deal of important attention and credibility to Wintersett House.

"The more Mrs. Fordyce denies her own gifts, the more I am convinced that she does indeed possess them," Durward mused aloud. "I must find a way to overcome her natural, entirely proper feminine qualms and convince her that she could make a tremendous contribution to the field of psychical research."

Elsworth shrugged. "She makes her living as a writer, not a medium. If you want to gain her attention, I suggest you offer her a contract for one of her novels."

Durward was briefly struck dumb by the cleverness of the suggestion.

"Good lord, man," he said when he could find his voice, "that is a brilliant notion. If I published her next book in *New Dawn*, I could attract an enormous number of new readers and a great deal of attention to the field. I must give this some close thought."

Inspired, he rushed off toward his office to ponder the details of the plan that was already taking shape in his mind.

No doubt about it, Elsworth was an enormous asset, even if he was decidedly unnerving.

CHAPTER
EIGHT

"It was all a great misunderstanding," Caroline said, looking both annoyed and resigned. "My so-called demonstration of psychical powers was meant to be nothing more than an amusing entertainment for Mrs. Hughes and her guests."

"An entertainment?"

"My aunts play cards with Mrs. Hughes and her friends several times a week. They asked me to stage the performance as a surprise. Emma and Milly were aware that in the course of my recent research, I had learned some of the tricks used by those who profess to possess psychical powers. They thought the ladies would enjoy a demonstration of how the practitioners achieve their effects."

"Mrs. Hughes, I gather, took your parlor tricks seriously?"

"I'm afraid so," she said. "It transpired that she has friends who are active in the Society for Psychical Investigations. One of them, in turn, spoke with a correspondent for the *Flying Intelligencer*." She widened her hands, palms up. "One thing led to another and the next thing I knew there was an item in the paper. It was all rather awkward, to say the least."

"Typical sensation journalism. Very few facts embedded amid a vast amount of melodramatic fiction."

She wrinkled her nose. "I will admit that at times the press does not always report events with the accuracy one would like." She broke off, glancing around with an air of abrupt concern. "Where are we going? I must return to Corley Lane. I have several more pages to complete today."

"I will see you home in my carriage, Mrs. Fordyce."

"Oh." She hesitated, looking taken aback, as though the notion of allowing him to escort her back to Corley Lane had disconcerted her.

Across the way, his coachman, Ned, saw them approaching. He jumped down from the box to open the door of the vehicle.

Caroline appeared to come to a decision. When they reached the far side of the street, she halted near the carriage.

"Thank you, Mr. Hardesty, but I took a hackney cab to Wintersett House today. I intend to return home in the same manner."

Her unwillingness to get into his carriage annoyed him more than he wanted to admit. He cast about for a lure he could use to entice her into the vehicle.

"Very well, Mrs. Fordyce, you must do as you please," he said, politely regretful. "I had hoped to take the opportunity to discuss our observations of Irene Toller's performance today while they are still fresh in our minds, but if you insist on returning home on foot —"

She looked startled. "You wanted to compare notes?"

"Yes. It had occurred to me that together we might come up with some conclusions that could well elude either of us independently."

Excitement sparkled in her eyes. "I see. I hadn't considered that possibility."

"However, if you do not wish to accompany me, I certainly understand. I realize that our association did not get off to a promising start. My fault entirely."

"Hmm." She glanced at the waiting carriage with an uneasy expression.

She could not have made it more plain that she did not trust him. He wondered if she would be equally reluctant to join Julian Elsworth in a carriage.

He tried another approach.

"Surely it is not gossip you fear, Mrs. Fordyce," he said dryly. "You are, after all, a respectable widow, not an unwed young lady who must avoid being seen getting into a carriage with a gentleman who is not her intended."

To his surprise the small taunt had a rather startling reaction. Caroline's hand tightened almost violently around the handle of the parasol.

"I am well aware of the dictates of propriety," she said coldly.

"Of course. Then may I ask where the problem lies?"

"It lies with the fact that I do not know precisely who you are, sir."

"I told you, my name is Hardesty. Adam Hardesty."

"Why should I believe that is your real name any more than Grove was?"

He reached into his pocket and withdrew a small white piece of pasteboard neatly imprinted with his name. "My card, Mrs. Fordyce."

She examined the card, unimpressed. "Calling cards can be forged."

She handed the card back to him as though it were a piece of trash. For the first time in a long while he felt his temper heat.

"I do not mean to give offense, madam," he said evenly, "but this coyness is a bit overdone, if you don't mind my saying so. You are, after all, an author of sensation novels."

"What of it?"

"Everyone knows what that means."

"Indeed? And just what does it imply about me personally, Mr. Hardesty?"

It occurred to him that he had painted himself into a very small corner. This sort of thing rarely happened to him in his dealings with women.

"It means that you write stories that rely upon a great deal of, well, *sensation*," he said, belatedly cautious.

"What is wrong with that?"

He gave the street a quick survey, making certain that there was no one near enough to overhear the deteriorating conversation. The last thing he wanted was a public scene.

"It is a fact that sensation novelists are noted for writing plots that involve what can only be termed extremely worldly subjects," he said in low tones.

"How would you know that, sir? You have made it clear that you don't read that sort of thing."

"True. But I did happen to peruse the most recent chapter of *The Mysterious Gentleman*. In that single episode there were unmistakable references to adultery, illicit love affairs, both a runaway marriage and a runaway carriage, and a murder. Clearly your plots rely on one sensation after another."

She gave him a steely smile. "I am impressed with your newfound knowledge of the genre, sir. But perhaps you should read a few more chapters before you make judgments about the author."

"There is no need to finish the story. It is obvious that Edmund Drake is going to meet a very unpleasant end. My uncle and my sister assure me that you are noted for bringing your villains to dreadful ends."

Caroline's expression underwent a sea change. "Your sister and your uncle read my work?"

"I'm afraid so."

"I see." She was delighted by that news. "It is always a great pleasure to learn that someone enjoys my stories."

"Yes, well, as I was saying —"

"I quite understand now why you are so concerned about the respectability of my novels." She smiled warmly. "Naturally you do not wish your sister to be exposed to inappropriate subjects. Rest assured that although my themes and plots are often mature in nature, my characters are suitably rewarded or punished depending upon the morality of their actions."

"That does not bode well for Edmund Drake."

"There is no need to be concerned about him. He is the villain, after all. Bear in mind that my heroes always save the day and marry the heroine."

He planted one hand against the side of the carriage and leaned over her just far enough to cast her into his shadow. "Tell me, Mrs. Fordyce, have you ever gotten your heroes and villains mixed up?"

"Never, sir. The difference between a hero and a villain has always been perfectly obvious to me."

He could see that there was not so much as a sliver of doubt in her mind on that score. Drake was doomed.

"How fortunate for you, madam," he said.

Understanding lit her eyes. "Oh, dear. You are taking this personally because I told you that I intended to use you as a model for the character of Edmund Drake." She gave him a contrite smile. "My apologies. I did not mean to insult you or injure your feelings, sir."

What in blazes was he doing standing here arguing about her villains and her heroes?

"Do not concern yourself with my feelings, madam. I assure you, they have endured far worse abuse." He straightened and took his hand off the side of the vehicle. "You can make amends by allowing me to see you safely home."

"Well —"

"If you still have doubts about my identity, Ned here can vouch for me."

Ned had been standing patiently beside the open carriage door, trying very hard to look as if he was not listening to the unusual conversation. He started violently at the sound of his name.

"Sir?"

"Please assure Mrs. Fordyce that my name is Adam Hardesty and that I am considered, by and large, to be a respectable gentleman who is not in the habit of kidnapping ladies and carrying them off in my carriage for immoral purposes."

Ned's jaw dropped in visible shock. He swallowed quickly and pulled himself together with an obvious effort.

"I can vouch for Mr. Hardesty here, ma'am," he said with touching sincerity. "Driven for him for years. Ye've nothing to fear from him and that's a fact."

Caroline smiled. "I have your word on that, Ned?"

"Aye, ma'am. And may I say, Mrs. Fordyce, that I find your new novel even more thrilling than the last one. The business with the fire and the rescue of little Miss Ann from the flames was very exciting. So was the bit with the murder."

Caroline glowed. "Why, thank you, Ned."

"It was a stroke of genius to keep Edmund Drake lurking about in the shadows, so to speak, until this new chapter. Very mysterious, he is."

Caroline blushed happily and walked to the steps that Ned had set down in front of the carriage door. "You are very kind to say so."

Ned grinned and handed her up into the vehicle. "I can't wait to see what happens to that rotten-hearted bloke."

Caroline laughed lightly. "I am working out his fate this very week, Ned."

Adam watched her bend elegantly at the waist to enter the carriage. The ridiculous green and gold velvet bow twitched enticingly and then vanished into the shadows.

Perhaps he ought to start taking lessons from Ned, he thought, climbing in behind Caroline. His coachman had had no difficulty whatsoever persuading her to get into the carriage. Hero material, no doubt.

CHAPTER
NINE

She had done it, Caroline thought, rather dazed by her own boldness. She had taken advantage of her status as a widow to climb into the carriage, and now she was sitting here sharing the vehicle's intimate confines with the most fascinating man she had ever met in her life.

It was unfortunate that the topic of conversation was to be murder.

She gave Adam an inquiring look, trying to act blasé, as though she was accustomed to riding through the streets of London with a gentleman.

"The rumors were correct, it seems," Adam said. He lounged in the corner, one leg outstretched, an arm braced on the window frame. "There was certainly no love lost between Irene Toller and Elizabeth Delmont."

"No, indeed." Caroline forced herself to concentrate on what she had observed at the demonstration. "Mrs. Toller made no secret of the fact that she feels justice was done."

Adam raised a brow. "I doubt if there was any justice involved, but regardless of the motive, Mrs. Delmont's skull was not crushed by manifestations from the Other Side. I cannot imagine that any self-respecting spirit would use something as mundane as a fireplace poker to commit murder."

Caroline shuddered. "I agree. That sort of violence is all too human, is it not?"

He meditated on the busy street scene. "Toller obviously possesses strong feelings about her dead rival. She may know something of the murder."

"It did occur to me that Mrs. Toller may have killed Mrs. Delmont. Professional rivalry is no doubt a very powerful motivation."

"I do not deny that." His eyes tightened faintly at the corners. "But the thing that interests me the most at the moment was what was not reported in the press."

"Did you see the papers this morning? They covered the crime in great detail. They all mentioned the overturned furniture and the watch that was stopped at midnight."

"Those were the least of the bizarre elements I found at the scene," he said quietly.

"I beg your pardon?"

"When I found Elizabeth Delmont, she was lying faceup on the carpet of her séance room. Someone, presumably the killer, had placed a wedding veil over her face. It was soaked with her blood."

She stared at him, shocked. "Good heavens."

"In addition, a black enameled mourning brooch had been left on the bodice of Delmont's gown. On the reverse side of the brooch there was a twist of blond hair and a small photograph of a young, fair-haired woman dressed as a bride."

102

"You say the brooch was placed on Mrs. Delmont's person? Not pinned to her gown?"

He shook his head. "It appeared to have been positioned very carefully on the body, just as the veil was."

Caroline folded her arms, hugging herself against the strange chill that his words had sent through her. "Bizarre is, indeed, the right word. The veil and the mourning brooch imply a very personal sort of murder. It certainly does not sound like the work of a housebreaker or a burglar."

"Nor does it sound like the actions of someone who killed Delmont simply to acquire the diary," he admitted, obviously reluctant to abandon that notion. "I cannot envision a potential blackmailer taking the trouble to create such a dramatic scene."

"Unless he wished to throw the police off the trail by making the murder appear to be the work of someone who had a personal reason for killing Elizabeth Delmont," she suggested.

He gave her a long, cool, assessing look. "That, Mrs. Fordyce, is a very interesting possibility. Distraction is the oldest trick in the world. Someone might well have stolen the diary and then deliberately left a variety of clues pointing in another direction. But if that is the case, why was there no mention of them in the papers?"

"Your problem would seem to be even more complicated than it appeared at the start. What do you intend to do next?"

"I would very much like to learn more about Irene Toller. Her intense dislike of Delmont makes her an

103

excellent suspect, to my way of thinking. But I doubt that she will respond helpfully to direct questions, especially if she has something to hide."

"You believe that she would lie to you?"

"I am more concerned that she will pack her bags and disappear if she thinks that she has been found out," he said. "I do not want to scare her off until I know for certain whether or not she is involved in this affair."

"What will you do?"

"If she is the one who killed Elizabeth Delmont and stole the diary, it is likely that she has the journal hidden somewhere in her house," he mused. "I believe my next step is to conduct a search of the premises."

She unfolded her arms very quickly. "You intend to break into her house? Good heavens, you cannot take such a risk, sir. If she has already killed once, she will not hesitate to do so again."

He appeared bemused by her protest. Then a strangely quizzical expression darkened his eyes. "Are you worried about my safety, Mrs. Fordyce?"

"I am merely trying to inject some common sense into your plan."

"A pity. For a moment, I dared to entertain the hope that you were concerned for my well-being."

"I do not appreciate being teased, Mr. Hardesty. Now, then, if you are determined upon this venture, would it not make more sense to at least learn something about the plan of the house before you break into it? Having some prior knowledge of that sort would enable you to conduct a more efficient search."

104

He gave her a speculative look. "What do you suggest?"

"You could schedule a séance," she said, thinking quickly. "Mrs. Toller made it obvious today that she was attempting to use her public demonstrations to promote her private business."

"What an imaginative notion." His brows rose. "Brilliant, in fact. Entering the house for the purpose of a séance would not only give me an opportunity to look around, it might provide me with other information about Toller as well. Do you know, something tells me that having a sensation novelist for a consultant in this affair is going to prove extremely useful."

His slow smile was as sensual and thrillingly intimate as it was unexpected. It transformed his appearance, giving her a brief glimpse of the complex man beneath the enigmatic façade that he presented to the world.

It also flustered her. She struggled to regain her composure.

"I must accompany you, of course," she said, trying to ignore the fluttery sensations in her stomach.

His smile faded as quickly as it had appeared. The remote, cryptic expression returned.

"I do not think that will be necessary."

"I disagree, sir," she said as forcefully as she could manage. "My presence will help allay any suspicions Mrs. Toller might have."

"What suspicions could she possibly entertain? Mrs. Toller and I have never met. Even if she does possess the diary and even if she is aware that a gentleman named Adam Hardesty is a potential target for blackmail, how could she recognize me as her intended victim?"

"She might have seen you at the demonstration today."

He moved one hand in an uninterested motion. "If she did, she will only know me as Mr. Grove, just as Reed and Elsworth do. Irene Toller is in the business of giving séances. I will be just another client as far as she is concerned."

Obviously she would have to come up with another argument to convince him that he must include her in his plan. She had no intention of allowing him to pursue his inquiries without her. *Tread cautiously*, she warned herself. Adam Hardesty would not appreciate any attempts to manipulate him. But manipulate him, she must.

She cleared her throat. "No offense, sir, but there is, shall we say, a certain aspect about you that might well make Mrs. Toller . . ." She paused, searching for a diplomatic word to finish the sentence. None came to mind. "Uneasy."

His jaw hardened. "Why the devil should I make her uneasy?"

She thought about taking out the small mirror in her pocket and letting him have a look at his fierce expression, but in the next moment, she decided against that tactic. He was unlikely to see what others saw when they looked at him.

Stick with logic and reason, she thought. Those were the tools she must employ if she hoped to prod Adam Hardesty into doing what she wanted him to do.

106

"If Irene Toller does, indeed, possess some knowledge of the murder, she will be on her guard," she said, striving for patience. "If, on the other hand, she is innocent of any knowledge of the crime, the murder of another medium will likely have made her quite nervous. I would not be surprised if she refuses all requests for sittings from strangers for a time. I would, if I were in her shoes."

"Would you?"

"Most certainly," she assured him.

He did not bother to conceal his skepticism of that statement. Nevertheless, she could see that he was giving her words some close thought.

"Are you acquainted with Toller?" he asked finally.

She was making progress, she told herself.

"We have not been introduced but I'm sure she will know who I am because I have been in Wintersett House several times recently to conduct my research. As you just witnessed in the case of Mr. Reed and Mr. Elsworth, my activities are no secret among the members of the Society for Psychical Investigations."

There was a wry edge to the curve of his mouth. "In other words, your name might be just what I need for an entrée to Irene Toller's house; is that it?"

"I do not think that it would seem odd to her if I requested a sitting. In fact, I might very well have done so in the normal course of events."

He contemplated that for a moment longer. Then he straightened in his seat and leaned forward, resting his forearms on his thighs.

"Very well, Mrs. Fordyce," he said in his midnight voice. "If you can arrange a séance with Irene Toller, we shall attend it together."

Relieved at having achieved her objective, she gave him an approving smile. "I will send a note to Mrs. Toller immediately. I'm sure there will be no difficulty."

"Will I be allowed to hold your hand?" he asked.

She froze. "I beg your pardon?"

He drew the curtains closed across the carriage windows with a few swift, efficient motions, plunging the interior into intimate shadow. He reached out and caught hold of her hand.

"I was under the impression that sitters at a séance often join hands." His fingers tightened gently around hers. "Something to do with strengthening or centering the power of the medium, I believe."

She looked down at his large, strong fingers and discovered that she could scarcely breathe. He was so very close.

"Yes, well, that is the usual explanation," she managed. "There are some who claim that mediums insist that everyone hold hands because that way a skeptical sitter is less likely to strike a light at an inopportune time or try to grab a spirit manifestation."

"And thereby expose the medium's tricks," he concluded.

"Precisely."

"I shall look forward to holding your hand at the séance, Mrs. Fordyce."

She could not move. She did not want to move.

108

He held her transfixed with some invisible force while he slowly, deliberately raised her hand to his mouth. Turning her fingers palm up, he eased the green glove down just far enough to expose the exquisitely sensitive inside of her wrist.

She stopped breathing altogether.

When he kissed the place where her pulse beat so swiftly, she thought she would fall apart into a million tiny fireworks.

"Mr. Hardesty," she whispered.

He raised his head but he did not release her hand. "Call me Adam."

"Adam." She tasted the name on her tongue and discovered for the first time in her life the exotic flavors of fire and ice.

He smiled as though the sound of his name on her lips pleased him. Then he leaned a little closer. She realized with shock that he was going to kiss her right on her mouth. Before she could deal with the monumental implications of the situation, his lips closed over hers and the world around her dissolved into mist.

A euphoric feeling welled up inside her; delight, excitement, curiosity and anticipation mingled, making her light-headed. Dazzled, she put her hands on his shoulders to brace herself. When she touched him, he made a harsh, urgent sound deep in his throat, gripped her shoulders and pulled her hard against his chest.

He deepened the kiss until she could no longer think, until she was lost amid a tumult of powerful sensations.

109

The well-sprung carriage clattered to a halt. Adam reluctantly eased her away from him, sat back against the cushions and opened the curtains.

"We appear to have arrived at your address." He gave her a heart-stoppingly intimate look. "I can only regret that the journey did not take a good deal longer."

She did not know what to say to that so she looked out the window instead. Two figures stood on the doorstep. They, in turn, were staring at her in open-mouthed astonishment.

She was instantly jolted back to reality.

"Oh, dear," she murmured. "This may prove to be a trifle difficult for you, sir."

Adam studied the pair on the step. "Your aunts, I presume?"

"I'm afraid so."

He reached for the door handle. "I told you that I am considered to be quite respectable. Surely they will not object to me bringing you home."

"The problem is that they will insist on inviting you in for a cup of tea."

"Excellent. I could do with a cup of tea."

"Wait, you don't understand," she said. "It won't be just the tea. There will be questions. A lot of them."

He smiled his mysterious smile and got out of the vehicle. "I don't mind a few questions," he said. "As it happens, I have a few of my own."

CHAPTER
TEN

Some twenty minutes later she was still wondering uneasily what Adam had meant by that last cryptic remark. She studied him covertly, uncertain of his mood. He should have been showing signs of impatience, she thought, but instead he seemed to have made himself quite comfortable in the little parlor at Number 22 Corley Lane.

He was seated in an armchair, legs stretched out in front of him, one ankle stacked casually on top of the other. On the table beside him there was a half-finished cup of tea and a plate of Mrs. Plummer's pastries. He had made great inroads on the latter.

"I'm sure your niece has explained to you both that I believe that Elizabeth Delmont was in possession of a certain diary at the time of her death," he said around a mouthful of jam tart.

Milly and Emma had been polite but wary at the start of the conversation. However they appeared to be falling very quickly under Adam's spell.

"Yes," Milly said. "Caroline told us about the diary."

Emma frowned. "I will admit that we are all quite curious about the contents."

"Naturally." Adam swallowed the last of his tart. "I regret to say that I cannot satisfy your curiosity entirely. I'm sure you will understand when I tell you that the diary contains some information of an extremely personal nature about other people of whom I happen to be very fond."

"How did you come to discover that Mrs. Delmont was in possession of the diary?" Caroline said.

He hesitated briefly. She knew he was deciding just how much to tell them.

"A fortnight ago I received word of the death of an old friend named Maud Gatley," he said. "I was saddened by the loss, but the news was not unexpected. Maud had been addicted to opium for a long time. In recent years the drug had taken control of her life. In the end, it killed her."

"How tragic," Milly whispered.

"A few days later I received a blackmail note threatening to reveal the contents of Maud's diary unless I left a very large sum of money in a certain location." Adam reached for another tart. "Until that moment, I had not realized that Maud had kept a journal. I immediately made some inquiries and soon discovered that what few possessions she had left behind had been claimed by a cousin."

"You tracked down the cousin?" Emma asked.

"Yes. Discovering that Maud had a relative was something of a surprise, too. She had always claimed that she had no family."

"Amazing how long-lost relations emerge from the woodwork when a person dies and leaves behind a few items of value," Emma said dryly.

Adam was amused. "Yes. In any event, I realized that, given the timing of events, the unknown cousin had no doubt found the diary among Maud's things, read it, saw the potential for profit and fired off the anonymous extortion note. I made a few more inquiries and identified Elizabeth Delmont as the woman who had come to Maud's lodgings and taken away what little was there."

"That was an excellent piece of detective work, sir," Milly said, impressed.

He reached for his tea. "Actually, it was not particularly complicated at all. A few questions here and there and I soon had an address in Hamsey Street."

He spoke casually, as though anyone could have achieved similar results, Caroline thought, but she knew that was not true. Those who moved in Adam Hardesty's circles did not associate with the Elizabeth Delmonts of this world. Judging by the few possessions she had left behind, the opium-addicted Maud had occupied an even lower rung on the social ladder. It was highly unlikely that the average gentleman in Society would have the sort of connections required to trace a link between someone like Maud and her cousin so quickly.

The more she learned of Adam, the more mysterious he became.

"Unfortunately, by the time I arrived on Delmont's doorstep to confront her the other night, she was dead and the diary was gone." He glanced at Caroline. "As you know, one thing led to another and that was how I happened to turn up here."

"Caroline explained about the list of sitters that you found," Milly said. "Her name was on it."

Adam switched his attention back to her. "I was soon satisfied that she had nothing to do with the affair and said as much to her." He drank some tea and lowered the cup. "Imagine my surprise when I walked into the lecture hall at Wintersett House today and saw that she had chosen to attend Irene Toller's demonstration of spirit writing."

Milly and Emma looked at Caroline.

"Not being a great believer in coincidences," Adam added, "I realized immediately that she had decided to conduct her own investigation. I do not feel that it is at all necessary, but I am under the impression that I cannot persuade her to leave this business to me."

Emma frowned. "I fear the three of us have excellent reasons for being extremely cautious about the potential for scandal, sir."

"Indeed," Milly said. "You appear to be sincere, Mr. Hardesty, and I believe you when you say that you no longer harbor any suspicions about Caroline's connection to the murder or the stolen diary. But what if you change your mind?"

"I am highly unlikely to do that." He turned back to Caroline with a nerve-shattering gaze. "Unless, of course, there is something you have not yet told me about this situation."

The teacup in her hand rattled gently against the saucer. She set both down very quickly and tried to organize her thoughts. He wanted some explanation for her stubborn refusal to step aside and leave the field to him. She sensed that he would not leave the matter alone until he was satisfied. She decided to risk giving him part of the truth but not all of it. The secrets were hers, she reminded herself. He did not have the right to demand all of them.

"I will be blunt, sir," she said, raising her chin. "I was involved in an extremely unpleasant scandal three years ago in, uh, Bath. The three of us simply cannot afford another such experience. It might well prove to be disastrous for my career. My aunts and I are dependent on the income from my writing."

"I see."

As far as she could tell, he had no reaction whatsoever to the news of her scandalous past. Of course, he did not know the precise nature of the sensation, she reminded herself. He no doubt assumed that she had been involved in some sort of illicit liaison. As a man of the world, he could overlook that sort of indiscretion. He considered her an experienced widow, after all. She had no intention of disabusing him of that notion.

If he were to learn the details of the events that had very nearly got her killed and had made it necessary for her to invent a new identity for herself, however, he might be far less inclined to view her in an innocent light.

She drew herself up determinedly. "I intend to remain involved in this matter until you have found that diary, sir. That is the only way I can look out for the best interests of my aunts and myself."

He contemplated the tips of his shoes for a moment before meeting her eyes. "Will it satisfy you if I promise to keep you informed of the progress of my inquiries?"

"No," she said. "I'm afraid not."

He gave her an unreadable smile. "You do not trust me, do you?"

She flushed. "It is not that," she assured him quickly. Too quickly, she realized.

"Yes, it is exactly that." He did not appear offended. "But I will not quarrel with you over the matter. If I were in your place, I too would hesitate to put my trust in a person whom I did not know well."

That was probably a veiled way of reminding her that he knew no more about her character than she did about his. Neither of them had any reason to trust the other.

Emma squared her already very straight shoulders. "We appreciate your understanding, sir."

He inclined his head and helped himself to another tart.

Milly smiled cheerfully. "Well, I'm glad that much is settled. I believe you will find Caroline's assistance quite helpful, sir. The world of psychical research is a difficult one for outsiders to penetrate. Caroline has become accepted within it, however, and knowledge of the community of mediums and the Society of Psychical Investigations will no doubt prove invaluable to you."

"At the very least, she can save you a great deal of time and make your investigations more efficient," Emma said.

Adam smiled his enigmatic smile. "It seems we are going to be associates in this affair, Caroline."

CHAPTER
ELEVEN

It was sheer luck that he had recognized Adam Hardesty today. Bloody damned luck, that was all.

But then his luck had always been better than that of most other men, Julian Elsworth thought. Or at least, it had been until recently.

He unknotted his silk tie, poured himself a restorative dose of brandy and dropped into the chair near the hearth. Another shudder went through him. He took a long swallow of the spirits to suppress it.

If not for that casual encounter the other evening with a patron who happened to be a member of one of Hardesty's clubs, a man who had pointed out Hardesty as they were leaving the theater, he would never have known that the formidable-looking Mr. Grove was flying under false colors this afternoon.

The questions came fast and furiously. Why was Hardesty in the company of the very attractive Mrs. Fordyce? Why had he used a name that was not his own? Why had he attended Irene Toller's demonstration of the planchette?

But there was only one logical answer. He could not escape it. Hardesty was on his trail. Unless he could be turned aside, it was only a matter of time before he stumbled onto certain secrets.

Julian closed his eyes and leaned his head against the back of the chair, summoning up an image of the death scene. So much blood. And the terrible odor of it all. Who would have thought that murder would have been such a messy business?

He opened his eyes and looked at his expensively furnished lodgings. After all these years he was finally where he deserved to be, mingling with the wealthy and the powerful in the glittering realm of Society. It was the world that should have been his from birth but that had been denied him because his highborn father had cast an inconveniently pregnant governess out into the streets.

He had worked hard to achieve the heritage that should have been his from the start, Julian thought. Damned if he would let Hardesty bring his carefully constructed life tumbling down around his ears.

CHAPTER
TWELVE

An hour later Adam walked into his study and sat down behind the large mahogany desk. His thoughts were consumed with Caroline. She was keeping secrets, he reflected. Fair enough. He understood the necessity. He held some closely guarded secrets of his own.

He admired her determination and tenacity. He had been right in his initial assessment of her character. She was a lady of resolute spirit.

Nevertheless, he did not like dealing with the unknown. In his experience, it never failed to lead to complications.

A knock sounded on the door.

"Enter."

Morton appeared in the opening. "Mr. Filby to see you, sir."

"Thank you, Morton. Please send him in."

Harold Filby — plump, bespectacled and fashionably attired in checkered trousers, a striped waistcoat and a dashing, cutaway morning coat — bustled into the room.

Harold dressed as well as — some would say a good deal more fashionably than — his employer. But then, Adam mused, when one hired a man to keep one's confidences, one paid him enough to ensure that he was inclined to do so.

Harold had served as Adam's man of business for more than six years. He could keep a secret.

"I received your message and came immediately, sir," Harold said.

"I appreciate your punctuality, as always. Please sit down."

Harold lowered himself into the chair directly across from the desk, adjusted his glasses and took out a small notebook and pencil.

"You said the matter was urgent, sir?" he prompted.

"I want you to leave immediately for Bath." Adam clasped his hands on the desk. "There you will make some extremely discreet inquiries concerning a certain scandal that took place there some three years past."

Harold made notes. "These inquiries concern a business venture, I assume?"

"No, they are of a more personal and private nature. I want you to discover whatever you can about a lady named Caroline Fordyce."

"Mrs. Fordyce?" Harold's head came up swiftly. "Would that by any chance be the author, sir? The Mrs. Fordyce whose novels are serialized in the *Flying Intelligencer*?"

A sense of resignation settled on Adam. "I appear to be the only person in all of London who was not familiar with her work until quite recently."

"Very exciting stuff," Harold enthused. "Certainly keeps one guessing. Her latest is her most thrilling yet, as far as I am concerned. It is called *The Mysterious Gentleman*."

"Yes, I know." Adam flexed his hands and deliberately relinked his fingers. "I believe the villain's name is Edmund Drake."

"Ah, I see you are following the story, sir. We haven't seen much of Edmund Drake yet but it's plain that he's a very menacing sort. Safe to say that he'll come to a nasty end, just like Mrs. Fordyce's other villains."

Adam tried and failed to suppress his morbid curiosity. "Doesn't the fact that you already know the identity of the villain and that he will meet with an unpleasant fate take all of the surprise and astonishment out of the story? What is the purpose of reading a novel if one knows the ending before one turns the first page?"

Harold regarded him with acute bewilderment. Then Adam saw the light of comprehension strike.

"I take it you are not a great reader of novels, sir," Harold said, sympathy as thick as cream in every word.

"No." Adam sat back in his chair and gripped the arms. "I do not count novel reading among my vices."

"Allow me to explain, if I may. Of course one knows that in a sensation novel, the villain will pay for his villainy, just as one knows that the hero and heroine will be rewarded for their good hearts and noble actions. Those things are givens, as it were. They are not the point of the business."

"Indeed? Well, what in blazes is the point?"

"Why, it is seeing how the characters arrive at their various fates that compels our attention." Harold spread his broad hands wide. "It is the series of startling incidents in the various chapters that entertains and amazes, all the twists and turns and emotional sensations. That is why one reads a novel, sir. Not to discover how it ends, but to enjoy the strange and exotic scenery along the way."

"I shall bear that in mind if I find myself tempted to read any more of Mrs. Fordyce's work." Adam narrowed his eyes. "Meanwhile, speaking of strange and exotic scenery, I think you had best go directly home and pack your bags. I want you on your way to Bath as soon as possible."

"Yes, sir." Harold got to his feet.

"Keep me advised of your progress by telegram."

CHAPTER
THIRTEEN

"I fear this may become a dangerous business for Caroline." Emma propped her slipper-clad feet on the small hassock in front of the reading chair and contemplated the cheery blaze that warmed the small parlor.

Milly lowered her book and removed her reading glasses. She was well aware that her companion had been brooding on recent events for hours. After all these years together, she had learned that she had to allow Emma time to digest things.

"I do not think you need to be overly concerned about Caroline's safety." She put her glasses on the table. "I am quite certain that Mr. Hardesty will take excellent care of her."

"But who will protect Caroline from Mr. Hardesty?" Emma asked in foreboding tones.

Milly opened her mouth to reply and then found herself hesitating. Her usual inclination was to take the most optimistic view of a situation. Emma, of course, could be counted on to take the opposite approach. In most cases they balanced each other very well.

Her first instinct was to defend Hardesty. She had respected him on sight and her intuition told her that he could be trusted. But what did she really know about him? She was forced to admit that Emma was right to be concerned. There were risks.

"Caroline is old enough and wise enough to deal with the likes of Adam Hardesty," she said, trying to sound assured. "It is not as if she is unaware of the dangers. After what happened three years ago, she knows she must be cautious."

"I'm not so certain of that. Did you see the way those two looked at each other this afternoon?"

Milly sighed. "Yes, I did."

"There was so much electrical energy swirling between them that it was a wonder we did not have a miniature thunderstorm right here in the middle of the parlor."

"Indeed."

Emma looked at her. "You know as well as I do that an intimate connection with a gentleman such as Mr. Hardesty can only end in misery for Caroline. Men of power and property marry for purposes of acquiring more power and property. Hardesty can look much higher than Caroline when he selects a wife, and he will most certainly do so. The most she can expect from him is a discreet affair."

Milly pondered her response very carefully. This was, after all, thorny ground.

"Would that be such a terrible fate?" she ventured finally.

Emma's face went taut. "How can you even ask such a question? It would be a disaster."

"You are thinking of your sister," Milly said gently. "But let us speak plainly here. Caroline is not her mother. Her temperament is quite different. We have both known her since she was in the cradle. Surely you do not imagine for a moment that she is the sort who would take her own life merely because a lover tossed her aside."

Emma closed her eyes. "I do not want to see Caroline hurt."

"We cannot protect her from that kind of pain. Sooner or later every woman must learn to deal with it. That is the way of the world."

"I know. Nevertheless —"

"Hear me out." Milly rose from the sofa and went to stand beside Emma's chair. She put her hand on her companion's shoulder. "When we took on the task of raising Caroline after your sister died, we vowed that we would teach her to be a strong and independent woman. To that end we gave her a fine education. We have taught her to think and reason logically and to manage her finances. We have made certain that she understands that she need not wed unless it pleases her to do so. Indeed, she has had at least two offers that we know of and she let them both go past."

"Because she was not in love," Emma burst out. She clasped her hands very tightly together on her lap. "That is the point, Milly. What if this time she loses her heart to a man who will never offer marriage?"

"She is no longer a girl. She has not been one for some time. She can look after herself. Only consider what she has accomplished. In spite of the dreadful

126

setback three years ago, she has succeeded in crafting a profitable career for herself. She would prefer to deal with the difficulties of making her own way in the world rather than be miserable in a loveless marriage. Any woman capable of arriving at that decision can certainly decide for herself whether or not to take the risk of having an affair with a man who is unlikely to marry her."

Emma smiled wearily and raised a hand to place it over Milly's fingers. "You are right of course, dear Milly. You usually are in such matters. But sometimes when I look at Caroline I can only think of what happened to Beatrice and of how I failed to protect her. I promised myself that I would not fail her daughter."

"We have discussed this often enough in the past. I can only repeat what I have said countless times before. There was nothing you could have done to save Beatrice. And you most certainly have not failed Caroline. She is the intelligent, sensible, high-spirited woman she is today because of you. She is your daughter in every way that matters, Emma."

Emma squeezed Milly's fingers. "I did not raise her alone. You were there at every step along the way. She is as much your daughter as she is mine."

They watched the fire for a while. There was no need to talk. They had been together a long time. They could read each other's thoughts.

CHAPTER
FOURTEEN

The response to the request for a séance came in a very speedy fashion the following morning.

Caroline was still at breakfast with Emma and Milly. All three of them were attired in their new dressing gowns. The fashion for wearing the comfortable, loose-fitting garments down to breakfast had arrived recently from France and was rapidly being adopted by women at every level of society. The ladies at 22 Corley Lane had been among the first to take up the style.

The gowns were modest enough but they were considered extremely daring because they were *loose-fitting*. Critics raged against the trend, seeing it as a harbinger of yet another decline in morals. Some went so far as to warn that husbands would soon lose interest in their wives' charms if those charms were carelessly draped in *loose-fitting* garments every morning at breakfast.

Few women paid much attention to such ominous prognostications. Certainly no one in this household, where there was a noticeable lack of husbands, cared a jot for the critics' opinions, Caroline thought. Given the discomfort of the stiff, tightly-laced corsets and bodices of modern dresses, not to mention the sheer weight of the heavy materials used in them, no female in her right mind was eager to don one any earlier in the day than necessary.

Caroline put down her fork and opened the message from Irene Toller.

"Ah-hah." She waved the note aloft in triumph. "I knew it would not take long to receive an appointment for a sitting. Did I not tell you that Mrs. Toller was eager for new business?"

Milly put down her teacup. "What does she say, dear?"

Caroline read the note aloud.

Dear Mrs. Fordyce:

Regarding your request to experience a proper séance, I am delighted to inform you that I will be conducting one this very evening at nine o'clock. I have room for two additional sitters. You and your assistant are welcome to attend. I assure you that you will not be disappointed.

Yrs. very truly,
I. Toller

P.S. My sitting fees are itemized below. Payment is due before the séance begins.

Emma put down her spoon very slowly. "Promise us that you will be careful tonight, Caroline. I am still quite apprehensive about this venture that you and Mr. Hardesty have undertaken."

"They will both be fine," Milly assured her cheerfully. "What can go wrong at a séance?" She turned back to Caroline. "Emma and I are engaged to attend the theater with Mrs. Hughes this evening. Afterward we will no doubt play cards until all hours. You will be sound asleep, I'm sure, by the time we get home. But tomorrow we will want to hear every single detail concerning Mrs. Toller's performance."

"Never fear," Caroline said. "I will take notes."

Emma frowned. "What was that business about your assistant? Is that how you identified Mr. Hardesty in your message to Mrs. Toller?"

"Yes." Caroline smiled, pleased with her creative solution to the problem of Adam. "I introduced myself as the author who has been making observations at Wintersett House and told her that I would be accompanied by my assistant. As you can see, she did not hesitate."

Milly raised her brows. "Does Mr. Hardesty know that you have described him as such?"

"Not yet," Caroline said. "I will explain it to him on the way to the séance this evening."

"Now that promises to be a most entertaining conversation," Milly said dryly. "A pity I will not be there to hear it."

Caroline reached for a slice of toast. "Why do you say that?"

"Something tells me that Adam Hardesty is not accustomed to taking orders from anyone."

★   ★   ★

130

At eight-thirty that evening Adam followed Caroline into the carriage and took the seat across from her.

"You told Irene Toller that I was your *what?*"

"My assistant," she repeated calmly. "What else did you expect me to say? I did not think it wise to claim you as a distant relation for fear that we might stumble over some casual inquiry concerning our pasts and give ourselves away."

"Surely you could have come up with a more elevated position for me."

"I was afraid that any other explanation of your presence might convey the impression that you and I shared an acquaintance of an, uh, intimate nature." She smiled very brightly. "I certainly did not want to embarrass you with that sort of suggestion."

"I see." His initial reaction to the news that he had been assigned the lowly role of assistant to a writer of sensation novels had been mild exasperation tempered by wry amusement. Discovering that Caroline had gone out of her way to ensure that no one mistook him for her lover, however, had a decidedly lowering effect on his spirits.

Evidently she had not responded to that kiss in the carriage yesterday quite the same way he had. The moment of surprising passion had left him with an abiding restlessness and a sense of longing that had only grown more intense with the passing of time.

Tonight Caroline looked enchantingly mysterious in the soft golden glow of the carriage lamps, he thought. Her gown was composed of an amber-colored bodice and reddish-brown skirts. The hem of the dress pooled around her feet. A tiny confection of a hat was tilted at a provocative angle on her gleaming hair.

He suddenly wished that they were not on their way to a séance. He wanted nothing more in that moment than to be en route to some snug, secluded room where they could be alone with a warm fire and a comfortable bed.

"I'm sorry if you are offended by the role I assigned you, sir," she said briskly. "I thought it was a very clever notion."

"It was certainly inventive," he allowed.

She frowned. "You did leave the matter of arranging the details of the séance to me, if you will recall."

"It seemed reasonable at the time. In hindsight, however, I cannot help but wonder if it was a rather glaring error in judgment."

Her mouth twitched at the corners. "But surely you see that the position of assistant is the perfect cover for you. It will also ensure that you are not the object of gossip or rumor concerning your connection to me."

So she was amused by her little joke, was she?

"As I said, it was creative." He smiled coolly. "And I do appreciate your concern for my reputation. But as it happens, it was unnecessary for you to worry about embarrassing me."

"I beg your pardon?"

"It would not have caused me any loss of sleep at all if you had chosen to imply that ours was an intimate connection."

Her eyes widened. Her lips parted.

"Oh," she said.

132

Satisfied that he had made her pay with a blush, he folded his arms. "What exactly does an assistant to a writer do?"

"I have no notion whatsoever," she admitted. "I've never had one before."

"Then I shall just have to make it up as I go along, won't I?"

"Well, yes, I suppose so," she said, obviously reluctant to place too much responsibility in his hands. "Now then, regarding the séance, you do realize that the sitters are expected to follow certain rules that are understood by everyone present, do you not?"

"Let me hazard a guess concerning séance etiquette. I'll wager that no one is to question the effects produced by the medium, no matter how bizarre or outrageous they might be. Am I correct?"

"Quite correct."

"Perhaps in my role as your research assistant, I could get away with striking a light or turning over the table to examine the fittings underneath," he mused.

"Do not even consider it, sir." She gave him a quelling look. "May I remind you that we are not attending the séance so that you can have the satisfaction of exposing the medium. We will be there for the sole purpose of providing you with a close look at Mrs. Toller and the interior plan of her house."

He inclined his head. "Thank you for reminding me of my priorities in this affair."

Irene Toller's house was located on a quiet street in a modest neighborhood. Adam noted that the upstairs and most of the ground floor were dark. A pale, eerie glow shone through the decorative glass panes above the door.

"Mrs. Toller evidently does not believe in wasting money on lighting," he said to Caroline.

"Hers is a business that thrives in poor light."

The housekeeper, a middle-aged woman of short stature and compact build, answered the door. She wore a dress of some dull, black fabric that lacked any hint of luster. A white apron and a cap completed her uniform.

"This way, please," the woman said. "You are the last to arrive. The séance will begin shortly. You can pay me Mrs. Toller's fee now."

Adam caught a whiff of lavender scent. There was something vaguely familiar about the woman, he thought as he handed over the money. He did not recognize her face but he was certain that he knew her voice and the set of those sturdy shoulders.

It came to him as he followed her into the parlor. He gave Caroline a quick glance. She nodded, letting him know that she, too, recognized the woman.

Toller's housekeeper had been the widow in heavy mourning at yesterday's demonstration at Wintersett House; the one who had asked about the location of her late husband's missing shares of stock. Evidently, in addition to her traditional duties, she worked as the medium's assistant.

Adam followed Caroline into a small, over-furnished parlor. A fire warmed the hearth. A photograph of the queen dressed in mourning hung above the mantel.

134

Two of the other sitters were women of a certain age. They introduced themselves as Miss Brick and Mrs. Trent. Both were gray-haired and dressed in sensible woolen gowns.

The third person was a fidgety man of about thirty-five who gave his name as Gilbert Smith.

Smith had pale blue eyes and lank, nondescript reddish-blond hair that was almost the same color as his ruddy complexion. His coat, shirt, waistcoat and trousers were ordinary in terms of quality and cut.

None of the three so much as blinked when Adam gave his name as Mr. Grove. He was satisfied that they did not recognize him. Not that he had expected any difficulty in that regard, he thought. This was not the world he inhabited.

There was, however, a small murmur of excitement from the two ladies when Caroline was introduced.

"I am delighted to make your acquaintance, Mrs. Fordyce," Miss Brick exclaimed, animated and energetic. "Mrs. Trent and I do so enjoy your stories."

"Yes, indeed." Mrs. Trent put her hands together in delight. "That Edmund Drake is such a dreadful villain. I cannot wait to see what happens to him. Perhaps you will have him fall off his horse and tumble down a huge cliff into the sea?"

Adam noticed that Gilbert Smith had stopped toying with his walking stick. He was studying Caroline with thinly veiled interest.

"I rather like the notion of having Drake get shot by the hero, Jonathan St. Claire," Miss Brick said eagerly.

"That way you could describe Drake's dying groans and the expression of agony and remorse on his face."

"Thank you for the suggestions," Caroline said in a light, polite way that did not invite further advice. "But I already have an end in mind for my villain. I trust it will prove to be a surprise for everyone." She smiled. "Especially Edmund Drake."

Adam felt his back teeth close tightly together. It occurred to him that every time Edmund Drake was mentioned, he clenched his jaw. It was becoming an exceedingly disturbing habit.

He forced a humorless grin. "Perhaps Mrs. Fordyce intends to astonish us all by having Drake avoid the usual unfortunate demise meted out to villains."

Miss Brick and Mrs. Trent stared at him as if he had gone mad.

"Talk about your startling incidents," he continued, warming to his own notion. "Only consider the effect on readers if she transformed Drake into the hero who saves the day and marries the heroine."

"I cannot imagine her doing any such thing," Mrs. Trent said with conviction.

"Of course not," Miss Brick added briskly. "Turn the villain into a hero? Unthinkable."

Gilbert Smith gave Adam a speculative look. "May I ask what your interest is in tonight's séance, sir?"

"Mr. Grove is my assistant," Caroline said very smoothly before Adam could respond.

Smith frowned. "What does a writer's assistant do?"

"You'd be amazed," Adam said.

Smith gave up on him and switched back to Caroline. "I confess that I am curious to know why an author would wish to attend a séance, Mrs. Fordyce."

"One of the characters who will appear in my next novel is a medium," Caroline explained. "I thought it would be a good idea to experience a few séances and observe some examples of psychical phenomena before I write those scenes."

Miss Brick was impressed. "You are here to do research?"

"Yes," Caroline said.

"How exciting."

Smith shot another veiled, searching look at Adam. "And you are assisting her in this research?"

"I find my work extremely interesting," Adam said. "Never a dull moment."

The housekeeper loomed like a spirit manifestation in the doorway.

"It is time," she announced with a suitably portentous air. "Mrs. Toller is ready to begin the séance. Please follow me."

They followed her down another shadowy hall. Adam used the opportunity to note the location of the rear stairs and the entrance to the kitchen.

Midway along the corridor, the housekeeper opened a door. One by one the sitters filed into a darkened room and took their places at a cloth-draped table.

A single lamp burned in the center of the table. It had been turned down as low as possible. The dim light did not begin to penetrate the thick dark shadows that draped the room.

Adam assisted Caroline into a chair and then sat down beside her.

He noticed at once that the heavy cloth that covered the table made it impossible to reach surreptitiously underneath to feel for hidden springs and other devices. In a similar fashion the general gloom prohibited a close survey of the walls, ceiling and floor. Nevertheless, there was something wrong about the proportions of the séance room. The space felt smaller than it should have been, judging by the distance they had walked down the hall.

A false wall and perhaps a lowered ceiling, he concluded.

"Good evening," Irene Toller said.

She stood in the doorway, silhouetted against the light. Adam knew that he was no connoisseur of ladies' fashions but, even from his limited perspective, Irene Toller's skirts appeared unusually voluminous. Caroline had explained that there was a common suspicion that fraudulent female mediums used wide, heavy skirts to conceal various apparatus designed to create the desired effects in a séance.

Irene moved into the room with a stately tread. Adam got to his feet. Gilbert Smith did the same and proceeded to hold the medium's chair for her.

"Thank you, Mr. Smith." Irene sat down and looked at the housekeeper. "You may leave us now, Bess."

"Yes, ma'am." Bess took herself out into the hall and closed the door.

The only light left in the room was the weak gleam of the lamp in the center of the table.

138

"Will you all please place your hands upon the table as I am doing," Irene instructed. She flattened both palms in plain view on the cloth-covered surface.

So much for having the opportunity to hold Caroline's hand, Adam thought.

"I ask that no one remove his or her hands from the table until the séance is completed," Irene continued. "This ensures that there is no trickery involved."

It did not ensure any such thing, Adam knew. But the others, with the probable exception of Caroline, seemed to accept that having all hands in view at all times was a guarantee against duplicity.

The rappings began immediately, faint pings and a loud thump that caused Miss Brick and Mrs. Trent to gasp.

The sounds came from a variety of locations around the room, including the corners and beneath the table.

"What is it?" Mrs. Trent asked in an awed voice.

"Do not be alarmed," Irene said. "It is only my spirit guide letting us know that he is present. His name is Sennefer. He was once a priest in ancient Egypt. He possesses a vast store of secret, arcane knowledge. I am his medium. Through me he will communicate with you as it pleases him. But first I must go into a trance."

She began to tremble violently, very much as she had at the spirit writing demonstration. She jerked and twitched. Her head twisted back and forth with sharp movements.

Adam watched her hands closely. They remained firmly planted on the cloth-covered surface. Utterly motionless.

The table suddenly shuddered and rose a few inches off the floor.

"Astonishing," Gilbert Smith whispered.

"Good heavens, it is floating in mid-air." Some of Miss Brick's enthusiasm had turned to anxiety.

"All hands must remain on the top of the table," Irene barked in a deeper, more resonant tone that presumably emanated from Sennefer.

Adam quickly counted hands. All were still clearly in view, including Irene's.

The table descended back to the floor. Irene Toller's fingers were all still in precisely the same position they had been in a moment ago, Adam noticed.

"Look," shrieked Mrs. Trent. "There is something up there."

Adam followed her shocked, wondering gaze toward the ceiling directly above the table. He could just barely make out a silvery, pale, faintly glowing shape floating in the darkness above their heads. It drifted about in a ghostly fashion and then vanished.

"Dear heaven, what is that?" Miss Brick whispered.

A corpse-pale hand had risen up beside the table next to Irene Toller. As they watched, it reached out and gently tapped Miss Brick on the shoulder. She gave a startled little screech.

"Do not be afraid," Irene said firmly. "The spirit means you no harm."

Miss Brick sat very still, her eyes huge in the shadows. The deathly white hand descended back out of sight beneath the table.

140

"It touched me." Miss Brick sounded awed. "The manifestation actually touched me."

Before anyone else could react, another series of raps and pings ensued. It was followed by the faint tinkle of chimes.

"Sennefer says that was the manifestation of a spirit who wishes to communicate with some sitters at this table." Irene broke off, squeezing her eyes shut. Her face contorted. And then her eyes popped open very wide in a disconcerting stare. "It wishes to send a message to Mrs. Trent and to Miss Brick."

Mrs. Trent was clearly unnerved. "I don't understand."

"Who is it?" Miss Brick asked, equally uneasy.

The chimes clashed.

"This message is from . . ." Irene spoke haltingly, in little bursts of words, as though she was attempting to interpret some sort of otherworldly telegraphy. "A friend. Yes, it is the spirit of a friend who made her transition sometime in the past year or so."

Mrs. Trent stiffened. "Oh, heavens, is it Mrs. Selby?"

Miss Brick stiffened and peered around the room. "Is that you, Helen?"

There was another series of raps and chimes.

"Helen Selby sends you both her regards," Irene said.

More pings and clicks.

"She says that she can offer you some useful advice concerning your finances."

"That would be wonderful," Mrs. Trent said, enthusiastic once more.

"What is it you want to tell us?" Miss Brick asked of the room at large.

Taps, raps and bells sounded.

"You will encounter a gentleman in the near future," Irene intoned. "He will offer you an investment opportunity. If you accept, you will become very rich within the year."

"What is the name of this gentleman?" Mrs. Trent demanded, dazed and excited.

A rapid series of raps ensued.

"I cannot say," Irene declared in her forceful voice. "But you will recognize him because he will tell you that he was once acquainted with Helen Selby. When you identify yourselves as two of her old friends, he will invite you to take advantage of the investment opportunity."

"Helen, we do not know how to thank you," Miss Brick whispered.

Gilbert Smith peered around eagerly. "I say, would there be any objection to my participating in the investment, Mrs. Selby? My name is Gilbert Smith. I realize we were never acquainted while you were alive, but we do seem to have met now, as it were."

A violent clashing of chimes and raps interrupted him.

The noise stopped suddenly.

Irene fixed Gilbert Smith with her grim, staring gaze. "Helen Selby's spirit is angered by your greed, Mr. Smith. She says that you will not be contacted."

"I see," Smith muttered. "Well, it was worth a try."

An eerie squeak that sounded to Adam suspiciously like a poorly oiled door hinge echoed from the corner of the room. All heads turned in that direction.

At that moment Adam felt the table once again elevate a few inches into the air. It trembled and then lowered itself back down to the floor. There was a series of quick taps followed by a ripple of the chimes.

"Another spirit wishes to communicate with someone at this table," Irene said. "This one has a message for Mrs. Fordyce."

Adam was aware of Caroline going still beside him.

"Who is the spirit?" she asked quietly.

Tiny raps and pings sounded.

"It is not very clear." Irene gave every appearance of concentrating fiercely.

More faint rappings.

"A man, I believe," Irene said hesitantly. "A gentleman . . . ah, yes, now I have it. It is the spirit of your late husband."

Caroline sat frozen in her chair.

Rage swept through Adam. The silly game had gone on long enough, he thought. How dare the fraud torment Caroline with so-called messages from her dead husband? He would put an end to this nonsense immediately.

"No, please," Caroline whispered, evidently having guessed his intent. "It is all right. I do not mind. In fact, I am eager to hear what my dear Jeremy has to say. His death was so sudden. We did not have an opportunity to say farewell."

Adam hesitated. His instinct was to take her away from this place at once, but he sensed that she would not come with him willingly. This was her decision, he reminded himself. If she insisted on staying here, he had no choice but to remain with her. She was an intelligent woman. Surely she understood that Irene Toller was playing a distinctly unpleasant parlor game.

On the other hand, grief for a beloved spouse lost to an untimely death could make even the most sensible, level-headed person easy prey for a charlatan such as Toller.

Damnation, he fumed. He had no one to blame but himself for what was happening. If he had not dragged Caroline into this affair, she would not be here tonight.

After another series of clicks, pings and chimes reverberated through the room, Irene looked across the table at Caroline.

"Your Jeremy says to tell you that he loves you and that he is waiting for you on the Other Side with open arms. Someday you will be together again and know at last the happiness that was denied you when he was taken away."

"I see," Caroline said in an odd voice.

A bell sounded.

Irene shuddered. Her hands trembled on the table. "The spirit says that he is unable to communicate any more tonight. He will try again in the near future." She stiffened and then writhed again in her chair. "It is over. The spirits have departed. Please leave at once. I am exhausted."

She collapsed forward, facedown on her motionless hands.

The door opened, revealing the housekeeper standing in the hall.

"The séance is over," Bess announced. "You must all leave now so that Mrs. Toller can recover."

CHAPTER
FIFTEEN

The carriage rolled back toward Corley Lane through fog-bound streets. The interior of the vehicle was drenched in shadows because Adam had not lit the lamps. He told himself that Caroline would appreciate a degree of privacy after what must have been a nerve-shattering experience.

His temper still smoldered. He looked at Caroline, trying to think what to say. She sat there across from him, a warm shawl draped around her shoulders, her face averted. She seemed lost in her memories.

Part of him wanted to offer sympathy but another part longed to remind her that she must not give credence to anything that had happened at the séance. On the other hand, what if the possibility that her lost husband had spoken to her from beyond the grave had provided her with some comfort? Who was he to rip that from her?

He could have strangled Irene Toller with no remorse whatsoever, he decided. How could the woman live with herself? It was one thing to stage a séance as entertainment or even as a cynical means of defrauding the foolish and the gullible. Business was business, after all. No one knew that better than he did. But to deliberately open the flood-gates of a woman's grief was intolerable.

Adam vowed to himself that before this affair was finished, he would see to it that Irene Toller was exposed as the charlatan she was.

"I regret that you were forced to endure that sad experience," he said eventually.

"Do not concern yourself, Adam." Her voice lacked all expression. "It was certainly not your fault."

"Yes, in fact, it was my fault." He flexed one hand on the seat cushion. "I should never have allowed you to talk me into taking you with me tonight."

"No, no, you must not blame yourself," she said quickly. "I am all right, truly."

"You are distraught."

"Not in the least." Her voice rose. "I assure you."

"No one could go through such a harrowing event and not be affected."

"It was all a bit . . ." She hesitated, as if unsure of the correct word. "Odd, I admit. But I promise you that my nerves are quite steady. I certainly will not sink into a fit of hysteria or melancholia."

"I do not doubt that for a moment." In spite of his simmering anger, admiration welled up inside him. "We have not been long acquainted, Caroline, but I must tell you that I am in awe of your fortitude and resilience."

She opened her fan, closed it and then opened it again in a nervous gesture that seemed quite unlike her.

"You flatter me," she mumbled.

147

He was making the situation worse for her by talking about it, he thought. But he could not seem to stop now that he had started.

"You must remind yourself that Irene Toller is a complete fraud," he said quietly.

"Yes, of course."

"She took advantage of your widowhood to resurrect strong emotions."

"I am aware of that." She folded her fan and then clasped her gloved fingers very tightly together in her lap. "It is a common trick of the medium's trade."

He clenched his hand into a fist and rested it on his thigh. "It is a cruel business, in my opinion. It rests entirely on deception."

She cleared her throat. "There has never been a noticeable lack of people who are only too happy to be deceived."

The carriage clattered past a row of gas lamps. The weak glare briefly illuminated Caroline's taut features. He worried that she might be about to burst into tears.

"You no doubt loved your husband very much." He groped for the proper words. "My condolences on your loss."

She stiffened. "Thank you. But it has been some time now. I have quite recovered from my grief."

The situation was deteriorating rapidly. If he had an ounce of sense he would close his mouth and keep it shut until they reached Corley Lane. But somehow the knowledge that she might be looking forward to someday joining her dead husband was turning a dagger in his belly.

148

"I suppose that the thought of your beloved Jeremy waiting for you on the Other Side offers a certain measure of consolation," he heard himself say.

"*Enough.*" She opened her fan with a violent snap. "Not another word, I beg you. I cannot abide any more of this conversation."

"Forgive me." He seemed to be repeating himself frequently tonight, he reflected. He could not recall having apologized as many times in the past year. "The subject is obviously quite painful for you. I give you my oath, you will not be subjected to any more séances. It was a mistake to allow you to become more deeply involved in this affair."

"It was not a mistake," she said brusquely. "It was my decision."

"I will expose Irene Toller at the first opportunity."

"No, you must not do any such thing." Caroline sounded genuinely horrified. "Only think of the risk, sir. You might well jeopardize your own secrets if you allow yourself to become distracted by such a small, unimportant matter. You must be cautious."

"Toller should be punished for the cruel deception she practiced tonight," he said, unmoved. "I cannot allow her to get away with what she did to you. To play upon your grief in such a fashion is unconscionable."

Caroline gave a small choked cry. She was, indeed, about to break down in tears, he thought. Alarmed, he reached for his handkerchief.

When she saw the square of white linen in his hand, she sighed, as if in surrender.

"That will not be necessary, sir," she muttered. "I am not prostrate with grief. I suppose I may as well come straight out with the truth. I can see that there is no other way to convince you."

"Convince me of what?"

"Irene Toller is not the only one skilled in deception. There was no Jeremy Fordyce. I invented him."

He sat there for a moment, ruefully amazed at his own amazement. He should have expected that she would surprise him yet again, he thought. Nevertheless, he had not anticipated this particular turn of events.

He knew very well why he had failed to perceive the fiction. He had wanted to believe that Caroline was an experienced widow. It had been so convenient to think of her as a woman of the world who was no longer confined by the rules that dictated the behavior of unmarried ladies under the age of thirty.

"You were never wed?" he asked carefully.

"I'm afraid not. After the disaster in Chillingham three years ago, I concluded that my life would be a good deal more comfortable if I were perceived to be a widow rather than an unmarried woman. After we moved to London, I adopted the name Mrs. Fordyce for both professional and personal use."

He made a mental note of the change in location of the scandal. "Would you mind telling me your real name?"

She hesitated. "Caroline Connor."

"I see." He contemplated the fact that it was late at night and he was alone in a carriage with an unmarried lady who should never have been allowed out of the house in the evening without a chaperone. Yes, it certainly had been far more convenient to believe that she was a widow.

"I realize that you are not pleased by my news, Mr. Hardesty," she said. "But surely you must know how dreadfully restricted life is for an unwed woman of my age. Things were easier in the country. The rules of propriety are somewhat more relaxed there. But here in town, a single woman is easy prey for those who would spread malicious gossip. When one adds to that my involvement in a great scandal and the fact that I am an author of sensation novels, well, you can see the enormity of my problem. It was so much simpler to let Caroline Connor disappear."

He thought about how often Julia, before her marriage, had railed against the restraints Society imposed upon young ladies. "I am aware that the proprieties can be annoying. But I would remind you that there are some very good reasons for those restrictions. The world is a dangerous place for women. There are any number of vicious rogues at every level of society who do not hesitate to take advantage of females."

Her gloved hand tightened fiercely around her fan. "And the most dangerous ones are those who move in the most elevated circles," she said in a voice that was barely above a harsh whisper.

There was a short, tense silence. He said nothing but the part of him that was always on the alert to take note of the unusual or the unexpected registered her vehemence. Evidently the scandal in which she had

151

been embroiled had involved a gentleman who inhabited exclusive circles.

She exhaled deeply. "You may trust me when I tell you that I am well aware of the realities of the world, sir. I appreciate your concern but you need not waste your energy lecturing me on the proprieties."

She had every right to call herself whatever she wished in order to live her life on her own terms, he reminded himself.

"I beg your pardon," he said quietly.

"Forgive me for snapping at you. As you can see, the subject is an unpleasant one for me."

"You have made your point. Unfortunately, this sudden change in your marital status only serves to make an already complicated situation considerably more difficult."

"Nonsense," she said hastily. "Nothing need change between us."

He almost smiled at that. "Come now, we both know that you are not that naïve."

She winced and turned her head toward the window. "Are you angry?"

Was he? He was not sure. "Let's just say that you have put me in an exceedingly awkward position."

"There is absolutely no need for you to take that view." She was anxious now. "The world believes me to be a widow and I see no reason to disabuse anyone of that notion. You may continue to treat me exactly as you did before I told you my secret."

"Do you really think that is possible?"

She made an exasperated little sound. "It is not as though I am a fragile flower. You said yourself that the subjects and themes of my novels imply considerable experience of the world."

"You may be a lady of some experience," he admitted, "but you nevertheless have a reputation to protect."

"On the contrary." Bitterness laced the words. "Caroline Connor had a reputation to protect. But it was ripped to shreds three years ago. Mrs. Fordyce has nothing to worry about in that regard."

"That is a matter of opinion."

She gave him a reproachful look. "Who would have thought that you would prove to be such a prig and a high stickler, sir?"

The accusation caught him off guard. He found himself smiling slightly. "I assure you, I am even more astonished than you are to discover that side of my nature."

She folded her arms beneath her breasts and tapped the pointed toe of one high-heeled shoe. "Well, I suppose that it is my turn to apologize. I never intended to place you in what you term *an awkward position,* sir."

"I realize that was not your objective." He hesitated. "You have a right to your secrets, Caroline, just as I have a right to mine."

"On that we are agreed."

He struggled to deal with the dangerous brew of passions she stirred within him. He felt an almost overwhelming urge to take her into his arms and kiss her until she was breathless, until she forgot the bastard who had ruined her in Chillingham. But he also wanted to do something that was far more reckless, something he had never done with any other woman. For some obscure reason that he could not explain, he felt compelled to balance the scales between them. He had unintentionally prodded her into revealing some of her secrets. He wanted to repay her by revealing one of his own.

"Will you come with me to another part of town?" he asked. "There is something I want to show you."

"Now? Tonight?"

"Yes." He did not know what had possessed him; he only knew that he could not turn back. "I promise you that you are in no danger from me."

She seemed startled. "I do not fear you."

Perhaps she would refuse to accompany him. Perhaps that would be for the best. Nevertheless, he found himself waiting as though his entire future depended on what she said next.

"Very well," she said quietly. "My aunts will be out quite late tonight. They will not be home to worry and fret if I am late."

Before he could change his mind, he stood, raised the trapdoor and gave Ned a familiar address.

CHAPTER
SIXTEEN

Accompanying Adam on this journey by night was far and away the most exciting thing she had ever done in her life, Caroline thought. A strange, feverish anticipation was building within her. Where was he taking her? What did he intend to show her?

But she did not ask any questions. She sensed that what he planned to reveal was extremely important and meaningful to him. He needed to go about the matter in his own way.

She pulled her wrap more tightly around her shoulders and looked out the carriage windows at the fog-shrouded streets. They were traveling into a less prosperous neighborhood. The gas lamps were spaced farther apart on these narrow streets. There were fewer lights in the windows and far less traffic. The dark entrances of the alleys were ominous enough to send small chills down her spine.

They passed a tavern. Through the grimy windows she could see men dressed in rough working clothes and a handful of women in shabby gowns. They sat at tables drinking from tankards and gin glasses.

"Do not be alarmed," Adam said, watching her face. "This is a poor neighborhood, but I know it well. You are in no danger."

"I am not afraid." *Not so long as I am with you,* she added silently.

The carriage turned a corner and went down a gloomy lane. A woman in a faded gown lounged in the light of a gas lamp. When she spotted the vehicle, she lowered her shawl to reveal her bare breasts and called out in a drunken, rasping voice, "I'll show you some fine sport 'ere, sir. The price is a bargain for what I'm offering." Then she scowled. "What's this? I see ye've already found some entertainment for the evening. Well, maybe next time. I'll be here, sir. Look for me. My name is Nan."

"I feel so sorry for that woman," Caroline whispered.

"You are not shocked?" Adam asked.

"I am aware that very little stands between a female with no resources and a miserable existence on the streets."

"You are right, of course." Adam reached into the pocket of his coat, withdrew a small packet and tossed it out the window with a casual, practiced motion of his hand. The prostitute hurried forward, seized the package and ripped it open.

"Thank ye, kind sir," she shouted as the carriage rolled past. "Ye're a generous man, ye are." She kissed the packet, whirled around and hurried away into the night.

Caroline knew from the manner in which the money had been wrapped and weighted that Adam had performed the same action on prior occasions.

156

"There was another woman under that lamp the last time I came this way," he said. "She had a bad cough. I wonder if she survived."

"Did you give her money, too?" Caroline asked.

"Yes. And directions to a charity house that would have provided her with a bed and a warm meal. But I expect she spent the money on opium or gin and dice, just as Nan will no doubt do tonight."

"You know this but you give the women money anyway?"

"Some of them have children to feed." His face was harsh in the shadows. "Sometimes it is the children I see waiting under the lamps."

She could feel his quiet anger swirling in the darkness around them.

The carriage turned another corner and halted in the middle of the street. Caroline looked out and saw an unlit doorway.

"Come," Adam said.

He climbed down and reached back to assist Caroline.

"We will be a while, Ned," he said. "Go and get something warm to drink from the tavern at the top of the street. I'll whistle when we're ready to depart."

"Aye, sir." Ned touched his cap.

Adam guided Caroline to the dark vestibule. There he removed a key from his pocket and unlocked the door.

They entered a small hall. Adam lit a small lamp. Carrying it in one hand, he took Caroline's arm and started up a flight of narrow steps.

"There is no one living here at the moment," he said. "I own the building and have scheduled some renovations."

She was more intrigued than ever. "What do you intend to do with it?"

"I have plans." He did not elaborate.

When they reached the landing, he drew her down the hall and stopped in front of a closed door. He took out another key.

Without a word, he unlocked the door and stood back to allow her to move past him into a dark, low-ceilinged room.

She entered slowly, keenly aware of the heavy weight of significance that imbued the atmosphere. This small, shabby room was very important to Adam.

The single window was covered with a simple curtain made of canvas. The furnishings were minimal. She saw a cot and a table. The floor was bare. There were no personal items of any kind lying about the place but the room was clean and well-dusted. A fire had been laid on the hearth.

Adam followed her across the threshold, closed the door and set the lamp on the table. He turned to look at her.

"This was where I lived until the beginning of my eighteenth year," he said.

He watched her with that enigmatic calm that was so characteristic of him but she sensed the powerful emotions simmering under the surface.

"You were not born into wealth?" she asked, feeling her way.

He looked wryly amused. "My mother worked in a milliner's shop. She married my father when she was eighteen. He was a clerk in a shipping company. He was killed in an accident on the docks two years after I was born. Mother was left with nothing except his ring and his books. She pawned the ring to pay the rent and buy food but she kept the books."

The terse summary was given in an emotionless tone, as though Adam were recounting some rather boring bits of ancient history.

"Your poor mother must have been quite desperate," she said quietly.

"Yes. She spent all day at the shop. At night she taught me to read and write using the handful of books that my father had left us."

She clasped her hands in front of her. "She was obviously a woman of great courage and determination."

"Yes, she was." His expression grew even more detached and distant. "She died of a fever when I was eleven."

"Adam, I'm so sorry. What did you do? How did you survive?"

"My mother had taught me to read and write, but I had also received another sort of education growing up on the streets in this neighborhood. It had begun to come in handy before Mother died. It kept me fed and paid the rent after she was gone."

"How did you make a living?"

"I bought and sold other people's secrets," he said simply.

159

"I don't understand."

"Remember Maud Gatley? The opium addict whose diary I am trying to recover?"

"Yes, of course."

He angled his chin toward the door. "She was a prostitute who lived across the hall. She frequently brought her clients upstairs to her room. Occasionally some of her customers whispered their secrets to her and she, in turn, told them to me."

"And you found a market for them?" she asked, incredulous.

His smile was cold. "There is a vast and lucrative market for secrets, especially when those secrets belong to gentlemen from the better social circles."

"I hadn't realized that."

"Maud was very beautiful in those days and she had not yet fallen completely under the spell of the drug. She counted a number of men of the Quality among her clientele. It was my job to find buyers for the gossip and rumors she picked up in the course of her work. We split the profits. The arrangements worked well for both of us for some time."

A rush of wonder swept through her. "Yours is an amazing story."

He raised one brow. "I am glad you find it intriguing. But I warn you, if a single word of it appears in one of your novels, I will be very displeased."

She gave him her most demure look. "I would, of course, change the names."

"A change of names would not be nearly enough to placate me," he warned.

160

"I was only teasing, Adam, as I'm sure you are well aware. Tell me the rest of the tale."

"Over the course of the next few years I acquired two sisters and a brother."

"How does one *acquire* siblings?" she asked.

"It varies. Sometimes one finds an orphan who is about to be auctioned off in a brothel that caters to gentlemen who prefer virgin girls under the age of twelve."

"Dear heaven."

"Sometimes one finds a girl abandoned at the age of three next to a pile of trash and sweepings."

"Adam, are you telling me —"

"Sometimes one finds a boy who, at the age of four, has been set out beneath a streetlamp to beg but whose parent never came back for him."

"You took them all in to live with you," she whispered. "I do not know what to say. I am quite stunned."

He shrugged. "I was making good money on the streets in those days. I could afford to feed a few extra mouths. It made for company in the evenings."

"Did you teach them to read and write as your mother had taught you?"

"There wasn't much else to do at night," he said.

She waved one hand to indicate the spare little room. "How did the four of you escape this place?"

"The situation changed in the middle of my seventeenth year. I came into possession of a particularly valuable secret. It involved a large-scale

161

financial swindle that affected a number of high-ranking investors. I sold the information to a new client, a wealthy, widowed gentleman. He used it to prevent himself and several associates from losing a great deal of money."

"Go on," she said, fascinated.

Instead of answering immediately, he straightened away from the wall, unfolded his arms and crossed the room to the fireplace. Going down on one knee, he struck a light and ignited the kindling.

He watched the small blaze take hold for a moment or two. She got the impression that he was reviewing scenes from the past and deciding which ones to reveal.

"The wealthy gentleman had lost his wife and children to a terrible fever several years previously," he said finally. "The gentleman was very rich but quite alone in the world. After the two of us had done some business together over the course of several months, he went so far as to offer me a position as a sort of unofficial man-of-business."

"You were only seventeen years of age. What sort of tasks did you perform for him?"

"As I told you, my mentor was very fond of secrets of all kinds and I had a talent for collecting them. I got them not just from Maud but from others who were in a position to learn them." Adam rose slowly. "Tavern keepers, chambermaids, footmen, hairdressers, washerwomen, men who work on the docks. The list of people who are in a position to provide useful information about others is endless."

"I see." She sank down onto the edge of the cot.

"My client's attitude toward me became almost paternal. He not only gave me a fine position, he offered to let me live in his great house. I told him that I could not leave my brother and sisters." Adam shook his head reminiscently. "So Wilson took us all in to live with him."

"It sounds as if you and your siblings filled up a portion of the empty space in his heart that had no doubt been created by the loss of his own family."

"He said something very much like that to me once a few years ago. It was his idea to claim us all as long-lost relatives. It was a bold scheme. I told him it would never work. But he had the power to put it into effect. He hired tutors, dancing instructors and a long list of experts to give us all a proper education and put a polish on us. In the end he made us the heirs to his fortune."

"What a fascinating series of startling incidents," she exclaimed.

"Perhaps it sounds that way in the telling, but I assure you, it did not feel that way while we were living through those incidents."

"No, of course not," she said gently. "So much sadness and loss. So much uncertainty and danger. Believe me, sir, I comprehend very well that your life does not feel like a work of fiction to you. I am honored by your confidence. I will not betray it."

He watched her very steadily. "If I had not believed that I could trust you, I would never have told you about my past."

"I think I can guess what is in that diary that you are trying to recover. It is the truth about your past and the pasts of your brother and sisters, correct?"

"Yes. Maud knew the facts. She evidently wrote them down in her journal. Elizabeth Delmont read that journal and tried to use the information to blackmail me."

"No wonder you wish to recover that diary."

"Wilson assures me that our family is sufficiently powerful to be able to deal with any scandal that may erupt. He is right. But I fear it will not be as simple as he believes. Julia is the Countess of Southwood. She has her husband to protect her. But Jessica is on the verge of making her debut into the Polite World. Who knows what kind of gossip she would face if it got out that she had been found in a heap of trash?"

"Scandal is always hard to handle. It would be especially difficult for a young woman who is facing all of the pressures that must come with moving into elevated social circles."

"As for Nathan, he is drawn to the world of academic writing and study. In order to pursue his interests he will find it necessary to join certain exclusive scholarly societies. I suspect he will not be readily accepted into them if it is discovered that he was once put out to beg on the streets."

"Naturally you wish to protect your brother and sisters. I am lost in admiration of your noble nature and determination to protect your family."

His mouth curved ruefully. "It is certainly true that I am determined to shield my family as much as

164

possible, but there is nothing noble about my intention. It is my responsibility to protect them."

She nodded. "Of course you would see it that way."

"You are the one who commands my admiration, Caroline."

She was taken aback by the seriousness of his tone. "Forgive me, but I was under the impression that you did not think highly of the manner in which I make my living."

He ignored that. "You have survived a great deal of loss and many difficulties yet you have triumphed resoundingly."

"I could not have done it alone," she said quietly. "If I had not had Aunt Emma and Aunt Milly, my life would have taken an entirely different turn, I assure you."

"Just as mine would have done had it not been for Wilson Grendon. But that does not lessen your own accomplishments. You have overcome a great scandal, and you have people who love you and to whom you are loyal. You have used your creativity and intelligence to craft an interesting career for yourself. All of those things add up to a great triumph, Caroline."

She did not know what to say. She could feel herself turning warm. No man had ever complimented her in such a touching, sincere manner. She knew that he meant every word.

And yet, she thought wistfully, those were not quite the sentiments that she wanted to hear from him.

"Very kind of you to say so," she managed in her most formal tones.

"You asked me why I brought you here tonight." He walked toward her. "I told myself that it was because I had more or less coerced you into revealing some of your own secrets and that it was only right to reciprocate. But that is not the whole of it."

The atmosphere in the room changed in some indefinable way, becoming more intimate and close. A deep sense of knowing swept through her, bringing her to her feet. Something important was happening between them, she realized.

When he reached her, he raised both hands and cradled her face between them.

"The truth is that I wanted you to know that I am not the man you believed me to be that first day when I descended on you in your study and tried to intimidate you into giving me information."

"I see." She could not think of anything else to say. She was so aware of the heat and power in his hands that she could scarcely draw breath, let alone form coherent sentences.

"I realize that I may strike you as merely another selfish, arrogant member of the privileged class. And I will admit that these days I move in those circles. But I was not born into them, Caroline. I wear the right clothes, belong to the right clubs and do business with the right people, but deep down, I will always be an outsider. I know that, even if those with whom I associate do not."

She lifted her hands and clasped his wrists. "I understand."

166

"I brought you here because I wanted you to comprehend that I do know what it is like to struggle and fight very hard to survive. Indeed, I have done things to achieve those goals that would shock you to the core of your soul."

"I cannot believe that."

"Believe it," he said harshly. "I will not burden you with those secrets. But what I want you to understand tonight is that I have not forgotten the lessons I learned while I lived in this room. I will never forget them. They are part of who and what I have become."

She sighed. "You may be arrogant. You are certainly strong-willed, even stubborn on occasion. But I am well aware that you are not one of those men who would take advantage of a woman, use her for your own selfish purposes and then call down shame and scandal upon her head when you have finished with her."

He tightened his hands very gently, tipping her head back a little. "Can I gather from that statement that you no longer believe that I am a threat to you and your aunts?"

"You would not destroy the three of us on a whim or a mere suspicion. I know now that you are a man who will settle only for the truth."

She felt some of the fierce tension in him ease. He stroked one thumb along the under edge of her lower lip.

"Thank you for that much," he whispered roughly. "Out of curiosity, what was it that made you conclude that I could be trusted?"

She wrinkled her nose. "If you must know, my intuition told me as much right from the start of this business, even though you gave me a false name. Logic and common sense held me back, of course."

"Of course," he agreed.

"There were others to be considered besides myself," she reminded him.

"Emma and Milly."

"Precisely. This evening, however, I feared that in your anger toward Mrs. Toller you might take the risk of trying to expose her prematurely. I did not want to be responsible for jeopardizing your investigation."

"So you told me one of your secrets."

"Yes."

"And now I have told you a few of mine." His gaze softened and heated like green glass in a furnace. "But there is another secret that I would confide in you tonight."

Anticipation sparkled and shivered through her. "What is that?"

He stroked the bones of her cheeks with his thumbs. "Although the fact that you are not a widow makes this situation extremely inconvenient, I am very glad to know that you are not mourning a lost love that you hope is waiting for you with open arms on the Other Side."

"Why does that matter so much to you?"

"Because I want to kiss you again more than I have wanted to do anything in my life and I did not relish competing with a ghost."

"Oh, yes. Yes, *please*."

168

He took her mouth with a fierce hunger that swamped her senses. She would have crumpled beneath the delicious onslaught had he not held her tightly against his chest.

The kiss burned through her, hot and intoxicating. But she was beyond all caution.

"Adam," she whispered, when he briefly freed her mouth.

"So passionate and so lovely." He kissed one of her brows and moved his hands intimately down her spine.

She put her arms around his neck and brushed her mouth tentatively against his, testing his reaction.

The delicate caress seemed to electrify him. He groaned and kissed her back, his mouth hard and urgent now.

A moment later she felt his fingers on the fastenings at the front of her gown. The stiffened bodice, which did double duty as a light corset, opened slowly like a suit of armor being severed down the centerline.

"I do not know how women tolerate these modern fashions," he said hoarsely. "Wearing a dress like this must be akin to walking around in a small, tight cage."

"But it feels so good when the cage is removed," she said earnestly. As soon as the words were out of her mouth, she was mortified. "Oh, dear, that did not come out quite as I had intended."

He gave a sensual, husky laugh and kissed her lightly. "Explanations are unnecessary. I think I understand."

"Perhaps it would be easier if I finished this for you?"

"Absolutely not. I forbid it." He resumed his work on the hooks of her gown. "Undressing you is like

169

unwrapping an elaborately wrapped gift. Never underestimate the pleasure of anticipation."

She clenched her fingers in the front of his linen shirt.

When he had opened the gown to a point just below her breasts, he paused again and rested his forehead against hers. "Damn. I don't believe this."

Her heart sank. Was he disappointed in what he had uncovered thus far? "Is something wrong?"

"Yes." He raised his head and looked down at her with a rueful expression. "My hands are shaking so badly it is all I can do to manage these hooks."

"Really?" She was entranced by the knowledge that she had such an effect on him.

"I intended to sweep you away on a romantic cloud of passion and pleasure. Instead, I feel like a great, clumsy oaf."

The confession emboldened her as nothing else could have done in that moment.

"Perhaps it would make things easier if I assisted you in this process," she suggested once more.

With trembling fingers she began to unknot his tie.

Adam's mouth crooked and his eyes gleamed in the lamp-light. "Yes," he said, "I think that will help considerably."

In a matter of moments she was left standing only in her chemise, stockings and drawers. Her heavy gown lay in a frothy heap on the wooden floor. Adam's tie, waistcoat and white linen shirt lay next to them. He stood before her, clad only in his trousers.

170

The firelight gleamed on his sleekly muscled body. Fascinated, she traced the strong contours of his chest with her fingertips.

"You are as magnificent as a statue of an ancient god," she whispered.

He uttered a half-choked laugh. "I trust you find me somewhat warmer and a bit younger."

"*Much* warmer and much younger. Perfect, in fact." She wanted to bask in the heat from his body.

"Ah, my sweet. You go to my head."

It had been difficult to undress Adam, owing to the fact that she had never before attempted to rid a man of his clothes. She had stopped after she had gotten his shirt off because she did not possess quite enough nerve to tackle the buttons of his trousers. Fortunately, he did not seem to find her hesitation odd.

He picked her up and settled her carefully on the cot. Then he straightened and freed himself from his remaining clothes with a few swift, impatient motions.

She was transfixed.

She reminded herself that unlike the carefully sheltered ladies of the city, she had been raised in the country. She was, therefore, not unfamiliar with the sight of male animals in this state. In addition, Emma and Milly had always been extremely modern in their notions of what was appropriate to a young lady's education. All in all, she ought to have had a fair notion of what to expect from this first encounter with a man. Nonetheless, she was astonished.

Adam hesitated at the side of the bed, his face shadowed in the flickering light. "Is something wrong?"

171

"No." She reached up and caught his hand in hers, squeezing tightly. "Nothing is wrong."

He lowered himself down onto the cot very carefully and pulled her into his arms. One by one, he took the pins from her hair. She trembled when she heard them click on the floorboards beside the bed.

"I did not plan on this tonight," he whispered, kissing her throat. "I brought you here on impulse and as a result, I have one great regret."

She held her breath. "If you have changed your mind —"

"Never." His fingers tightened in her hair. "I am consumed by my desire for you. I could not turn aside now if my life depended on it. No, my regret is that I did not take you to more elegant surroundings. You deserve better than this barren room."

She relaxed and touched his face. "This room is perfect, Adam. Everything tonight is perfect."

He put one hand on her stocking-clad leg. When he stroked her inner thigh, the world as she had always known it was forever changed. The intimacy of his touch was almost unbearably exciting.

It was as if she had been walking through a garden all of her life, turned a corner around a high hedge and suddenly found herself in an exotic, tropical jungle.

"You are so beautiful." He undid the buttons of her chemise and kissed the curve of her breast.

She was not beautiful, she thought. But tonight he made her feel as though she were the direct descendent of Cleopatra, Helen of Troy and Venus.

172

When he took one nipple between his teeth, waterfalls of sensations crashed through her. A wild, fiery tension built deep inside her. The weight of Adam's leg anchoring her thigh to the bed was an exquisite pressure.

When his fingers found her secrets through the open seam of her drawers, she almost screamed. Shock and astonished pleasure played havoc with her breath and pulse. Nothing she had ever experienced felt quite like the touch of Adam's hand on the most delicate portion of her anatomy.

"You are already damp and ready for me," he whispered into her ear.

She was vaguely embarrassed that he had noticed the wet heat between her legs but she could not retreat from his touch. She wanted more of whatever he was doing to her.

And then somehow he had undone the tapes that secured the drawers. He moved on top of her and kissed the place between her breasts. Her head fell back across his arm. She felt tight and hot and desperate.

"Please," she whispered, urgently curving one leg around his muscular thigh.

He shifted his position slightly. She felt pressure.

"Yes," she said. "It feels so good."

"*Caroline*."

He drove himself into her in a single, searing thrust.

Be careful what you wish for, she thought.

She had been expecting something of the sort, but the pain still came as a shock because a few seconds ago she had been glorying in the most amazing pleasure.

"What on earth?" She jerked violently and shoved instinctively at his shoulders. "Wait. Stop. I believe there is something wrong."

Adam froze.

She tried to gingerly ease away from him. "Forgive me. This is my fault. I didn't realize, you see. I mean, I thought I did but clearly I didn't."

"Caroline, stop moving, I beg you."

"Would you mind very much getting off of me?"

He groaned. She could see sweat on his brow. His jaw clenched as though he was in agony. His eyes were half-closed. With an obvious effort of determined will, he began to ease himself out of her body.

The sensation was not unpleasant.

"Wait," she ordered. She clamped her hands on his back, holding him still. "Maybe that won't be necessary."

"Caroline, you are going to drive me mad."

"Actually, it does not feel quite so uncomfortable now." She wriggled again and got a satisfactory feeling in return. "Perhaps if you continued very slowly."

"Very slowly?" He rested his weight on his elbows and imprisoned her face with his hands. Every muscle in his body seemed to be sculpted of steel. His eyes were those of a man who is fast approaching some inner limit. But his mouth curved slightly in a sensual smile that could have set fire to the entire city. "Like this, do you mean?"

He began to move again. Slowly.

174

Her body relaxed. He reached down and did something to her with his fingers. Everything inside her clenched as tight as a fist. But not in resistance this time; rather in a frantic, demanding manner.

"Yes," she whispered. "Oh, yes, just like that."

"Draw up your knees, my sweet," he whispered.

She obeyed. The exciting sensations intensified.

"Ah, Caroline," he said against her mouth. "I am well and truly lost."

Before she could ask him what he meant by the strange words, he began to move more quickly.

The delicious friction tightened her insides until she could no longer tolerate the intense sensation. She convulsed.

The release sent her flying into the night.

Adam gave a muffled groan and went rigid.

At the last possible instant, he pulled free of her body and collapsed beside her, spending himself into the bedding.

CHAPTER
SEVENTEEN

A long time later Adam folded one arm behind his head and pulled Caroline close beneath the old blanket. She snuggled and seemed to settle against him, as if preparing to go to sleep. A pleasant prospect, he thought, but not possible tonight.

"When did you plan to tell me?" he asked.

He knew he sounded brusque and unromantic; so be it. He was trying to balance a chaotic mix of emotions that had shaken him to the core.

In hindsight he knew that he had not wanted to heed the small clues that had pointed to Caroline's lack of experience. He had been only too pleased to believe that she was a widow. When that convenient fiction had evaporated earlier this evening, he had comforted himself with some equally handy assumptions concerning a shady past and a scandalous affair.

But Caroline was one surprise after another.

She yawned delicately and stretched out one leg like a small cat beneath the blanket. "Tell you what?"

He felt her toes brush against his calf. The small caress had a stirring effect.

"That you were a virgin," he said.

176

Caroline went still. Then she levered herself up on one elbow and looked down at him with a puzzled frown.

"Was I supposed to inform you?" she asked.

"Yes," he said unequivocally. He was as annoyed with her as he was at himself. "You were supposed to tell me. I have a rule against bedding innocents."

"Ah, so that is the problem." Her face cleared instantly. "You had a rule."

"You mock me at your peril, Caroline," he warned gently.

"Let us examine this situation logically. By innocents, I assume you refer to very young ladies with no experience of the world and who are expected to guard their reputations until marriage. Am I correct?"

"Close enough," he allowed carefully. Her glib response made him cautious. She was going to try to manipulate him. He knew it as surely as he knew his own past.

She gave him a brilliant, smug smile. "Then you have nothing to be concerned about. I do not fit into the category of innocent and therefore you have not broken your rule."

He caught a tumbled lock of her hair, curled it around his fingers and tugged gently. "No?"

"No, indeed. Only consider the facts." She held up her hand and ticked off her arguments, one by one. "First, I am no longer a *young* lady. I am twenty-seven years old, well past the age that the world considers either innocent or marriageable."

"Caroline —"

"Second, in the highly unlikely event that I did meet a man who could be considered potential husband material, I would feel obligated to tell him about the dreadful scandal three years ago, and that would be the end of the matter. No proper, well-bred gentleman would want to wed a woman whose reputation had been destroyed as thoroughly as mine was, even if she took an assumed name. Therefore, I see absolutely no reason whatsoever why I should have saved myself for a wedding night that will never occur."

"Your logic has a major flaw," he began.

"And last but not least," she said, interrupting him, "although I was, technically speaking, a virgin until quite recently, I am not lacking in experience of the ways of the world. I knew very well what I was about when I returned your kisses tonight, Adam. You did not take advantage of me. If anything, it was the other way around."

"The other way around?" Stunned by that assessment of events, he yanked his arms out from behind his head and sat up. "Are you trying to convince me that you deliberately set out to seduce me?"

She pursed her lips. "Well —"

"Because I do not believe it. Not for a moment."

"I am only saying that from the first moment we met, I was attracted to you." She waved one hand negligently. "Granted, there were some initial problems because I feared you might be a threat. But once I concluded that I could trust you, I admit I did hope that you might return my feelings."

"I see."

"I will allow that matters proceeded at a much brisker pace than I had anticipated," she continued blithely. "I certainly never expected that we would find ourselves in a passionate embrace after such a short acquaintance."

"Nor did I." He threaded his fingers through her hair and pulled her face closer to his. "Tell me, Caroline, if you were so eager to taste of physical desire, why did you wait this long? Surely there have been other opportunities."

She shook her head, smiling as though she found his question amusingly naïve. "There are any number of risks involved for a woman. I did not want to take them with the wrong man."

A thrill of gut-deep satisfaction momentarily distracted him. "You thought that I was the right man?"

The laughter vanished from her eyes, leaving certainty. "There was no doubt in my mind at all tonight."

He brushed his mouth slowly, deliberately across hers. "And did you find the experience as interesting and exciting as you had expected?"

"Absolutely. Quite satisfying, indeed."

"You leave me speechless, to say nothing of what you are doing to my nerves."

"Get hold of yourself, sir," she said bracingly. "If you fear that your nerves may fail, fortify them by reminding yourself of my great asset and most excellent shield, the sturdy bulwark that will protect me from the worst effects of scandal and ruin."

"And what is this asset, shield and bulwark?"

179

"Why none other than my late husband, Jeremy Fordyce, who so conveniently made me a widow."

He pulled her back down onto the bed. "I will concede that the man's spirit does have his uses."

CHAPTER
EIGHTEEN

Irene Toller sat alone in the séance room, a large glass of gin on the table in front of her, and contemplated her vengeance. She had been a gullible fool, she thought, but no longer. The scales had fallen from her eyes at last.

"Here's to you, Elizabeth Delmont, wherever you are." Irene hoisted the glass of gin in a mocking toast and took a long swallow. The potent spirits burned all the way down.

She wiped her mouth with the back of her hand. "Conniving harlot that you were, you did me a tremendous favor by showing me the truth. Do you know, if I actually did possess the ability to summon phantoms, I would call yours up from hell just so that I could thank you properly."

She drank more gin, vaguely aware that the house was growing cold around her. The fire had begun to die after Bess had left.

"Unfortunately, I won't be able to tell you how much I appreciate what you did for me, Mrs. Delmont, because when it comes to séance work, I am just as much of a fraud as you were," she muttered to the empty room. "But then all of us in this line are charlatans and tricksters, are we not? It is the great secret that unites those of us in the profession."

She lapsed into a moody contemplation of the past. She had begun her career nearly a decade ago. She had been young and pretty, both extremely useful attributes in a female medium, but the competition had been fierce nonetheless. In order to make a living she had been obliged to resort to the tried-and-true tactic of holding private séances for gentlemen who desired to meet the spirits of long-dead courtesans and temptresses.

Night after night, in darkened rooms, she had pretended to be possessed by the phantoms of women whose carnal natures had made them legends. For a price she had allowed her male clients to use her body to satisfy their fantasies of passionate encounters with the lusty queens and famous mistresses of antiquity.

It was not an uncommon practice among those who eked out a living at the lower end of the profession. And there was no denying that it had the great advantage of allowing the medium to maintain an aura of innocence. After all, she was not the one having sex with the client; she was merely the conduit the spirit employed for the purpose.

She had disliked the nature of the work involved, but it was not as if she'd had a great deal of choice, she reminded herself.

Eventually she had added the planchette, some rappings and the odd manifestation to her repertoire. Those techniques had brought her a different, less demanding clientele.

Then a few months ago *he* had come into her life and she had found herself back in the old role. In the beginning she had assured herself that their relationship was purely a business matter as far as she was concerned. But she had made a devastating mistake. She had fallen in love.

How could she have been so foolish? It was as if she had been entranced, she thought. But the spell had been broken at last by the spilling of blood, the oldest magic of all. Not that she believed in that sort of superstitious nonsense, she reminded herself, shuddering.

But she did believe in revenge, and soon hers would be fulfilled.

Somewhere in the house a floorboard creaked. The eerie groan echoed loudly in the stillness, startling her. She took a deep breath and told herself to be calm. The sound was nothing more than the familiar squeak of wood on wood that one often heard when one was alone at night.

She forced herself to concentrate on other matters. The séance had gone exceptionally well tonight, she thought. It had been particularly gratifying to have Mrs. Fordyce present. The author was certainly one of the most important people she had ever attracted to a sitting. Granted, Caroline Fordyce did not move in Society, but she was becoming quite well known and there was no doubt that many people in high circles read her novels.

Irene's only regret was the inspiration that had made her summon the author's dead husband. There was always an element of risk involved in contacting the spirit of a departed spouse, she reflected. A medium had to be careful with that sort of thing, especially when she was not acquainted with the nature of the relationship between the client and the deceased. She still recalled all too vividly that one dreadful evening when she had summoned up a dead husband only to discover that the widow had hated him intensely and had very likely speeded him on his way to the Other Side.

Pretending to make contact with Jeremy Fordyce had seemed harmless enough, though, until she had looked across the table and glimpsed the cold fury in Mr. Grove's hard eyes. In that unsettling moment, a chill of dread had shot through her from head to toe. She shuddered again just thinking about it. She had sensed immediately that she had miscalculated badly.

For a few terrible seconds she had feared that Mr. Grove might strike a light and expose all her tricks, including the false wax hands she had placed on the table so that her real hands were free to manipulate the various devices she employed.

It had been an unnerving moment, to be sure. Luckily Mrs. Fordyce had managed to keep a tight rein on her so-called assistant.

Irene made a note not to mention the departed husband again in Mr. Grove's hearing.

She certainly intended to promote the association with Mrs. Fordyce, however. The author could open new doors for her, Irene thought with satisfaction. It was a fact that the social rules were just as rigid when it came to communicating with the Other Side as they were in every other aspect of life. The inhabitants of the Polite World were as fascinated with spiritualism as everyone else, but they preferred to patronize mediums who at least appeared to come from their own ranks. True, they occasionally amused themselves by attending séances given by those whom they considered their social inferiors, but they would never for one moment consider allowing an Irene Toller into their exquisitely furnished drawing rooms.

Even if she did manage to work her way up to such lofty heights, she knew she would be nothing more than a carnival entertainer in the eyes of the elite. They would never see her in the same light as Julian Elsworth.

She snorted softly and gulped more gin. If only those rich, arrogant Society types who doted on Elsworth knew the truth about him. She grimaced. The things she could tell them about that man.

Another eerie groan emanated from somewhere in the cold house. She glanced uneasily toward the secret compartment where she had hidden the damning evidence of her crime. There had been no opportunity to dispose of it yet but she intended to do so first thing in the morning. She would put the bloodstained gown into a sack, add a few rocks for weight and toss it into the river.

She was sorry about the dress. It had been a lovely one. He had bought it for her. She simply hadn't expected that there would be so much blood.

A draft of air sighed somewhere in the darkness of the hallway. Irene's fingers tightened around the glass. It was as if the spirit of the dead woman had just called her name.

Stop this nonsense at once.

"You were as big a fool as I, Elizabeth Delmont," she whispered into the shadows. "We both should have understood from the outset that neither of us could compete with *her* phantom."

She swallowed more gin to steady her nerves. He would be here soon. She must remain focused on the second part of her vengeance.

A short series of soft, muffled knocks sounded hollowly from the front hall. Irene lurched to her feet, pulse racing in spite of the gin.

He was here at last. The time had come to exact the remainder of her revenge.

The house felt so very strange tonight. She suddenly wished that she had not sent Bess away after the séance. But what she had planned could hardly be done in front of witnesses.

The light raps sounded again, reminding Irene of the tappings that the spirits made in the course of a séance.

For some inexplicable reason she had to force herself to go down the hall to the door. What was the matter with her? Why was she suddenly so frightened? There was no reason for this irrational terror. She had a plan, one that would not only exact vengeance but would make her far more money than the investment schemes.

She paused in the hall, breathed deeply and opened the door.

186

"I got your message," he said.

"Come in."

He crossed the threshold. "You have made things very difficult for me, Irene."

"Did you really believe that I would let you use me and then betray me as if I was nothing more than a cheap whore?"

"Actually you are worse than a cheap whore. You are a fraudulent whore. But let's not quarrel over details. Tell me what it is you want from me."

She smiled through her rage. "Follow me and I will tell you precisely what you must do unless you wish me to expose your secrets to the press."

"This sounds remarkably like blackmail."

"Think of it as a business proposition."

She led the way back down the hall to the séance room. When she walked into the chamber, he was a few steps behind her.

"Something tells me this conversation is going to be most unpleasant," he said. "Do you mind if I help myself to some gin?"

"You will help yourself to nothing more of what is mine," she replied, turning her head to give him a scornful look over her shoulder.

Too late she saw that he had picked up one of the pair of heavy brass candlesticks that sat on the hall table. That was when she knew that she had miscalculated for the second time that night.

She opened her mouth to scream and instinctively whirled around to run. But there was no place to flee in the small space.

He struck so swiftly and with such force that the only sound she made was a soft grunt.

She collapsed under the first blow but he hit her again and again until the carpet was soaked with blood. Until he knew for certain that she was dead.

When he was finished he was breathing heavily. Sweat beaded his brow. He looked down at his victim.

"Fraudulent whore."

He took his time creating the effect he wanted in the séance room. When he was satisfied, he removed the pocket watch and checked the time. Twelve-fifteen.

He carefully repositioned the hands and then placed the watch on the floor beside the body. He brought the heel of his shoe down with great force, shattering the glass and the intricate works inside the case.

The hands of the watch stopped forever at midnight.

CHAPTER
NINETEEN

He did not just want her, Adam acknowledged to himself sometime later. He craved her.

Seated in the carriage once more, he looked at Caroline in the shadows. Between the two of them they had managed to get her back into her petticoats and gown and put her hair to rights. She looked quite presentable once more. But nothing could dim the sparkle of newfound knowledge that illuminated her face.

He was not accustomed to this kind of edgy, restless passion. Even now, after he had made love to her twice and spent himself completely, all he wanted to think about was how and when he could arrange for another rendezvous with Caroline. The seemingly fathomless depths of his desire for her should worry him greatly, he thought. But for some reason he could not manage to summon up the energy or the will to be even mildly alarmed.

Caroline had said very little on the journey back to Corley Lane. She seemed happily lost in her own musings. He wondered if she was contemplating the pleasures of passion or if she was using the experience as fodder for the next chapter in *The Mysterious Gentleman*.

The latter possibility was truly chilling, he thought. If he really wanted to rattle his own nerves with dire concerns about what had happened this evening, the notion of Caroline incorporating her observations into her novel should do the trick nicely.

When the carriage slowed to a halt, she emerged from her reverie with a visible start and peeked through the curtains.

"Good heavens, I am home and we have not even discussed the next step in our investigation," she said.

He cracked open the door of the carriage and turned to step down onto the pavement. "Obviously we were occupied with other, more pressing matters."

Her laughter was as light and refreshing as a spring shower.

"Oh, yes, I see what you mean." She followed him out of the carriage and grew more serious. "I do hope you will not attempt to search Mrs. Toller's house tonight."

"No." He took her arm and started toward the steps. "I plan to wait until she and her assistant take themselves off to Wintersett House tomorrow afternoon for another demonstration of spirit writing."

"You know her schedule?" she asked, sounding surprised.

"I made inquiries this afternoon."

"Ah, yes, your infamous inquiries. Well, I am relieved to hear that you do not intend to go sneaking about her house tonight."

He came to a halt at the top of the steps. "I would like to talk to you about the events that occurred at the séance this evening. There was one thing in particular that made an impression, aside from the mention of Mr. Fordyce. May I call upon you tomorrow?"

"Yes, of course." She reached into the pocket of her gown for her key. "What was it that caught your attention?"

"The investment opportunity that one of the spirits mentioned to the two ladies."

"I remember. But I do not think it means much. I told you, it is quite common for mediums to predict that some of their sitters will come into a surprise inheritance."

"But this struck me as an unusually precise prediction." He took the key from her hand and fitted it into the lock. "There were certain specific details, such as the fact that the man who approached them would identify himself as a friend of their deceased acquaintance."

"Yes, that's true."

"The first time we spoke you mentioned that one of the sitters at Elizabeth Delmont's last sitting received investment advice."

"Yes, you're right," she said. "And it was of a similar nature, now that you mention it. One of the spirits that Delmont summoned told Mr. McDaniel that he would soon be contacted by a gentleman who would mention the phantom's name and provide him with information concerning a lucrative investment. But what does that have to do with murder and the missing diary?"

"Perhaps nothing at all." He opened the door. "But I admit that I find it very interesting that Toller and Delmont made such similar predictions to their sitters."

She stepped into the shadowed front hall and turned to look at him. "Do you think it suggests a link between the two mediums?"

"It's possible, yes."

"But Irene Toller and Elizabeth Delmont were rivals."

"Money makes for strange bedfellows. Just ask any of the husbands and wives in Society."

"That is a very cynical remark, Adam."

"I discovered long ago that one can answer a great many questions about anyone, high or low, if one first examines the source of his or her income."

"An intriguing observation. That reminds me, you said you had plans for that building in Stone Street. What are you going to do with it?"

He hesitated and then decided that there was no reason not to tell her of his intentions. "I am making arrangements to turn it into a charity house for street children. It will be a place where they will be safe and well fed. They will be taught to read and write so that they can make their way in the world."

She gave him a soft, mysteriously knowing smile. "Of course. I should have guessed."

Surprised at the comment, he frowned. "How the devil could you have possibly —"

"Never mind. It's not important. Good night, Adam."

"Good night, Caroline."

"I cannot wait to get back to my new chapter in the morning," she said. "I am suddenly brimming over with fresh ideas for my story."

The door closed very gently in his face.

He stood there for a moment, bemused. At a time like this, some women would be worrying about their reputations or the possibility of pregnancy. Caroline appeared to be concerned only with the plot of her novel.

He wondered if that should give him cause for alarm.

CHAPTER
TWENTY

Shortly after nine-thirty the following morning, Caroline put down her pen and looked at the paragraph that she had just finished writing.

Lydia began to suspect that Edmund Drake was not as he appeared on the surface. The hard, unyielding exterior he presented to the world concealed not just only his secrets but perhaps a certain innate nobility of soul as well. He was not the sort to reveal his true nature easily, but she had learned enough about his character in the wake of the recent, disturbing events to cause her to question her original assumptions.

Drake was most certainly a man of strong passions, she concluded, but those passions were held in check by a powerful will and a sense of honor that would put to shame the shallow code embraced by so many wealthy, well-born gentlemen.

Drake made his own rules, and he lived by them.

Satisfied, Caroline reached for another sheet of paper. The story was coming along nicely. The surprising twist in the character of Edmund Drake

194

would certainly astonish her readers. Now all she needed was another startling incident with which to end the chapter and she would be finished with this week's episode.

She picked up her pen and tapped it lightly on the desktop. A runaway carriage, perhaps? No, that would be much too similar to an earlier incident. That sort of thing had to be spaced out carefully in order to create the desired effect.

What was needed now was a scene of thrilling passion, she decided, Something along the lines of what she had experienced in Adam's arms last night would be perfect.

The exciting memories flooded back. She indulged herself in them once again, aware of tingling warmth in her lower body.

Yes, a passionate embrace would be just the thing to end this chapter. Inspired, she started to write.

In the shadowy light cast by the carriage lamps Lydia could see Edmund Drake's eyes glowing like emerald coals taken from some supernatural fire. He took her into his arms, crushing her against his powerful chest.

"My sweet, beautiful Lydia," he whispered. "When I am with you I cannot seem to control —

"Mrs. Fordyce?"

Caroline started in surprise. Her pen slipped, marring *control*. She looked up quickly and saw Mrs. Plummer standing in the opening.

"Yes, what is it?" she said, trying not to let her impatience show.

"I'm sorry to disturb you while you're writing but this just came for you." Mrs. Plummer walked into the room. She held an envelope in one hand. "A lad brought it around to the kitchen door a moment ago."

"A note?" Caroline was instantly wary. "It's not from Spraggett, is it? He knows very well that the new chapter is not due until the end of the week. I vow, if he does not stop pestering me I am going to lose all patience and look for another publisher."

"No, I don't think it's from Mr. Spraggett. He always sends that young red-haired lad, Tom, when he wants to deliver a message to you. The boy who gave me this was a stranger."

Adam, Caroline thought. It had to be him. No one else had any reason to send her a message. Her pulse sparked and a pleasant sense of euphoria bubbled through her. Then it occurred to her that Adam might have dispatched the note to let her know that he had changed his mind about calling on her today.

"Thank you, Mrs. Plummer."

Snatching the envelope from the housekeeper's fingers, Caroline ripped it open.

Dear Mrs. Fordyce:

I must see you immediately. It concerns a message from the Other Side that was communicated to me last night after you left my house.

Yrs.,
I. Toller

196

"How curious," Caroline said, rereading the note. "It is from the medium."

"Which medium would that be, ma'am?"

"Irene Toller. The one who gave the séance that I attended with my, uh, friend Mr. Hardesty last night." She put the note down, rose quickly and started around the desk. "I wonder what on earth this is all about."

"Will you be going out, then, ma'am?"

"Yes. This is a very interesting turn of events. I do not want to miss the opportunity. I am going straight upstairs to change into a walking dress." She whisked through the door and then paused in the hall. "When my aunts return from their morning constitutional, please tell them that I had to pay a hasty visit to Mrs. Toller and that I shall be back in time for lunch."

"Yes, ma'am."

Caroline hurried toward the stairs and then paused again when another thought struck her. "One more thing, Mrs. Plummer. Mr. Hardesty mentioned that he would pay a call sometime today. If he arrives before I return, will you please tell him that I will be back shortly and ask him to wait?"

"Yes, ma'am."

She was forced to let two dashing hansom cabs go past before a lumbering hackney presented itself. It was really most annoying not to be able to use a hansom, she thought, climbing up into the aging carriage. Not only did the design, with its open front and the driver up behind, appear as though it would provide the passenger with a marvelous view, the hansoms were

197

considerably faster and more agile in the London traffic than other vehicles.

Unfortunately, any lady, even a widow, who was seen riding in a hansom was considered to be fast in more ways than one.

Sometime later the hackney stopped in the street in front of Irene Toller's address. The house appeared just as bleak and gloomy this morning as it had the night before when it had been shrouded in fog and darkness, Caroline thought, alighting.

She was concentrating so intently on wondering why Irene Toller had sent the message that she did not immediately take note of the small cluster of people standing about in the street in front of the house. When she realized that a crowd had gathered, a trickle of alarm coursed through her. Something was very wrong here.

She caught snippets of conversation when she went up the steps.

"The villain broke into her house while she was asleep is the way I heard it," announced a woman who wore a housekeeper's apron.

"Can't believe it happened right here in our street," a maid whispered.

"Never had any trouble like this in all the years I've lived here," a matronly-looking female declared. "This is a respectable neighborhood."

Caroline's alarm intensified. All she could think about in that dreadful moment of realization was Adam and his plan to search the premises. Had he changed his mind after he had taken her home? Had he come directly here instead of waiting until later today as he had planned?

"Who's that woman on the front step?" someone hissed behind Caroline. "Never saw her around here before."

Caroline ignored the curiosity and banged the knocker. *Please don't let this have anything to do with Adam.*

Heavy footsteps sounded in the narrow hall. The door opened. She found herself gazing at a large burly man in a constable's uniform.

"What would you be wanting at this address, madam?" he demanded.

Panic shot through her. Had Adam been caught in the act of searching Toller's house? Visions of him being clapped in irons and hauled off to a damp, dark prison seared her brain.

She forced herself to speak calmly. "I received a message from Mrs. Toller a short while ago. Is something wrong?"

"A message, you say?" The constable squinted a bit. "From the medium?"

"Yes. I came immediately."

A short, spindly, thin man in an ill-fitting suit appeared behind the first man. There was a shrewd, no-nonsense air about him.

"What's going on out there, Constable?"

"There's a lady here, Inspector." The policeman glanced back over his shoulder. "Says she got a message from the medium a short time ago."

"Well, now, isn't that interesting?" The inspector came forward. "Very interesting, indeed. And who might you be, madam?"

"My name is Mrs. Fordyce," Caroline said. She managed to keep her voice firm but she could scarcely breathe. "I do not believe we have met."

"Inspector J. J. Jackson, at your service. What is your business here, Mrs. Fordyce?"

The situation was growing worse by the second, Caroline thought. "As I just told the constable, I received a message. It sounded quite urgent."

A third figure emerged from the dark hallway behind the inspector.

"Good morning, Mrs. Fordyce," Adam said. He spoke in an extremely polite, very cool manner, as though they were on only the most formal of terms. "It is certainly a surprise to see you here."

Her stomach clenched. Her worst fears were confirmed. Adam had been caught inside Irene Toller's house. There was no mistaking the message that he was sending her now with his chilly, impersonal air. He wanted her to pretend that they barely knew each other.

She managed what she hoped was a bright, polite smile. "How nice to see you again, sir," she said smoothly. She did not dare to address him by name because she had no way of knowing if he was using Hardesty or Grove. "I gather that you also received a message from the medium asking you to call this morning?"

"Yes," Adam said without any inflection whatsoever. "When I arrived I found Inspector Jackson and the constable here."

"I see," Caroline said. She felt as though she were making her way through a field of nettles. "Was anyone hurt?"

"You could say that Mrs. Toller was badly hurt," Inspector J. J. Jackson announced solemnly. "She's dead."

"*Dead.*" Unnerved, Caroline sat down hard on a small chair set against the wall directly beneath a row of iron coat hooks. "Dear heaven."

"Murdered in her séance room. The place was ripped apart. Furniture upended. Lamp broken. That sort of thing."

"Same as the other one," the constable said with a knowledgeable nod.

"Mrs. Toller appears to have been struck several times on the back of her head," Inspector Jackson continued, remarkably matter-of-fact.

"Just like the other medium," the constable offered ominously.

Caroline forced herself to think. "She cannot have been dead for very long."

J. J. Jackson rocked on his heels. "Murdered at midnight."

"Just like the other one," the constable mumbled again.

"Midnight? But that's impossible. I just had a note from Mrs. Toller." Caroline checked her watch. "It was delivered less than forty minutes ago."

201

Jackson raised one narrow shoulder in a shrug. "She must have written it last night and given it to her housekeeper to dispatch this morning."

Caroline looked around. "And just where is the housekeeper?"

"She hasn't turned up yet," the constable said.

"How did you learn of the murder?" she demanded.

"Got an anonymous message," Jackson said. "A tip, you might say. We depend on that sort of thing."

"What makes you so certain that Mrs. Toller was killed at midnight?" Caroline asked.

Jackson cleared his throat and looked at Adam. "As it happens, we found a gentleman's pocket watch on the floor beside the body. Mr. Hardesty and I were just discussing it when you arrived."

Mr. Hardesty. So Adam had given the inspector his real name. She did not know if that boded ill or not.

"A watch?" she asked carefully.

"Same as happened with the last one," the constable said with another wise nod.

Caroline recalled Adam telling her that he had seen a broken pocket watch next to Elizabeth Delmont's body.

"I don't understand," she said evenly. "What does the watch tell you about the time of the medium's death?"

"It appears to have been smashed in the course of the struggle." J. J. Jackson moved one hand in a dramatic fashion, a magician unveiling a new trick. "The hands are stopped at twelve o'clock precisely."

"Do you believe that the watch belonged to the killer?" she asked, her curiosity resurfacing.

202

The inspector and the constable looked at her as if they found the question exceedingly strange. Another chill went through her.

Adam folded his arms and leaned one shoulder against the wall. "The pocket watch in question is engraved with my name, Mrs. Fordyce."

"*What?*" She leaped to her feet, horrified. "But that's not possible."

This was far worse than she had believed. This was a case of murder. Adam might hang. The image that came to mind made her feel quite faint.

Struggling to conceal her panic, she gave Adam a quick, searching glance, silently asking for guidance. But his face remained grimly unreadable.

"Those are the facts, ma'am," Jackson announced. "No mistaking the name on the watch. Spelled out clear as a bell."

Caroline swung around to confront him. "I can assure you that Mr. Hardesty had nothing to do with the death of Irene Toller."

Inspector Jackson arched thick brows.

"Mrs. Fordyce," Adam said flatly, "I think it would be best if you refrained from commenting further on this affair."

It was an order, but she had no intention whatsoever of obeying it.

"Inspector Jackson," she said in her most forceful tones. "I cannot explain how Mr. Hardesty's pocket watch came to be at the scene of the crime, but I can assure you that Mr. Hardesty himself was nowhere near this house at midnight last night."

Adam's jaw jerked in annoyance. "Mrs. Fordyce, you've said quite enough."

"And how does it happen that you are so certain of Mr. Hardesty's whereabouts last night?" Jackson asked, politely curious.

"Because Mr. Hardesty was with me at midnight, Inspector." She raised her chin. "We attended a séance here at Mrs. Toller's house earlier in the evening and then we left together in Mr. Hardesty's carriage. The other sitters will confirm that."

Jackson nodded. "Mr. Hardesty claims the séance ended around ten o'clock."

"That is correct," she said.

Jackson regarded her with keen interest. "How far away is your address, Mrs. Fordyce?"

"About half an hour, depending on traffic."

"In that case, you would have been home well before midnight, leaving Mr. Hardesty plenty of time to return to this house and commit the murder," Jackson observed.

Outraged, Caroline looked down her nose at the short man. "Mr. Hardesty and I did not go to my address directly after the séance. We spent a number of hours together. He did not deliver me home until nearly two o'clock in the morning."

"Is that a fact?" The inspector took a notebook out of his pocket. "Well, now, that is very interesting, Mrs. Fordyce. Did the two of you attend a party or the theater, perhaps?"

"No, Inspector, we were alone together in a room in Stone Street. Mr. Hardesty's coachman drove us there and picked us up a few hours later."

Adam exhaled heavily and appeared to resign himself to some inevitable fate.

"Alone together in a room in Stone Street," Jackson repeated softly, making some notes. "Very interesting, Mrs. Fordyce." He gave Adam a speculative look. "Didn't realize that the two of you were so closely acquainted."

Caroline reminded herself that she actually was an experienced woman of the world as of last night. She gave the inspector her most polished smile. "Yes, indeed, Mr. Hardesty and I are very good friends, Inspector. Intimate acquaintances, as it were. And I will be happy to testify in a court of law that he was with me last night at the time of the murder."

Adam wrapped strong fingers around her arm. "If you will excuse us, Inspector, I will escort Mrs. Fordyce home. If you have more questions for me, you know my address."

Jackson pocketed his notebook. "Thank you, sir."

Adam steered Caroline through the front door and down the steps. A familiar face lunged out of the crowd and hurried toward them. He had a copy of a newspaper tucked under one arm.

"Mrs. Fordyce. Mr. Grove."

Caroline looked at him in surprise. "Mr. Smith. What are you doing here?"

"Actually, the name is Otford. Gilbert Otford." He whipped the newspaper out from under his arm and held it aloft like a banner. "When we met at Toller's séance last night, I was not free to inform you that I am a correspondent for the *Flying Intelligencer*."

"I recognize your name," Caroline said, suddenly incensed anew. "You did that dreadful piece on me, didn't you? The one about my supposed demonstration of psychical powers at a certain tea."

"Yes. It was all very interesting, but I fear that it is old news." Gilbert's cunning eyes shifted back and forth between Caroline and Adam. "I have been informed that Mrs. Toller was murdered sometime during the night. Is it true?"

"How did you come to learn of the murder of Mrs. Toller?" Adam asked before Caroline could respond.

A secretive expression pinched Otford's features. He put a bony finger alongside his sharp nose. "Let us just say that information reached me a short time ago. We correspondents depend on informants, you know. I'm pleased to say that mine are among the swiftest and the most accurate."

"Given your decidedly misleading piece on me, perhaps you should review the accuracy of your informants," Caroline snapped.

Adam contemplated him as though deciding whether to set a rat trap or simply fetch a broom and sweep Otford into the gutter. "Why were you at the séance last night?"

Otford lowered his voice and looked around quickly, making certain that no one could overhear him. "Between you and me, sir, I am conducting an investigation of mediums with the intention of exposing their deceptive practices. Public's right to know and all that sort of thing. That is why I did not reveal my identity last night. I was incognito, as it were."

"What a coincidence." Adam produced a card. Rather than handing it to Otford, he contrived to drop it into the correspondent's palm in a not-so-subtle manner that made it clear he disdained any physical contact. "I neglected to tell you my true identity also. Adam Hardesty. I am not Mrs. Fordyce's personal assistant. I am her friend."

Caroline watched Otford stare at the card, eyes widening. She could tell that the Hardesty name registered immediately. When it all finally came together, Otford's eyes glittered with barely restrained excitement.

"I say, sir, this is all extremely unusual." Otford took out a small pad of paper and a pencil. "False identities and what-not. Very curious. Would you care to explain what the two of you were doing at the scene of a murder this morning?"

Caroline could almost see Otford writing his next crime sensation story in his head. Disaster loomed.

Adam casually reached out and jerked the notepad from the correspondent's fingers. "Confidentially, Otford, Mrs. Fordyce and I were aiding the police in their inquiries. If her name appears in any piece written about this murder, I assure you that you will hear from me very soon thereafter. Do I make myself clear, Mr. Otford?"

Otford's mouth opened and closed twice. He took a step back. "I say, sir, you cannot threaten a gentleman of the press."

"I do not see any of that breed in the vicinity," Adam said. "I only see you. For the sake of your continuing

207

good health, I strongly recommend that you keep in mind the fact that I never make threats, Mr. Otford. I only make promises. Good day."

Adam drew Caroline down the street to a waiting hackney cab.

CHAPTER
TWENTY-ONE

Caroline did not speak during the entire trip back to Corley Lane. She could scarcely order her thoughts, let alone voice them aloud. Adam lounged beside her, one foot braced on the opposite cushion, his attention on the scene outside the window. He made no attempt to shatter the brittle silence inside the cab. She had no clue at all to what he was thinking.

When they arrived at Number 22, she was deeply relieved to discover that Emma and Milly had not yet returned from their morning exercise. She stormed into her study and flung herself down into the chair behind her desk.

"That," she announced, "was a very near thing. I am still shivering in my shoes."

Adam strolled into the room behind her and stopped in the center of the carpet. He put his hands in his pockets and contemplated her thoughtfully.

"It was somewhat dicey there for a moment or two," he agreed.

"This is no time for bad jests, sir." She frowned. "You do realize that your threats will very likely not keep Otford from writing a piece on the murder and our connection to it for the *Flying Intelligencer*?"

"I admit I am not hopeful on that point."

"I assure you, an item that involves another murdered medium, a powerful gentleman and a sensation novelist will prove utterly irresistible to Otford and Mr. Spraggett." She raised a finger in warning. "Mark my words, the story, in one version or another, will appear in print sooner or later."

"I suspect you are right." He looked around expectantly. "Have you got any brandy, by chance?"

She closed her eyes. "We seem to be dealing with an ever-widening scandal. How can you be so calm about this situation?"

"Do not mistake my mood. I'm not entirely unconcerned. I do recognize that we have a few problems on our hands."

She opened her eyes. "I'm pleased to hear that."

"About the brandy? I know it is rather early in the day, but I could use a restorative. It has been a trying morning."

"There is some sherry in that cupboard," she said grudgingly.

"Thank you." He opened the cabinet and removed the decanter of sherry. "Not quite the strong tonic I would have preferred but it will have to do." He selected a glass. "I am sorry if you are distressed at the notion of having your name linked with mine in the press, Caroline. But I would remind you that you were the one who insisted on informing Inspector Jackson that we spent a good portion of last night together in extremely intimate circumstances."

She spread her hands. "There was no help for it. I had to tell him that you were with me at the time of the murder."

"Actually," he said with grave precision, "you did not have to tell him any such thing. You must have realized that I had not given him your name or mentioned the nature of our association."

"Yes, I gathered that much. You were trying to protect me. I appreciate your intentions, Adam, but I simply could not remain silent under the circumstances."

"I see." He drank some sherry and lowered the glass. "A prudent woman who had a proper concern for her reputation would have had the sense to remain quiet and thereby avoid being dragged deeper into an unpleasant scandal."

"We have both agreed that my status as a widow gives me a great deal of freedom."

He raised his brows. "You know very well that if it gets out that you are not really a widow, your reputation will be ripped to shreds."

"You are worrying about an extremely unlikely possibility. I suggest that you save your energy for more pressing concerns."

He gave that a moment's consideration and then inclined his head. "Perhaps you are right. What's done is done. We must go forward from here."

"Quite right." Relieved that he was not going to lecture her further, she folded her arms on top of the desk. "Did you have an opportunity to examine the scene of Mrs. Toller's murder?"

"To some extent. Inspector Jackson did not object to my looking around the séance room."

"No sign of the diary, I take it?"

"None."

"Aside from the pocket watch, were there any other similarities to the scene of Mrs. Delmont's murder?"

"The scene in Mrs. Toller's séance room duplicated the scene at Mrs. Delmont's house in every particular that was reported in the press," he said softly. "And I find that fact quite interesting."

"Every particular reported in the press?" Understanding dawned. "You mean there was no wedding veil and no brooch?"

He shook his head. "Whoever killed Toller evidently used the newspaper reports of Delmont's death as a guide to setting the stage for the second murder."

"That implies that he or she is not the same person who murdered Mrs. Delmont."

"So it seems." Adam contemplated his sherry. "Which brings us back to the question of what happened to the veil and the brooch."

"Perhaps a neighbor or even one of the constables stole them."

"No." He turned the sherry glass in his hands. "Do you recall that the papers mentioned the jewelry that Delmont was wearing at the time of her death?"

"That's right. There was a necklace and a pair of earrings according to the piece in the *Flying Intelligencer*."

"I saw them," Adam said. "They looked far more valuable than the ruined veil and an inexpensive brooch. A common thief would have seized them."

212

She reflected on that briefly. "What about the pocket watches?"

"The watch I saw next to Delmont's body was inscribed with her initials, so I assume it belonged to her. It may have simply fallen out of her pocket when she was killed. As for the one that was found next to Toller's body, all I can say is that, although it was engraved with my name, it does not belong to me."

She stared at him in mounting horror. "The killer must have purchased it, had your name put on it and then deliberately left it at the scene of the crime to implicate you."

"That would seem to have been his intention, yes."

"Adam, this is dreadful."

He finished the sherry without comment.

She glowered. "May I ask why this development does not appear to concern you greatly?"

He gave her a slow cold smile. "Because it implies that I am making progress."

"I am not at all certain that I agree with your interpretation of progress." She paused. "I wonder who sent those messages summoning us to Mrs. Toller's address this morning."

"I don't know but it would appear that someone wanted us to be in the vicinity when the police began their investigation," he said.

"But why?"

"We will find out eventually." He paused. "Caroline?"

"Yes?"

"It was very noble of you to provide me with an alibi for last night," he said quietly. "Thank you."

His gratitude made her blush. "It was nothing. I'm sure that eventually you would have convinced the inspector that you were telling the truth."

"One would hope so but the fact that you vouched for my whereabouts at midnight last night certainly makes things a great deal more simple and straightforward. I am in your debt, Caroline."

"Nonsense. The thing that worries me the most at the moment is that given the great sensation that will be made in the press, rumors will be flying all over town. Everyone will be talking about us, not about finding the real killer. By the time the scandal quiets down, the trail will have gone quite cold."

"Perhaps that was the villain's intent." Adam's mouth twisted in a feral way. "You have to hand it to him, it is a rather ingenious scheme, especially when you consider that it had to be concocted on such short notice."

She rubbed her temples with her fingertips. "What is our next step?"

"I find myself returning again and again to the fact that both Delmont and Toller summoned spirits who gave financial advice to some of the sitters but not to others. There is some link there. I can feel it."

"I agree there are several questions to be answered."

"Yes, but before we pursue them, there is another little matter that must be dealt with."

She looked up uneasily. "What is that?"

"You must meet my family, at least those who are present here in town, and you must do so before they read about you in the newspapers."

214

CHAPTER
TWENTY-TWO

Adam found Wilson in his club, sitting alone in a corner, drinking coffee and reading the day's edition of the *Flying Intelligencer*.

"Where the deuce have you been?" Wilson peered at him over the top of the paper. "Thought you'd be back hours ago." He took an envelope out of his jacket. "This telegram came for you while you were out."

Adam sat down and ripped open the telegram. It was from Harold Filby.

REGRET TO INFORM YOU NO PROGRESS IN
INVESTIGATION STOP.

Adam looked up. "Have you ever heard of a village called Chillingham?"

Wilson pondered briefly. "There's a Chillingham not far from Bath, as I recall."

Adam motioned to one of the elderly servants. "Pen and paper, if you please. I want to send a telegram."

The man returned with the requested items. Adam dashed off a message.

TRY NEARBY VILLAGE OF CHILLINGHAM STOP.
TRY LAST NAME OF CONNOR STOP. DISCRETION
CRUCIAL STOP.

He noted Filby's address in Bath and then gave the message to the porter, who hurried off to dispatch it to the telegraph office.

Wilson raised his brows. "What was that all about?"

"I will explain later."

"Well, then, did Irene Toller try to extort money in exchange for the diary as you suspected she would when you got her message this morning?"

"No. Toller was murdered last night in a manner very similar to that in which Delmont was killed. Several violent blows to the head. Séance room torn apart again."

"Good lord. Are you serious?"

"Yes."

"Astonishing." Wilson reached for his coffee with a troubled expression. "This is most extraordinary. A second murdered medium will certainly heap more fuel onto the fires that have been ignited in some of the more colorful newspapers." He nodded toward the copy of the *Flying Intelligencer* that he had been reading. "I just finished a piece by some fool named Otford who hinted that Delmont's murder might be attributable to supernatural forces. Of all the damnable nonsense. I can only imagine what he will have to say about a second similar killing."

"Otford may prove to be a problem in other ways, as well." Adam put his fingertips together. "I will deal with him if necessary. Meanwhile, I am pursuing the possibility that Toller and Delmont were perpetrating some sort of fraudulent financial scheme."

"Ah, yes." Wilson nodded sagely. "Follow the money."

"I thought your advice was *cherchez la femme*," Adam queried.

"Women and money often go together."

"Forgive me, sir, but that piece of wisdom is not terribly helpful in light of the fact that men and money often go together, as well."

"I will allow you that much." Wilson laced his hands over his belly. "Were you able to conduct a search for the diary at Toller's house?"

"Not a very thorough one. By the time I got to her address this morning, the police had already arrived. I managed to make a casual examination of the séance room and portions of the downstairs hall while I chatted with the inspector but I could hardly start opening drawers or lift up the carpet. No matter. I am certain the diary is gone."

"You believe that the killer took it?"

"It is one possibility, but there are others."

"Such as?"

"Mrs. Toller had a housekeeper who also served as her assistant and partner in some ways. She seems to have vanished. I got her name from one of the neighbors. I hope to locate her." He paused. "As it happens, Toller's death is only one of several recent events that will no doubt interest you."

"Indeed?"

"The police found a pocket watch with my name on it at the scene of the Toller murder, the time stopped presumably at the very moment the act of violence was carried out."

Everything about Wilson seemed to sharpen with alarm. "Was it one of your watches?"

"No. It was a cheap timepiece. The engraving work was poorly done, but quite legible."

"This means the killer knows that you are searching for him. He used the watch to point the finger of guilt at you."

"So it appears." Adam tapped his fingertips twice. "Matters have become more complicated. I did not want to alarm Julia, but I think the time has come to tell her and Southwood what is going on."

"Indeed. This situation has become extremely worrisome. It would be best if they were made aware of events." Wilson narrowed his eyes. "I assume the police consider you a suspect?"

Adam shrugged. "The inspector had some questions but most of them were put to rest when he discovered that I had an excellent alibi. A close acquaintance verified my claim that I was otherwise occupied when Toller was murdered."

"I am relieved to hear that." Wilson relaxed visibly. "That should make things a good deal less dire. What time was Toller killed?"

"Midnight."

Wilson nodded. "That was well after the séance had ended. You were no doubt at your club. You probably have a dozen witnesses." He gave a disdainful snort.

"The killer should have had the sense to confirm your whereabouts before he tried to implicate you."

"I was not at my club."

"Where were you? The theater?"

"No. I went to the rooms in Stone Street."

"At midnight?"

"Yes."

"I don't understand." Wilson scowled. "When you go there, you always go alone. Who is this acquaintance who vouched for your whereabouts?"

"My very good friend, Mrs. Fordyce."

"Fordyce? Fordyce." Wilson's expression was puzzled. "Do you refer to the author Mrs. Fordyce?"

"Yes."

Wilson looked stunned. "The deuce, you say. This is no time to exhibit your eccentric sense of humor, Adam."

"It is not a joke. Brace yourself, sir. I am about to become embroiled in a shocking scandal involving murder and an illicit liaison with a famous sensation novelist."

CHAPTER
TWENTY-THREE

"Brace yourselves." Caroline folded her hands on top of her desk and faced Emma and Milly. "A number of startling incidents occurred last night and early this morning while you were out."

"How exciting." Enthused, as always, by the promise of entertaining news, Milly bustled to the nearest chair and sat down. "Do tell us everything, dear."

Predictably, Emma did not appear nearly so enthusiastic. She lowered herself into one of the reading chairs and examined Caroline with the air of a physician watching for signs of a high fever. "Are you all right?"

"I am quite fit, I assure you." Caroline paused. "So much has happened in the past few hours that I am not certain where to begin."

"Just start anywhere, dear," Milly advised with an airy wave of her hand.

"Very well. Another medium has been murdered in a manner that is strangely reminiscent of the way in which Elizabeth Delmont was killed."

The clock ticked into the astounded hush that followed that announcement.

"This is shocking news." Emma looked dazed. "Absolutely shocking."

Milly had clearly been jolted out of the first flush of excitement. "Another dead medium, you say? Which one?"

"Irene Toller," Caroline said.

"Delmont's rival?" Milly frowned. "But I thought that you and Adam had concluded that Toller was very likely a suspect in the murder of Elizabeth Delmont."

"Mr. Hardesty and I certainly considered that a distinct possibility. But we may have been wrong."

Before she could launch into a more thorough recitation of events, she was interrupted by the muffled clatter of hooves, harness and carriage wheels.

The rumble in the street ceased abruptly as the heavy vehicle halted in front of Number 22.

"I wonder who that can be," Emma said, distracted.

Someone banged the brass knocker. The sound was followed by the patter of Mrs. Plummer's footsteps. The door opened in the front hall. Voices could be heard.

A short time later Mrs. Plummer loomed in the doorway of the study. Her ruddy features were redder than usual. She held herself in a self-consciously erect, square-shouldered manner: a woman with a message of great importance.

She cleared her throat portentously.

"The Earl of Southwood, Lady Southwood, Mr. Wilson Grendon and Mr. Hardesty have called. Shall I say that you are home?"

Milly shot to her feet. "Oh, my. An earl and a countess? And Mr. Grendon, as well? What will the neighbors think?"

Emma lurched out of her chair. "Why would Mr. Hardesty bring his relatives here? They must have got the wrong address, Mrs. Plummer."

"No," Caroline said wearily. "I fear they have come to the right address." She nodded to Mrs. Plummer. "Please show our guests into the parlor."

"What is going on?" Milly demanded.

"Why would the Earl of Southwood and his wife call on us?" Emma asked. "And Mr. Wilson Grendon, too."

Caroline rose. "It has to do with another startling incident that I have not had a chance to relate to you."

"What is it?" Emma asked.

"The police viewed Mr. Hardesty as a possible suspect in the murder of Mrs. Toller."

Emma and Milly stared at her, open-mouthed.

"Do not concern yourselves," Caroline said hastily. "All is well. I was able to provide him with a firm alibi. But unfortunately, I fear that the entire affair is about to erupt into a sensation in the press."

"I must tell you that I am a great admirer of your stories, Mrs. Fordyce." Julia accepted a cup of tea from Milly. "It is so exciting to meet you."

"Yes, indeed." Wilson enthusiastically helped himself to a tart from the tea tray. "Don't mind saying that you make a delightful change from the usual run of Adam's acquaintances."

222

"Very true," Richard, the Earl of Southwood, said. He was a quiet, thoughtful man who stood directly behind his wife as though casting a protective shadow over her. He gave Adam a dryly amused look. "But then Hardesty rarely reads anything other than *The Times*, so it stands to reason that his circle of associates is usually equally dull."

Adam, positioned near the window, ignored his brother-in-law. He seemed content to let his relatives conduct the interview with Caroline, Emma and Milly.

Caroline managed a smile. In truth, she was feeling overwhelmed. Given what Adam had told her about his family's odd past, perhaps it should not have come as a surprise that Richard, Julia and Wilson did not exhibit the cold, supercilious behavior one would have expected. They were not, after all, typical members of the Polite World. Nevertheless, she was secretly astonished at how comfortable the elegantly dressed visitors appeared in their modest surroundings.

Julia's expression became more serious. "Adam has told us something of your recent adventures."

Wilson nodded somberly. "We are aware that you have assisted him in his search for a certain diary. The two of you have certainly had an exciting time of it."

"Indeed they have." Emma leaned forward tensely, pinning Adam with her sharp gaze. "I do not like to pry and if it were not for the fact that Caroline is quite intimately involved in this affair, I would not dream of doing so. But my niece appears to be in this thing up to her neck and I feel it is only right that we should know

223

why you consider it so important to retrieve that diary, Mr. Hardesty."

Milly abruptly ceased smiling, allowing everyone a clear glimpse of the sturdy, purposeful character that lay directly beneath her cheerful, optimistic exterior. "I am in complete agreement with Emma. The situation has become distinctly menacing, what with two women dead. I think we deserve to be given some notion of the nature of the threat if only so that Caroline can be protected."

"The details are not necessary," Caroline said, quickly. "Mr. Hardesty has told me enough to satisfy me that it is very important to recover the diary."

Julia smiled gently. "Your aunts deserve to know the full particulars, Mrs. Fordyce."

"No, really," Caroline began.

Julia looked at Emma and Milly. "The long and the short of it is that my brothers and sister and I are not related by blood. We have no family connections to Uncle Wilson except those created by affection and loyalty."

"I don't understand," Emma said, frowning slightly.

"We were all abandoned to our fates in the streets many years ago," Julia continued. "If it had not been for Adam, who rescued each one of us, Jessica, Nathan and I would likely have perished."

Richard put a reassuring hand on her shoulder. Julia reached up and lightly touched his fingers with her own. The aura of intimacy and love that enveloped the pair was unmistakable. Theirs was a love match, Caroline realized. How fortunate they were.

"The truth about our pasts is in that missing diary," Julia concluded. "Adam is determined to find it and destroy it. He is most concerned for Jessica and Nathan, who are both still quite young. Jessica, especially, is vulnerable. She is only eighteen and on the verge of her debut into Society."

"Astonishing," Milly whispered, wide-eyed.

Julia looked at Caroline. "Adam said that he took you to the rooms in Stone Street last night."

Caroline was acutely aware of Emma and Milly watching her in veiled surprise. She tried to suppress the heat that rose in her cheeks. She really was a woman of experience now. She must act like the widow she purported to be. Widows who were having affairs with powerful gentlemen did not allow themselves to be easily embarrassed.

"Yes," she said, trying to keep her tone equally calm and cool. "He told me something of your past there and of how the four of you came to make the acquaintance of Mr. Grendon."

"If Adam trusted you with the secrets of Stone Street, then I have no qualms whatsoever about trusting you," Julia said simply.

Wilson reached for another tart. "I agree with Julia."

Richard shrugged. "Hardesty has his irritating little quirks but I must admit that he is generally quite accurate when it comes to judging the trustworthiness of others."

Adam's mouth kicked up at the corner. "Thank you, Southwood. I had no idea that you thought so highly of me."

Richard grinned unexpectedly. "You approved me as a husband for Julia, did you not? Obviously you know sound character when you encounter it, even if you do occasionally require convincing evidence."

"You proved your character when you refused to be put off by the truth about my past, Richard," Julia said.

He gripped her shoulder gently. "How could I not fall in love with such a brave young woman?"

Julia smiled, her love clear in her eyes.

Milly dabbed the corner of her eyes with a lace handkerchief. "How romantic."

Wilson cleared his throat. "I have assured Adam that any gossip that resulted from a revelation of the contents of the diary could be lived down, but he is determined to find the thing, if possible, and burn it. Must admit, it would be simpler if he got rid of it before anyone else reads it. I do worry a bit about how Jessica might fare next Season if there are rumors about her past going around."

"Yes," Richard said, his expression hardening. "And I, too, would much prefer that Julia not become the subject of that sort of gossip."

"Blackmail is essentially a business matter," Wilson assured them. "No one is better at such dealings than Adam."

Julia, Richard and Wilson got into the earl's gleaming coach a short time later. Adam stood with Caroline, Emma and Milly and watched the liveried footman close the door of the vehicle.

"Heavens, what with all the excitement, I almost forgot." Julia leaned out the window to look at Caroline, Emma and Milly. "Richard and I are hosting a ball the night after next. You must all attend, of course."

Alarm spiked through Caroline. "Impossible. Can't possibly make it."

"Other plans? I know this is awfully late notice."

Emma shook her head. "Caroline is right. The three of us cannot attend. It is very kind of you to ask."

"But you must come," Julia said. "The rumors of Adam's connection to Caroline will be all over town by then. It will look very odd if you are not there."

"Can't be helped, I'm afraid," Milly declared, not bothering to conceal her regret.

Adam studied the three women in turn.

"Why not?" he asked.

"Well," Caroline began and promptly floundered to a halt.

"Difficult to explain," Emma murmured.

"Gowns," Milly announced baldly. "To be blunt, none of us possesses any dress suitable for such an occasion. True, we have some very nice clothes, thanks to Caroline's new contract, but they are not at all the sort of gowns one would wear to an elegant social affair."

"Yes, of course," Julia replied. "I should have realized. Do not trouble yourselves with the problem of gowns. I shall call for you first thing tomorrow morning, if that will be convenient. We will pay a visit to my dressmaker. She will take care of everything."

"But," Caroline managed weakly, "the cost —"

"The cost will not be a problem, either," Wilson assured them. "Have the dressmaker send the bill to Adam."

"But," Caroline said again.

"Consider the gowns as the fee I am paying you for your assistance in the recovery of the diary," Adam said.

A business arrangement, Caroline thought. How depressing.

CHAPTER
TWENTY-FOUR

"I am very uncomfortable with the notion of attending your sister's ball," Caroline said.

It was not the first time she had made the remark.

Following the departure of Julia, Richard and Wilson, she and Adam had avoided further questions from Emma and Milly in favor of taking a hackney cab to this quiet, tree-shaded street. Their intent was to interview Miss Brick and Mrs. Trent, the two women who had been promised a visit by a man who would offer them an excellent investment.

"Stop worrying about the damned gowns," Adam said. A trace of impatience edged his words, probably because this was not the first time he had uttered his assurances. "Julia will see to it that you are perfectly turned out for the ball."

"But three ball gowns and all the trimmings will cost a fortune, Adam."

He looked amused. "Please believe me when I tell you that I am well aware of how much gowns cost. I paid for Julia's for years before Southwood took over the task and I am still paying for Jessica's." The carriage halted. Adam checked a note he had made. "This appears to be the address we are looking for. I suggest we cease this rather repetitive discussion and proceed with business."

"Repetitive? I am not repetitive. Are you implying that I repeat myself?"

He smiled. "Wouldn't dream of even hinting at such a thing. Are you ready to talk to Miss Brick and Mrs. Trent?"

She forced herself to concentrate on the matter at hand. "Yes, of course. You had better let me ask most of the questions. Remember, they know you as my assistant, *Mr. Grove*."

"I shall try to remember my place."

They descended from the cab and went up the steps. Adam banged the knocker twice. The door opened a moment later. A young, frowsy-looking housekeeper in a worn apron peered out.

"What can I do for ye?" she asked.

"We are here to see Miss Brick and Mrs. Trent," Adam said. "You may tell them that Mrs. Fordyce and Mr. Grove wish to speak with them."

The housekeeper frowned. "Wait here, please."

She returned a moment later and ushered Adam and Caroline into a tiny, gloomy parlor.

Miss Brick and Mrs. Trent were delighted to see them.

"This is, indeed, an honor, Mrs. Fordyce," Miss Brick exclaimed. "We have never had an author call on us. Will you take tea?"

"Tea would be lovely," Caroline said and sat down on a squat sofa covered in green velvet. The fabric was thin and shiny from long years of wear. "Thank you for seeing us. Mr. Grove and I have some questions concerning the events that followed Mrs. Toller's séance."

Adam went to stand near the fireplace, one hand braced on the mantel. Caroline knew that he was watching the expressions on the faces of both women closely. Neither betrayed any indication that they had yet heard of the murder of the medium.

"It was certainly a very satisfactory sitting," Miss Brick said.

"It was so good to speak with our generous friend on the Other Side," Mrs. Trent added.

Caroline smiled. "As I told you last night, I am researching the business of séances and mediums with the assistance of Mr. Grove. One of the most important questions one must ask is how much of what a medium predicts comes to pass."

Mrs. Trent made a tut-tutting sound. "There are so many frauds about these days. But we can assure you that Mrs. Toller's talent is quite genuine."

Adam moved slightly. "Then you did, indeed, receive a visit from a gentleman offering the opportunity of a lucrative investment?"

"Oh my, yes," Miss Brick said. "He showed up early this morning. We were still at breakfast when he called."

"Can you describe him?" Adam asked.

Caroline could see that the ladies were taken aback by the question.

"A description would be quite helpful for my research," she said quickly.

That seemed to ease the concerns of both women.

"Yes, well, let me think," Miss Brick said. "His name was Mr. Jones. He had a most unfortunate limp. His entire body was somewhat twisted. I suspect he suffered some dreadful illness as a child that affected his posture."

"Very sad." Mrs. Trent sighed. "Such a pleasant gentleman. Excellent manners. Oh, he wore gold-rimmed spectacles."

Miss Brick narrowed her eyes. "Too many whiskers, if you ask me. He could have done with a trim."

Caroline glanced at Adam.

"You say Jones limped?" Adam asked.

Miss Brick nodded. "Rather badly, I'm afraid."

"Which leg?" Caroline asked.

"I beg your pardon?" Miss Brick frowned. "Oh, I see what you mean. I can't recall if it was the right or the left. Can you, Sally?"

Mrs. Trent pursed her lips, brows wrinkling. "Left, I believe. No, wait, it may have been his right leg that appeared weak. Oh, dear, I'm afraid I can't be entirely certain on that point."

"But he identified himself just as Mrs. Toller told us he would, and he offered us a very fine investment," Miss Brick said eagerly.

"You gave him some money?" Caroline asked, fearing the worst.

"It was a golden opportunity," Mrs. Trent said cheerfully. "We would have been foolish not to take advantage of it."

"Oh, dear," Caroline whispered.

"What sort of investment did this Mr. Jones offer to you?" Adam asked.

For the first time, the ladies hesitated, looking at each other.

Miss Brick cleared her throat in an apologetic manner. "We don't wish to seem rude or unhelpful, but Mr. Jones made it clear that we were not to discuss the exact nature of the investment."

"For fear of starting a mad scramble to obtain shares, you see," Mrs. Trent explained. "He said that if it got out that such an excellent opportunity was available, any number of people would try to take advantage. He said secrecy was imperative."

"Of course," Adam said, looking wise. "You must keep the shares in a safe place."

Miss Brick's eyes twinkled. "Never fear, we have them well hidden."

"I'm delighted to hear that." Adam caught Caroline's eye. "Well, I think that is enough research for today, don't you, Mrs. Fordyce? Shall we be on our way?"

Miss Brick and Mrs. Trent stared, stricken.

"But you haven't had tea yet," Miss Brick said in a pleading sort of way.

Caroline glared at Adam. "We haven't had tea, Mr. Grove."

He drummed his fingers on the marble mantel and gave her a thin, steely grin. "Right. Tea. How could I forget?"

Twenty minutes later, Caroline decided that they could finally take their leave without hurting the ladies' feelings.

Outside on the street, Adam seized her arm. "Thought we'd never get out of there."

"Now, Adam, I realize that you are impatient, but it would have been very unkind to rush off. Miss Brick and Mrs. Trent would have been crushed."

"They are no doubt going to be completely flattened, financially speaking, at least, when they discover that those shares they were issued are worthless."

She winced. "I was afraid you were going to say that. Do you think there is any chance at all that Mr. Jones offered them a legitimate investment opportunity?"

"No."

Nothing ambiguous about that response, she noted. "While you spoke with Miss Brick and Mrs. Trent, a question occurred to me."

"What was it?"

"Stock certificates are printed documents, are they not?"

He glanced at her, curious. "Yes. They are often quite ornate with a good deal of fancy lettering and pictures of the railroad or the mine or whatever project the shares represent. Why do you ask?"

"My publisher, Mr. Spraggett, is a printer who grew up in the business. From my dealings with him, I can assure you that printers take great pride in their art." She paused. "In fact, Mr. Spraggett told me once that printers often sign their work with something called a printer's mark."

Adam halted, forcing her to stop so quickly that she almost stumbled. He looked as if he had just had a revelation.

"What a brilliant notion, madam." He kissed her quite fiercely, looking very pleased. "Absolutely brilliant. If I could track down the printer who produced the shares, I might be able to learn something about the man who commissioned them."

Breathless, Caroline blushed and then quickly checked the street to make certain that no one had witnessed the outrageous spectacle of a gentleman kissing a lady in public. She was relieved to see that there was no one about.

Adam glanced back toward the little house shared by Miss Brick and Mrs. Trent. A decidedly calculating expression darkened his features. "I would very much like to take a look at those shares."

"No, please," she said hastily. "Adam, every time you search a house, you come across dead bodies."

"That is very unfair of you, Caroline. It only happened once in the case of Elizabeth Delmont."

"It very nearly happened again with Irene Toller." She shuddered. "You had every intention of searching her house. If you had gone there only an hour or two earlier this morning, the police might well have discovered you *inside* the house. That would have made them a good deal less inclined to believe your alibi."

"Nonsense. I was perfectly safe so long as I had you to vouch for my whereabouts at the time of the murder. Who could possibly doubt the word of the famous author Mrs. Fordyce?"

A short time later they were ushered into the lodgings of Mr. McDaniel, the elderly sitter who had been promised a financial windfall at Elizabeth Delmont's last séance.

McDaniel was as delighted with his unexpected company as Miss Brick and Mrs. Trent had been. He proved even more willing to chat about his good fortune.

"Yes, indeed, the man of affairs Mrs. Delmont described showed up, just as the spirit promised. Name of Jones." He raised his cup using a hand that shook so badly, tea splashed onto his trousers. He did not seem to notice. "Very polite. Very knowledgeable. Pity about the dreadful limp."

"Do you recall anything else about him, sir?" Adam asked.

"Not really. Too many whiskers. Fellow ought to have a chat with his barber." Mr. McDaniel hesitated, thinking. "Wore spectacles." He raised his brows. "Why do you ask?"

"A man very similar to the one you describe approached me with an interesting financial opportunity," Adam said with the air of one shrewd investor to another. "Mentioned your name. Thought I'd inquire into his references, as it were."

Caroline made a note of the fact that Adam could spin a web of fiction as easily as she did.

McDaniel brightened. "He offered you a similar proposition, I take it? Shares in a mining company?"

"I'm looking into it," Adam allowed. "But, to be frank, he did not show me any actual stock certificates. That worried me somewhat so I have been reluctant to hand over my money."

"Odd. He certainly had no hesitation in presenting me with a certificate."

"I wonder if I might have a look at them," Adam said. "Just to see if they appear legitimate."

"Don't see why not. Jones said not to talk about the project with anyone who was not involved in it. But in view of the fact that you are considering the same investment, I can't imagine that he would object to me showing you the shares."

"Thank you," Adam said.

Mr. McDaniel heaved himself out of his chair with the aid of a cane and tottered to the desk in the corner. He unlocked a drawer and withdrew a sheet of heavy paper. Adam crossed the room to examine it. Caroline followed quickly.

The stock certificate was an impressive-looking document with a light blue background. It was decorated with flamboyantly executed lettering that read *Drexford & Co.* and featured a vignette of a mine, complete with miners and their tools. The detail was very fine and the printing was superb.

"It certainly looks genuine," Adam said, casually handing the certificate to Caroline. "What do you think, Mrs. Fordyce? As one who is involved in the world of publishing, you are more expert than I in such matters."

Mr. McDaniel looked anxious as his precious certificate was passed to a third party. She gave him a reassuring smile and quickly held the document up to the light.

Amid the flourishes, curls and fancy work, she could clearly discern the small figure of a griffin entwined with the letter B.

"The printing is quite elegant," she said, giving the certificate back to Mr. McDaniel.

"What did Mr. Jones tell you about the firm?" Adam asked.

"The company owns a gold mine somewhere in the American West," McDaniel said, relaxing now that the certificate was safely back in his hands. "The founder died before he could begin operations. Left everything to his heir, a young man who is determined to open the mine and make it productive."

"But the heir requires capital to finance the expenses involved in starting up the mine, correct?" Adam asked.

Caroline could hear the grim edge on the words but McDaniel was oblivious.

"Precisely." McDaniel bobbed his head with a sage expression. "Can't go wrong with gold, I always say."

"Words of wisdom, sir." Adam said. "I shall certainly give close consideration to the investment. I appreciate your assistance."

"Not at all, not at all." McDaniel tucked the certificate securely back into the drawer. "I must say, I was somewhat skeptical when the spirit advised me to be on the lookout for Mr. Jones, but when he showed up the very next day I realized that the medium was the genuine article."

"As genuine as that stock certificate you just put into that drawer, Mr. McDaniel," Adam said.

CHAPTER
TWENTY-FIVE

It was after five by the time Mr. McDaniel ushered them out of his house. A thick fog was closing in fast, leaching the light from the fading day. Adam could feel the angry tension shimmering through Caroline. Her shoulders were rigid.

"Well?" he prompted. "Did you see a mark on the certificate?"

"Yes. I can describe it to Mr. Spraggett. But he will have left his office for the day. I will not be able to talk to him until tomorrow."

She fell silent.

"Try not to take this matter to heart," he said after a while. "It is certainly not your fault. There was nothing you could have done to protect Jones's victims."

"All three of them are going to lose their money."

"*Caveat emptor.* Anyone who is foolish enough to take financial advice from the Other Side —"

"Rubbish. That is very easy for you to say, sir, but Miss Brick, Mrs. Trent and Mr. McDaniel lack your financial skills. You know very well that none of them can afford to have that gold mine investment fail."

"It will be a great hardship on them, no question."

A hansom cab clattered past and disappeared into the fog. Awareness shivered across the nape of Adam's neck. The sensation was one he recognized all too well. He had experienced it often enough in the old days when he had been in the business of selling other people's secrets in narrow lanes and dark alleys. The survival instincts that he had learned as a youth persisted within him still. It required a great deal of discipline to fight the urge to look back over his shoulder.

"You saw their homes," Caroline continued, voice ringing with the force of her feelings. "It is obvious that they are all barely getting by as it is. I do not want to think about what will happen when they discover that they have been duped. They will be devastated."

"Very likely," he admitted.

He turned his head partway toward her, bending forward slightly, making it appear that he was paying earnest attention to Caroline's conversation. Out of the corner of his eye he glimpsed a shadowy figure in the fog.

Caroline raised one gloved hand. "We must do something, Adam."

He almost smiled. "By *we*, I conclude that you mean I must do something?"

"Ideally, of course, that dreadful Mr. Jones should be forced to reimburse his victims. But if that does not happen, we cannot let those poor people lose everything."

"Do not concern yourself, Caroline." He risked another glance and saw that their follower was still there, still maintaining the same distance. "I will see to it that Brick, Trent and McDaniel get their money back, one way or another."

She tilted her head slightly. Beneath the brim of her clever little hat he could see that she was glowing with approval.

"Thank you, Adam. That is very kind of you."

"I can only hope that Jones's list of financial victims is not long."

"I wonder how many people he has fleeced with those worthless mining shares."

"Caroline, we have a small problem."

"I beg your pardon?"

"Someone is following us."

"*What?*" She tried to stop and spin around.

"Keep moving." He used his grip on her arm to force her to continue forward. "Do not give any sign that you are aware of him."

"Yes, of course." She continued along the pavement, walking at her usual brisk pace. "Who do you think is back there?"

"I intend to find out."

He studied the mist-shrouded street for a moment, looking for a place to set a snare. The houses along each side of the pavement were placed side by side with no convenient walks or paths between them. The best option was the small park. The fog would provide a convenient veil.

"Here is what we will do," he said to Caroline. "Listen closely and do exactly as I say."

CHAPTER
TWENTY-SIX

They walked into the park together. When they reached the first suitable tree, however, Adam signaled Caroline to continue on across the grass alone. He took up a position under the low-hanging boughs and waited.

From his vantage point he could see what the man behind them saw: a woman dressed in a rust-colored gown disappearing eerily into the heavy fog. It was impossible to tell that she was alone, and the follower would have no particular reason to think that the lady's escort had abandoned her in the park.

That was, at any rate, the line of reason that Adam hoped the man would follow.

He was not disappointed. A few minutes after Caroline walked through the park, Adam heard stealthy footsteps on the pavement. The sounds ceased abruptly when the man moved onto the grass.

A moment later, a figure in a gray coat and a low-crowned hat hurried past the spot where Adam stood, waiting.

Adam took two strides, caught his quarry by the collar of his coat and yanked hard, tugging him off balance. The man squeaked in shock and fear and landed hard on his rear.

Adam looked down and saw a familiar face. "Mr. Otford. What a surprise it is to meet up with you here."

Gilbert Otford sputtered, red-faced with outrage. "How dare you assault me in this rude fashion?"

"Do you know, Otford, I'm inclined to show you just how ill-mannered I can be."

Caroline appeared out of the fog, holding her skirts in both hands so that she could run in what Adam suspected was an unladylike manner.

"Mr. Otford," she exclaimed, halting in front of him. "You were following us, weren't you? Whatever did you think you were about?"

"I have every right to walk down a public thoroughfare." Otford climbed awkwardly to his feet, brushing ineffectually at the mud and grass on his coat. "Look what you've done to my clothes, Hardesty. You may be able to afford an unlimited number of coats, but I assure you the rest of us are not so fortunate."

Adam took a step forward. Alarmed, Otford retreated, coming up hard against the tree trunk.

"Don't touch me," Otford yelped. "I shall summon a constable if you so much as lay a finger on me."

"What did you hope to learn by following us?" Adam asked, genuinely curious.

"I told you, I merely happened to be on the same street." Otford cast a beseeching look at Caroline. "You and I are colleagues of a sort, Mrs. Fordyce. Surely you do not doubt my professional intentions."

Caroline sighed. "I believe him, Mr. Hardesty. I really do not think that Mr. Otford had any intention of perpetrating mischief."

"Well, I am not convinced of that." Adam took another step, deliberately closing the distance. "Furthermore, I have no patience for your lies, Otford. I thought I told you to stay out of my way."

Otford swallowed several times but he managed to pull away from the support of the tree and stand upright. Adam could see that Caroline's presence and air of concern had renewed his confidence. The correspondent had concluded that Adam would not do him any grave damage while a lady stood by watching.

"I am a professional, sir," Otford snapped. "A correspondent has a solemn duty to the public. You and Mrs. Fordyce are involved in a matter of murder. I have an obligation to my readers to ferret out the truth and convey it to them."

"You work for a newspaper that specializes in sensations of all types," Adam said. "The truth is the least of your concerns."

"I resent the implications of that statement, sir. You have no right to abuse me in this manner. I insist on an apology."

"Really . . ." Adam sneered.

Otford took a quick step back, eyes widening. "Now see here, sir."

"I can see that you are going to continue to plague me, Otford. You leave me little choice."

Otford panicked. He lurched forward, intent on escape. Adam caught him by his coattails, hauled him back and shoved him hard against the tree.

"Adam," Caroline said softly. "Please don't hurt him. I do not deny that he is very irritating, but he is a

244

correspondent and he is right when he claims that he has a job to do."

"There, you see?" Otford said quickly. "I am a professional going about my business."

"You call your line a business?" Adam asked. "Very well, I will strike a bargain with you. Answer my questions and I will let you continue on your way in one piece."

"What questions?" Otford asked, wary.

"How did you obtain your descriptions of the scenes of the Toller and Delmont murders?"

"I have an excellent source for that sort of information," Otford said, looking smug. "One with whom I have worked on several occasions. I trust him completely."

Adam tightened his grip on Otford's lapels. "And what is the name of this trustworthy source?"

Otford hesitated. "A correspondent never reveals his sources."

Adam looked at him, saying nothing.

Otford coughed. "His name is Inspector J. J. Jackson. Not that it is any of your affair."

"You say you trust him?"

Otford attempted a shrug. "I have always found him to be extremely reliable."

"And you put every interesting detail of Delmont's murder into that story that you wrote for the *Flying Intelligencer*?"

"Of course." Otford made a face. "I will confess that I had to liven it up a bit for the sake of creating interest — skirts pushed up above the dead woman's knees in a

245

lewd manner, supernatural forces at work and so forth — but there is nothing unusual about that. Done all the time in my business."

"Yes, I gathered as much."

Otford gave him a sly look. "If it's details you want, perhaps you will get them from Julian Elsworth tomorrow afternoon."

Caroline's expression sharpened. "What do you mean?"

"Saw a notice posted at Wintersett House today. Elsworth is going to give a special consulting demonstration of his psychical powers to Inspector J. J. Jackson and members of the Society for Psychical Investigations."

"How is Jackson involved?" Adam asked.

"Elsworth claims that he may be able to use his gifts to assist in the investigation of Delmont's and Toller's murders." Otford snorted. "Should be amusing, don't you think? Imagine the police turning to a person who claims to possess psychical powers to help solve a crime."

Adam released him. "Off with you, Otford. Do not let me find you following me again. I will not be so good-natured about it the next time."

Otford straightened his tie, adjusted his hat and stalked away into the fog.

Caroline looked at Adam. "It seems certain now that the bloodied wedding veil and the mourning brooch were not left out of the press accounts by accident. And you have convinced me that they were unlikely to have been stolen by a common thief."

246

Adam watched Otford vanish into the mist. "There is only one explanation for this. Someone found Delmont's body after I did and removed the veil and brooch. The question is why?"

"Can I assume that we will be attending Julian Elsworth's consulting demonstration of psychical powers tomorrow afternoon at Wintersett House?"

"I would not dream of missing it. You have told me that I must keep an open and inquiring mind when it comes to this psychical nonsense."

CHAPTER
TWENTY-SEVEN

The lecture hall was filled to overflowing the following day. Caroline and Adam barely managed to secure the last two seats in the back row.

"Elsworth certainly knows how to draw a crowd," Adam growled, settling into the chair next to Caroline. "I will give him credit for his theatrical talents."

"I told you that he was highly regarded among those who study psychical matters," Caroline said. She surveyed the murmuring audience and saw a familiar face. "Look, there's Mr. Otford. He is standing on the side, together with a number of other gentlemen. They are all holding notebooks and pencils. They must be correspondents."

Adam followed her gaze and shook his head in mild disgust. "This ridiculous séance is going to be a waste of time as far as the police are concerned but it will no doubt sell a great many newspapers."

"Stop grumbling, Adam. You wanted to come here today."

"I could hardly ignore the opportunity to watch Elsworth in action."

Something in his voice caught her attention. "You do not like him, do you? Why is that? You only met him on one occasion and he did nothing to offend."

"I don't trust him. Blame it on masculine intuition."

An odd thought struck her. "Adam?"

"Yes?" He did not look at her. He was occupied with an examination of the crowd.

"Are you by any chance *jealous* of Mr. Elsworth?"

There was a short, disturbing pause.

"Do I have reason to be?" he asked in a very neutral manner.

"No, of course not."

"I'm pleased to hear that. Might be difficult to compete with a man who can levitate chairs and read minds."

The slight change in his tone allowed her to relax. If not actually jealous, Adam had, at the very least, been concerned about the possibility that she possessed warm feelings for Elsworth. She must not place too much stock in that. Nevertheless, she felt her mood lift.

"Never fear, sir," she said. "I have no doubt that if it proved necessary, you could levitate a chair or read a mind."

He gave her a quick, searching look. But whatever he might have said in response was lost forever because at that moment the curtain parted and a man walked out onto the stage.

"Ladies and gentlemen," the announcer intoned. "Your attention, please. As you know, Mr. Elsworth has generously agreed to make his unique psychical gifts available to the police for the purpose of attempting to solve the recent shocking murders of two mediums. He is willing to allow those of you in the audience to witness his efforts but he insists that there be no talking

249

or unnecessary noise during the séance. No one is to enter or leave the room. The unique nature of the psychical forces Mr. Elsworth employs are extremely delicate and fragile. They can be severely hindered by loud sounds or too much activity."

The crowd hushed immediately. An air of expectation gripped the room. Although she privately shared much of Adam's skepticism, Caroline realized that she was tense with curiosity. What if Elsworth could obtain some clues through the use of psychical forces?

The lights dimmed, just as they had at the start of Irene Toller's demonstration of the planchette but not quite so dramatically. They went down slowly this time, creating a gradual heightening of excitement in the chamber. Eventually only the lamp on the table at the front of the room still burned.

"Allow me to introduce Inspector J. J. Jackson, who will conduct the interview with Mr. Elsworth," the announcer said.

The curtains opened again. Inspector Jackson walked out onto the stage. Caroline thought he looked decidedly ill at ease. Jackson acknowledged the audience with a curt nod and sat down on one of the two chairs at the table.

"I believe Mr. Elsworth is ready now," the announcer said reverently. "Please, no applause. He has spent the past several hours preparing himself for this séance. He must maintain his concentration."

Elsworth walked slowly through the curtains. The silver streak in his dark hair gleamed in the dim light. Although it was mid-afternoon, he was dressed in formal evening wear. His black tail coat and trousers were faultlessly tailored. His white shirt and bow tie were crisp and elegant.

The man knew his stage lighting, Caroline thought. In the glow of the single lamp, his aristocratic features were strongly etched and made even more dramatic.

She leaned forward, trying to get a better view. There was something odd about his eyes. She couldn't be absolutely certain from this distance but it looked as though he was wearing theatrical makeup.

Adam touched her arm, making her start slightly. She turned her head. There was just enough light left to allow her to see his cold, scornful expression. He must have noticed Elsworth's makeup.

When Elsworth approached the table, J. J. Jackson seemed to feel that some action was required of him. He stood quickly and then sat down just as abruptly. *He is nervous*, Caroline thought. She did not blame him.

"Inspector." Elsworth's deep, resonant voice rolled effortlessly through the room.

He greeted Jackson with a bow that, to Caroline's mind, bordered on mocking. Then he took his seat.

"Mr. Elsworth." Jackson's voice was thin and self-conscious. "Appreciate your assistance in this matter."

Elsworth inclined his head again, reached out and turned the lamp down so low that his starkly illuminated face was the only thing clearly visible to the audience. J. J. Jackson was reduced to a stiff shadow.

"I will do my best to aid the police in their search for the person who murdered Mrs. Toller and Mrs. Delmont, Inspector," Elsworth said. "I consider it my duty. Please ask your questions."

Jackson cleared his throat several times, pulled out a notebook and flipped through the pages.

"Can you, ah, speak to the spirits of Mrs. Toller and Mrs. Delmont, sir?" he asked, sounding awkward. "Perhaps ask them to identify their killer?"

"No," Elsworth said. "I do not work that way. I am not a traditional sort of medium. I cannot contact the spirit world in the manner that Toller and Delmont claimed to be able to do. Frankly, I do not believe that it is possible to summon phantoms and ghosts from the Other Side."

In spite of the announcer's admonition, there were several murmured gasps of astonishment from the audience.

"My psychical powers are quite different from those of the average medium," Elsworth continued. "I cannot fully describe my metaphysical gifts to those who lack such talents themselves. Suffice it to say that, when I go into a trance, I am able to perceive things in a manner that goes far beyond the normal senses."

"Well, then, sir, can you perceive the face of the killer?" Jackson asked.

"Not as though I were looking at a photograph," Elsworth said. "But if you have the items that I asked you to procure for me, I might be able to tell you something of the individual who perpetrated these crimes."

"Yes, sir." Jackson reached into his pocket and withdrew a small object. "This is one of Mrs. Delmont's earrings." He plucked a square of embroidered linen out of a second pocket. "And this handkerchief belonged to Mrs. Toller."

"Thank you." Elsworth picked up the earring and the handkerchief and closed his eyes. "Please give me a moment to focus my powers."

Silence throbbed heavily in the room. After a moment, Elsworth opened his eyes and stared intently out across the crowded chamber as though he could see through the heavy shadows.

As she watched, Caroline could have sworn that his features seemed to grow more taut. His eyes darkened into eerie pools.

"Rage," Elsworth whispered. "The killer is a man in the grip of a great mad fury. I see him now in Mrs. Toller's house, striking blow after blow. He has killed once before. It has given him a dreadful courage. He knows that this time it will be easier and more satisfying."

He stopped speaking abruptly.

An audible shudder went through the audience.

Inspector Jackson seemed uncertain about how to proceed. "Can you, uh, tell me why the killer is so enraged with Mrs. Toller, sir?"

"He believes that they deceived him," Elsworth said in mesmeric tones.

Caroline felt Adam shift slightly in the chair beside her. He leaned forward, arms resting on his thighs, suddenly very intent.

"In what way did the mediums deceive the killer?" Jackson asked, sounding more like a policeman now.

"Both claimed that they could communicate with the spirit world but both lied."

Jackson took out a pencil. "Can you supply any of the particulars concerning these lies, sir?"

Elsworth sat perfectly still for a long moment.

"In the course of the séances they gave him he asked questions that only the spirit could have answered correctly," he said at last. "Toller and Delmont gave the wrong responses, so he knew for certain that they were frauds. In his fury, he decided to punish them."

"The killer attended sittings with each of the mediums, sir?" Jackson displayed real eagerness for the first time. "Is that what you're saying?"

Elsworth hesitated. "So it appears."

Astonishment whispered across the room.

Caroline could feel Adam's alert tension. He and Jackson were both displaying similar reactions to the clue that Elsworth had just offered. Both men reminded her of hunters who had caught the spoor of their prey. It occurred to her that, had he not found his way into Polite Society, Adam might have made an excellent detective.

"Would this have been a recent sitting?" Jackson pressed. "Can you provide a date?"

"I'm afraid not." Elsworth appeared abruptly overcome with weariness. Raising his hands, he massaged his temples. "That is all I can do for you today, Inspector. I regret to say that I cannot provide more information. But the exercise of my powers in this extremely intense manner drains me of strength quite rapidly."

"You've been very helpful, sir," Jackson said. "Very helpful, indeed. If you're correct, we're looking for a sitter who attended séances with both Mrs. Toller and Mrs. Delmont. That should help narrow the list of suspects."

"Not bloody likely," Adam said half under his breath. The air of keen attention left him as quickly as it had come. He relaxed back into his chair. "The man's a complete fraud, just as I thought."

The audience buzzed softly as people discussed the revelation. On stage, the announcer stepped forward.

"Mr. Elsworth has concluded his exhibition of psychical powers. He thanks you all for your attention."

A round of applause went up across the room. Caroline saw Otford and the other gentlemen of the press surge toward the doors. On stage, Elsworth rose, bowed to the crowd and then vanished through the curtains, leaving Jackson alone.

The inspector glanced around, as though not sure what to do next. Then he rose and hurried away off stage.

The lights came up. Caroline noticed that Adam was studying the empty stage with a pensive expression.

"What are you thinking?" she asked.

"It occurs to me that Mr. Elsworth has just provided an interesting distraction for the police. I expect that Inspector Jackson is about to waste a great deal of time trying to obtain the names of all of the male sitters who attended séances conducted by both victims. If he does manage to identify some, he will then have to carry out extensive investigations to see if any of them had motives or alibis. It will be a very lengthy and no doubt futile process."

"You are assuming that Mr. Elsworth's psychical powers are not genuine."

"Very insightful of you, my dear. That is precisely what I am assuming." Adam got to his feet and reached down to draw her up alongside him.

"But why would he go to the trouble of inventing clues? Surely the falsehoods will come back to hurt his credibility when the real killer is found."

He took her arm and guided her toward the door. "There are two possibilities. The first is that Elsworth is going with the odds."

"Which odds?"

"The ones that favor the unlikelihood of the police ever catching the murderer. After all, it won't be Elsworth's fault if the inspector never finds his man, will it? He did his best as a psychical consultant."

"Good point. What is the second possibility?"

Adam's expression hardened. "That Elsworth knows something about the murders and used today's entertainment to create confusion and misdirection."

She was shocked to the core. "Are you suggesting that Mr. Elsworth is involved in the murders?"

"Mrs. Fordyce. Please wait a moment. I must speak with you."

Julian Elsworth spoke from somewhere in the hallway behind Caroline and Adam. They stopped quickly. Caroline was very aware of Adam's hand tightening reflexively around her arm, as though he wanted to pull her out of the reach of the other man.

Julian strode toward them, handsome features set in an urgent expression. He had managed to remove most of the makeup around his eyes, Caroline noticed, but he had obviously rushed the task. There were slight traces and smears left.

He halted in front of them and gave Adam a mocking inclination of his head. "Mr. Hardesty, I believe. I don't know how it came about but I somehow managed to get your name wrong at our last meeting. I could have sworn that you called yourself Mr. Grove."

"No need to concern yourself with the mistake, Elsworth," Adam said dryly. "These things happen. I assure you I took no offense."

Julian smiled derisively. "I am relieved to hear that. I expect you had your reasons for ensuring that the mistake got made in the first place." He turned to Caroline. "I am honored that you chose to attend my demonstration this afternoon."

"I found it quite fascinating," Caroline said.

"Thank you," Julian said. He lowered his voice. "I became aware of your presence in the course of my trance a few moments ago. I sensed you out there in the darkness and I realized that I had to warn you."

"Warn her of what?" Adam asked.

Julian ignored him. "When I saw you in my trance, Mrs. Fordyce, I became aware that you are in grave danger."

"I beg your pardon?" she whispered.

Adam took half a step forward. Caroline sensed the controlled menace emanating from him.

"If you have something important to say, Elsworth, be specific," Adam said.

Elsworth's mouth thinned. "I regret I cannot provide you with any other details. I can only tell you that during the trance, I became aware of an aura of great danger closing in upon Mrs. Fordyce." He looked at Caroline, clearly troubled. "I only wish that I could define the threat more precisely for you, madam."

"That would certainly be a good deal more helpful," Adam said, still speaking far too softly. "It would also make you appear somewhat less of a fraud."

Elsworth paid no attention to him. He focused intently on Caroline. "I can only urge you to be extremely cautious, Mrs. Fordyce. Do not trust anyone with whom you have not been well acquainted for a very long time."

He slid his gaze toward Adam in an unsubtle, insinuating manner. Then, turning on his heel, he strode rapidly away down the corridor.

Adam watched him go. "Bastard. He was warning you off me."

"Yes, along with anyone else I do not know well, which includes any number of people." She tapped her fan idly against her palm. "What reason could he have for doing that, do you think?"

"Distraction."

She did not like the way he said the single word. "Do you really believe that he may be the killer?"

"I think it is a distinct possibility, yes."

258

"But what motive would he have had for murdering Mrs. Toller and Mrs. Delmont?"

"There is money involved in this thing. I have always found that it provides a near-universal motive for any sort of crime."

She pondered that briefly. "But he certainly does not fit the description we have been given of the mysterious Mr. Jones. Mr. Elsworth certainly does not walk with a limp. He also lacks the excess of whiskers and the spectacles that were described to us."

"All of those attributes could be affected by a skilled actor, and it is clear that Elsworth has a great talent for the stage."

CHAPTER
TWENTY-EIGHT

"Good day to you, Mr. Spraggett." Caroline swept into the office ahead of Adam, trying to ignore the strong odor of stale cigar smoke. "I would like you to meet my very good friend, Mr. Hardesty."

"Mrs. Fordyce." Spraggett hastily stubbed out his cigar and surged to his feet. "This is a surprise." He nodded at Adam, peering at him from beneath his eye-shade. "Mr. Hardesty. An, uh, unexpected pleasure, sir."

"Spraggett." Adam closed the glass-paned office door with a solid *kerchunk*, leaned back against it and folded his arms. "Never had the opportunity to visit the offices of a newspaper publisher. So this is the source of all those sensation pieces one reads in the *Flying Intelligencer*."

Spraggett glowered through his spectacles. He was a wiry, balding man of middle years who exuded the nervous energy of a terrier. His hands were permanently stained with ink. A number of dirty coffee cups and half-eaten pastries and sandwiches littered the place.

"We take our responsibility to keep the public informed very seriously at this paper, sir," Spraggett declared.

"Do you, indeed?" Adam's mouth twisted in cold amusement. "The piece on the murdered mediums in this morning's edition was certainly revealing."

"Especially the part describing how a watch with Mr. Hardesty's name on it was found at the scene of the second crime," Caroline said.

"Facts are facts."

"Indeed." Caroline whipped open the copy of the paper she had brought along and read aloud. "'The noted author claimed that she was secluded together with Mr. Hardesty in a private location at the time of the murder. It was clear to this correspondent that an air of romantic intimacy surrounded the pair, leaving no doubt as to the nature of their association. It would seem that fiction and reality have become closely entwined for Mrs. Fordyce.'"

"It's unfortunate, Mrs. Fordyce, but you and Mr. Hardesty have become news." Spraggett assumed a virtuous air. "That is what we publish here at the *Intelligencer*."

"You also publish my novels, sir." Caroline tossed the paper down onto the desk. "At least until the conclusion of my current contract. After that I may decide to look for another publisher."

Spraggett's voice jumped in alarm. "Now, Mrs. Fordyce, you must not take that piece Otford wrote personally."

"I do take it personally." She dumped a pile of newspapers off a chair and sat down, adjusting her skirts with a flourish. "I will not forget that I was made the subject of a great scandal in this very newspaper the next time you wish me to sign a contract for a new novel, Mr. Spraggett."

"What's this? Have you had another offer from Tillotsons's Fiction Bureau? Damned upstart syndicators. I vow, if they try to steal you away from this paper, I'll sue."

"Perhaps Tillotsons would be more inclined to treat my reputation with proper respect."

Spraggett bristled. "What do you expect me to do when every other paper in town is printing the news of your connection to Mr. Hardesty and the murders? I can hardly ignore the situation, given that I am publishing *The Mysterious Gentleman*."

"You may not have been able to ignore it, but you could have avoided the colorful references to an intimate love bower and the delicate blush that stained my cheeks when I was seen leaving the murder house in the company of Mr. Hardesty."

"Now, Mrs. Fordyce —"

"The least you can do is compensate me in some small way for the manner in which you are using me to sell papers."

Spraggett scowled. "If you are suggesting that I pay you an additional fee for your novel, I would remind you that we have a contract, madam."

"Calm yourself, sir." She adjusted her gloves. "I am not asking for more money. What we want from you is some of your professional expertise and advice."

Spraggett looked wary. "I beg your pardon?"

She reached into the pocket of her gown to retrieve the slip of paper on which she had sketched the printer's mark. "I noticed this little figure of a griffin and the letter B on a stock certificate. Mr. Hardesty and I would like to know if you can identify the printer."

"Huh." Curiosity replaced the caution in Spraggett's face. He took the paper from her, studied it for a few seconds and then frowned. "Saw it on a stock certificate, you say?"

"Yes. Do you recognize it?"

"Bassingthorpe used this mark for years. He did beautiful work in the old days, but there were always the rumors."

"Bassingthorpe," Adam said, frowning slightly. "Thought he'd retired."

"I was under the same impression." Spraggett glanced again at the certificate. "But that is most certainly his mark."

"What were the rumors?" Caroline asked.

Spraggett shrugged. "It was said that if you happened to need a handsome certificate attesting to a stint in a medical school or a degree in law, whether or not you had actually attended the college in question, you could purchase a very satisfactory one from Bassingthorpe."

"I see." Caroline rose. "Thank you, Mr. Spraggett."

"Hold on here." Spraggett jumped to his feet again. "What's this all about? Is Bassingthorpe connected to the murders in some way?"

"We don't know," Adam said, opening the door for Caroline. "But if I were you, I would not bother to send a correspondent out to find him."

263

"Why not?"

"Unless Bassingthorpe has changed his ways, which is doubtful, you will not get any information out of him. From what I have heard, he did not achieve his reputation by being indiscreet."

Adam ushered Caroline through the opening and closed the door before Spraggett could ask any more questions.

Out in the hallway, Caroline looked at him with great interest. "What, exactly, is the nature of Mr. Bassingthorpe's reputation?"

"It was said that Bassingthorpe not only created the occasional fraudulent medical license, but that he could create reproductions of banknotes that were indistinguishable from the real thing."

"In that case, I can see why he would be a very cautious man." She hesitated. "But if Mr. Bassingthorpe is not given to gossiping about his clients, how do you intend to persuade him to talk to us?"

"Bassingthorpe was still actively working when I was selling secrets on the streets. I did him a couple of favors. If we're fortunate, he will remember them."

"We must go to see him immediately."

Adam shook his head. "One does not show up unannounced on Bassingthorpe's doorstep. There are certain proprieties to be observed. I will send a message to him. With a bit of luck he will agree to meet with me at a place and time of his choosing."

264

CHAPTER
TWENTY-NINE

The interior of the drawing room never failed to amuse Adam. It was lush, overwrought and extravagant beyond belief. The decorator had obviously felt free to cast aside the restraints of good taste in favor of dramatic impact.

Red was the predominant color. The massive sofa and chairs were upholstered in crimson silk. Vermilion velvet draperies pooled on the floors in front of the windows. The carpet was patterned in scarlet and gold.

As was the case in so many homes across the breadth and width of the nation, a large, ornately framed photograph of the queen, dressed in her perpetual mourning, hung in a place of importance over the hearth. But the theme of the other pictures that cluttered the walls was quite different. Every painting featured a bold knight in gleaming armor who was in the process of rescuing — or being rescued by — a lovely woman clad only in the filmiest of clothing.

Florence Stotley was very fond of chivalric motifs.

Florence was a pleasantly plump, gray-haired woman who was rapidly approaching her sixth decade. With her warm, bright eyes, dimpled features and charming eccentricities, she could have been mistaken for someone's beloved grandmother or doting great-aunt. Few would believe that she had made her fortune as the proprietor of one of London's most exclusive brothels.

She was officially retired now, but she continued to employ her entrepreneurial talents in a variety of profitable ways. Any number of people had underestimated Florence Stotley over the years, Adam reflected. But he had known her since his days on the street, and he had nothing but the most profound respect for her.

In a sense, they were business associates, but the focus of their interests varied slightly. While he concerned himself with the affairs of those in Society these days, Florence continued to steep herself in the murky activities of those who operated in London's underworld.

It was not uncommon for one of them to call upon the other for assistance. After all, the doings of the rich and powerful in Society intersected with the business activities of their counterparts in the city's less legitimate spheres far more frequently than most people wished to acknowledge.

"How delightful to see you again, Adam." Florence poured tea from a fanciful silver pot designed to resemble a flamboyant dragon. "It has been some time since we last visited. All is well with Julia and the children, I trust?"

"They are happy and in excellent health, thank you." Adam settled into a large wingback chair and stretched out his legs. "At the moment, my sister is busily engaged in the task of outdoing herself with another memorable ball."

266

"I'm sure she will produce a spectacular event this year." Florence chuckled and handed him a cup of tea. "The talk of her great success with the Camelot theme last spring went on for weeks after the event."

"She was greatly indebted to you for the inspiration." He examined the delicately rendered illustrations of scenes of the Round Table on his cup. "New china, I see."

"Yes. I am pleased with it." Florence arranged her skirts and looked expectant. "Now, then, I am always delighted to have you call, Adam, as you well know. I did get your message asking for assistance in locating the medium's missing housekeeper and I assure you I am making inquiries, but thus far I have not had any luck."

"If anyone can find Bess Whaley, it will be you, Florence. I have complete confidence in your sources. But as it happens, I am here on another matter tonight. I did not want to send a message in this instance. Thought it should be handled personally."

Florence nodded. "I understand. What is this other item of business?"

"I wish to convey a message to that old forger Bassingthorpe. At one time he was a client of yours. Are you still in touch?"

Florence smiled fondly. "Of course. He is a friend as well as a former customer. I will let him know that you would like to speak with him."

"Thank you."

"Is that all?"

"For now," Adam said.

Florence poured more tea. "Very odd, this affair of the murdered mediums. There are rumors going about that both were killed by dark forces from the spirit world that they accidentally set loose."

"I assure you that whoever murdered those two came from this world."

"May I ask what your interest is in this matter?"

"Do you remember Maud Gatley?"

"Yes. Such a sad situation." Florence shook her head. "The poor woman never succeeded in getting free of her addiction. I know how much you tried to help her, Adam. You paid for so many cures and they all failed."

"The opium was always stronger than her will," he said. "It seems that she kept a diary that she left to Elizabeth Delmont. Delmont tried to use it to blackmail me. But it disappeared the night she was murdered. And now Irene Toller is dead in a similar fashion."

"Ah. That explains a great deal. Maud knew the truth about you and Julia and Jessica and Nathan, didn't she?"

He nodded. "The man who appears to have been involved in the fraudulent investment scheme that Mrs. Toller and Mrs. Delmont operated is said to walk with a severe limp. The witnesses tell me that he is heavily whiskered and wears gold-rimmed glasses."

"You suspect those are attributes of a disguise?"

"They are all too obvious and memorable."

"I agree." She frowned. "But if he now possesses the diary, I wonder why he has not yet contacted you to attempt blackmail."

268

"Biding his time, I expect."

"I do not blame him," she said dryly. "If he knows anything at all about you, it will be plain to him that he must be exceedingly careful. He must know that if he makes a mistake and gives himself away, you will find him and that will be the end."

Adam looked at her. "I will find him. It is only a matter of time."

"I am aware of that. I have known you since you were a boy, Adam. You are relentless. But I urge you to be extremely cautious. Two people have been murdered in this affair."

"I appreciate your concern." He reflected briefly on Florence's extensive connections throughout every level of society. "I find myself involved in the world of psychical research these days. Can you tell me anything about the crowd at Wintersett House that might be useful?"

"Not a great deal. Psychical researchers, in general, strike me as misguided but relatively harmless." She paused, thinking for a moment. "I have heard that Mr. Reed, the president of the Society for Psychical Investigations, is a grieving widower who dreams of someday contacting the spirit of his dead wife."

"What happened to her?"

"She was murdered several years ago. I do not recall all of the details, although it created quite a sensation in the press for a time. I believe Mrs. Reed's body was found in a park a short distance from the couple's home. Evidently she went for a stroll a day or so after the wedding and was attacked. The reports claimed that she was raped and strangled."

"Did the police find her killer?"

"No." Florence drank some tea and lowered her cup. "Perhaps that is one of the reasons why Durward Reed is so determined to contact her. He no doubt wants to ask her the name of the villain who murdered her so that he can bring the man to justice."

"I would have chosen a more direct approach to finding the killer," Adam said.

"Yes, of course. But not everyone has your connections and few are as comfortable with the thought of violence as you are."

He let that pass. "I wonder what makes Reed believe that he can contact her."

Florence's brows rose. "Perhaps he is convinced that she can be reached on the Other Side because she claimed to possess psychical powers while she was on this side. He no doubt reasons that if any spirit can make contact through the veil, it will be one who had a gift for doing so while she was alive."

"Mrs. Reed was a medium?"

"Yes, indeed. A decade ago, before her marriage, she was very fashionable. Gave séances to some of the most exclusive people."

"She moved in elevated circles?"

Florence nodded. "She was the last member of a prominent family that had made a fortune in shipping. I had a number of clients who attended séances given by her."

"Thank you, Florence. Once again I am in your debt."

She assumed a familiar expression, one that told him that she was ready to transact some business.

"You can repay me easily enough with some information from your world," she said.

"If I can answer your questions, I will do so."

"You recall that little establishment in Marbury Street? The one that caters to gentlemen who enjoy the pleasures of discipline and bondage?"

"Yes. I heard that Mrs. Thorne had sold the business."

"She did. But her successor, who goes by the charming name of Mrs. Lash, is quite ambitious. She has taken a notion to expand into a new and much grander location. To that end, she has come up with a very ingenious plan to acquire the necessary financial capital. She is putting together a consortium of investors from among her regular clients."

"Is she?" He was intrigued. "That is certainly creative of her. These investors are gentlemen who move in Society, I assume?"

"Yes. She has commissioned me to make some inquiries into the financial standing of each of them. A woman in her position who decides to do business with gentlemen cannot be too careful."

"That is true," he agreed.

"I'll show you the list." Florence rose, went to a nearby table and opened a drawer. "Two of the names were familiar to me but three are not. I trust you will be able to tell me something about them."

He got to his feet, took the list from her and studied it for a moment, memorizing the names out of long habit. This sort of information was always useful.

"I had not realized that Ivybridge and Milborne had a taste for the whip," he said absently.

"All of them do. That is why they became clients of the establishment in the first place. I am interested to hear what you know about any of the men on that list."

He shrugged. "It appears to be the usual assortment of insufferable prigs and hypocrites. They are the type who affect superior airs and pretend to sterling moral characters while, behind the scenes, they routinely force themselves on their chambermaids and patronize brothels." He paused. "But you said that it is the state of their finances that particularly interests you?"

"Yes. Given her position, Mrs. Lash will not have much recourse if it turns out that any of these men proves to be unreliable in that regard."

He gave her a short, concise summary of what he knew of the men's financial positions.

"Thank you." Florence put the list back into the drawer. "I shall inform Mrs. Lash that none of her potential investors appears to be on the verge of bankruptcy."

"Remind her that there are other risks involved. None of those men can be entirely trusted."

"I'm sure she is well aware of the nature of their characters."

"If that is all, I must be on my way." He took her hand and bowed over it. "Good evening, Florence. As always, it has been a great pleasure."

272

"So very gallant," Florence murmured. A wistful expression lit her eyes. "I vow, when I see you these days with your elegant clothes and fine manners, I can scarcely believe that you are in any way related to that ragged boy who used to come to my back door offering to sell secrets and gossip obtained from Maud's customers. I always knew that you would become successful one day."

He grinned. "Did you?"

"Yes. The only question in my mind was whether or not you would make your fortune legally or illegally."

"One of the many lessons I have learned, madam, is that there is often very little distinction between the two approaches."

"Bah. You make a point of presenting a cold and ruthless face to the world, but I have known you for a very long time, Adam Hardesty. I am aware of how you saved your brother and sisters. I know about the charity houses for children that you have established in the stews. Underneath that decidedly rusty armor, you possess a sense of honor and a measure of nobility that would have done credit to any of the knights of the Round Table."

Amused, he surveyed the nearest painting. It showed a knight in elaborately wrought armor enjoying the solicitous attentions of a group of scantily clad nymphs. "Then why is it that I very seldom find myself under attack by scores of beautiful, nude females?"

"Most likely because thanks to your infamous rules, you have been obsessed with avoiding scandal for the past several years."

He studied another picture, which depicted a lovely nude woman in the arms of a knight in gold armor. Memories of the hot, sweet passion he had found with Caroline heated his blood.

"I seem to have shattered a number of my own rules lately," he said.

"You have indeed, and managed to become the subject of a great sensation in the papers." Florence laughed. "Which reminds me, is your connection with Mrs. Fordyce a serious matter or merely a wild, tempestuous fling for you? I am hoping it is a bit of both."

"You know her work?"

"Yes, of course. I adore Mrs. Fordyce's novels."

"You force me to reveal the humiliating truth, madam. I have reason to believe that Mrs. Fordyce may be using me as her muse. In particular, she has informed me that I have become her model for the character of Edmund Drake in her new novel."

"How exciting. I cannot wait to see if you will escape the usual fate meted out to a Fordyce villain."

CHAPTER
THIRTY

Adam went down the broad marble steps in front of Florence Stotley's elegant town house and found himself confronted by a wall of fog and night. Gas lamps glowed in front of the elegant front doors that lined the street, but for the most part they provided balls of useless, glaring light that reflected eerily off the mist.

Earlier in the evening he had noticed the dense vapor gathering in the streets. Aware that the stuff would slow traffic, he had elected to walk to Florence's address.

At the foot of the steps he turned and started back in the direction he had come, relying on the secret web of hidden walks, lanes and alleys that constituted his private mental map of the city.

Now and then the shadowy shapes of tentatively moving carriages and hansom cabs rattled past. Figures came and went like wraiths in the thick mist. They appeared briefly silhouetted against a flaring gas lamp and then vanished, leaving only the echoes of footsteps.

Halfway across a small park in a quiet square it occurred to him that he was not all that far from Corley Lane. It was just going on ten o'clock. Caroline had mentioned earlier in the day that she intended to write tonight. Perhaps she would like to hear about his visit to Florence Stotley.

It was a transparent excuse to call upon her. Then again, he did not actually need a good excuse, he decided. After all, they had embarked upon an affair. That gave him certain privileges.

In any event, there would be no harm in walking past her little house tonight. If he saw lights in the windows, he would knock. If not, he would continue on his way.

He moved silently along a tiny walk that separated two rows of town houses, cut through another park and started along a narrow street.

A short time later, he ducked into a crooked lane. The stones of the darkened buildings that loomed over the passage dated from medieval times. It was a route he had used often enough in his younger days when he had come to this part of the city to sell his wares.

The all-too-familiar shiver of ghostly electricity touched the back of his neck. A second later he caught the unmistakable scrape of shoe leather on pavement behind him.

As startling incidents went, this was a particularly interesting one.

He kept moving, not altering his stride or giving any other indication that he knew he was being followed.

Several of the doorways along the lane had been built with deep vestibules and entranceways. The pools of darkness offered a variety of hiding places. He chose one at random and moved noiselessly into a well of shadows created by ancient stones.

The footsteps stopped a few seconds later. Whoever had followed him into the lane had just realized that his quarry had disappeared. Adam breathed slowly and waited, motionless. He willed his pursuer not to abandon the chase. He had some important matters to discuss with whoever was out there.

A few seconds later the footsteps started up again, hurrying now.

Adam watched for movement in the tiny lane. The single gas lamp at the far end provided barely enough light to reveal shifting shadows. But that proved sufficient for the task at hand.

The figure of the pursuer materialized as a dark shape in the greater darkness that drenched the passage.

Adam vaulted out of his hiding place. He slammed into the man with enough force to send them both sprawling on the pavement. The pursuer landed on the bottom, taking most of the shock of the fall. A metallic object clattered on the stones.

The man's hoarse, astonished shout of fear and rage ended abruptly. Adam heard a wheezing sound as the villain fought to regain the breath that had been knocked from his lungs.

"Don't move," Adam ordered.

He rolled to his feet, stepped back and slid one foot along the paving stones until it contacted an object. He bent and picked up the knife.

"I see you came armed," he observed. "Therefore, I must assume you did not follow me with the intention of inviting me to join you for a pint at the nearest tavern."

The man made a gulping sound and found his voice.

"Message. Just trying to give you a message. That's all. No cause to attack me like that, you bloody bastard."

"What was the message and who sent —"

He broke off when he felt the hair on the nape of his neck stir a second time. Another set of footsteps sounded, pounding toward him out of the shadows.

He swung around and tried to move aside but he came up hard against an iron railing. The second villain was upon him in an instant, lashing out with a heavily booted foot. Adam turned away from the blow, trying to limit the damage that was going to be done.

He succeeded to some extent. The boot caught him in the ribs but it did not land with the force that the attacker had intended. Off balance, Adam slammed down onto the pavement.

"This is the message," the attacker hissed. He closed in swiftly and prepared another jolting kick to the ribs.

Adam managed to grab a pant leg. He hauled on it with all his strength.

"Bastard." The assailant danced wildly, trying to stay erect and retrieve his foot.

He failed, hitting the stones hard.

The first man was on his feet. Adam heard him coming up fast from behind and turned to face him, knife in hand.

The man froze a few steps away.

Holding the confiscated blade in his left hand, Adam reached inside his overcoat.

The second man scrambled awkwardly to his feet.

"What are ye waitin' for, Georgie?" he whined. "Stick him. He deserves it after what he done to us."

"He's got me knife, Bart."

"True," Adam said. "But I prefer to use my own." He slid the blade from the hidden sheath inside his jacket, letting the men hear the whisper of steal on leather. "I'm more familiar with it, you see."

A short silence greeted that announcement.

"Now see here, we didn't bargain for any knife play." Georgie edged away.

"He's right," Bart assured him hastily. "Been a misunderstanding here, I believe. We were paid to deliver a message, that's all."

"Then why assault me?" Adam asked.

"The cove what commissioned us to give you the message said you would pay more attention to it if we roughed you up a bit."

"This cove you mentioned. Would he, by any chance, have been heavily whiskered and walk with a limp?"

There was another short silence.

"How'd ye know that?" Bart asked, sounding deeply uneasy.

"Never mind. Now, as you have gone to all this trouble, why don't you deliver the message?"

Georgie coughed. "You're to stop poking around in certain financial matters what don't concern you." He sounded as if he were reciting a school lesson. "And if you keep prying into other people's business affairs, a certain diary will be turned over to the press."

"Thank you," Adam said. "You have confirmed my suspicion. The killer evidently does have the diary."

"What killer?" Georgie demanded nervously. "What are you talking about?"

"The man who sent the pair of you to deliver his message has recently murdered at least once and quite possibly twice."

"Ye're mad, ye are," Bart snarled. "The cove what hired us was no murderer. He were a man of business."

"So am I," Adam said.

He held the knife up slightly. There was just enough light to glint evilly on the blade.

Bart and Georgie turned and fled away down the lane.

CHAPTER
THIRTY-ONE

"Edmund," Lydia whispered frantically. "You must not do this. You know you will regret it when the terrible fever of your rage has passed and you discover the truth. You are wrong about me, I swear it."

Edmund responded with ruthless kisses, plundering her senses with the determination of a marauding pirate intent only on gaining the abject surrender of his victim.

Trapped beneath him, her skirts a tumbled sea of delicate blue silk, she looked up into his savagely set features. She knew at once that she was powerless to stop him. He was so lost in his fury and despair that he was likely not even aware of her puny struggles.

When sanity returned, he would be horrified by his own actions. But by then it would be too late for both of them.

Desperate to save herself and Edmund as well, she placed her dainty hands against his broad shoulders in a vain attempt to check his rash assault.

Caroline paused and put down her pen. She was not entirely satisfied. It was certainly a very exciting scene but Edmund Drake seemed to be out of control. That did not fit his character.

The muted clang of the door knocker sounded just as she made to pick up her pen for another attempt. Emma and Milly were home early. Evidently the play they had attended that evening had failed to live up to expectations. They must have left during the intermission.

Mrs. Plummer was in bed upstairs, having taken her usual sleeping tonic: a mix of laudanum and gin. The combination was guaranteed to ensure that she slept like the dead until morning.

Caroline listened closely and then got to her feet when she did not hear the scrape of iron in the lock. Perhaps her aunts had neglected to take their keys.

She crossed the carpet and went along the corridor to the front hall. There she paused to peer through the small panes of beveled glass that framed the door. Shock snapped through her when she saw Adam. He seemed to be leaning rather heavily against the jamb.

Hastily she unlocked the door and yanked it open. "What are you doing here at this hour?"

"It is a long story." He braced one hand against the doorjamb and looked at her with a veiled expression that did nothing to conceal his prowling tension.

She was suddenly very conscious of the fact that she was garbed only in a dressing gown and slippers.

"Something is wrong," she said, trying to read his hard face. "What is it?"

"May I come in?"

"Yes, of course." She stepped back to allow him into the hall.

He shoved himself away from the doorjamb. When he walked through the opening, she saw that he was not moving with his customary masculine ease.

"Are you all right?" she asked. She noticed the beginnings of a dark bruise under his right eye and answered her own question before he could speak. "No, I can see that you are not. You have been hurt."

"I could do with a glass of your aunts' sherry," he admitted, tossing his hat onto the hall table. "Make that two glasses."

He winced when he started to peel off his overcoat.

"Let me help you." She reached up to ease the garment off his shoulders. "Please tell me what happened."

"Could I have the sherry first?"

She led him back along the hall to the study, sat him down in a reading chair and poured out a large measure of sherry.

He took a long, grateful swallow and lowered the glass with a sound that was somewhere between a sigh and a groan.

"It has occurred to me this evening that I am not as young as I used to be," he said. "No wonder everyone is pressing me to get married."

"You are making me very anxious, Adam. Kindly tell me what has happened."

He leaned his head against the back of the chair and closed his eyes. "A message was delivered to me a short time ago by two gentlemen of the criminal class. It was

283

made clear that if I did not cease my inquiries into the matter of the fraudulent investments and, presumably, the murders, the diary would be turned over to one of the more flamboyant newspapers."

Horrified, she leaned down and gently touched the incipient bruise. "You could have been killed."

He opened his eyes. She saw the predator in him and shivered.

"As it happens, I wasn't," he said.

She had never seen him in this strange, unpredictable mood. Whatever had occurred tonight, it had been dangerous and violent, she thought.

"I noticed that you favored your ribs when you removed your coat," she said, trying to maintain an air of Florence Nightingale calm. "Do you think you have broken any bones?"

"No." He touched his side somewhat tentatively and then shook his head with more certainty. "Nothing is broken. Just a few bruises."

"Wait right here." She hurried toward the door. "I will fetch a clean cloth and some of the salve that Aunt Emma uses for bruises."

He frowned. "There is no need —"

She ignored him and went down the hall to the kitchen to find the things she needed.

When she returned a few minutes later with the cloth and salve, she discovered that he was no longer seated in the chair where she had left him. Instead, he was standing behind her desk, reading the scene she had been working on when he had arrived. She noticed that he had helped himself to another glass of sherry.

"What the devil is going on here?" Adam looked up, scowling. "Drake is attacking Miss Lydia?"

"There has been a dreadful misunderstanding," she explained, opening the jar that contained salve. "Edmund Drake believes that Miss Lydia has lied to him. In his anguish and rage he has lost control of his passions."

"Only a brute or a madman is allowed that excuse," Adam said flatly. He swallowed more sherry.

She paused in the act of applying the salve to the cloth. "You are right. I knew there was something wrong with that scene. I shall have to come up with some other reason to explain his behavior."

"Why? I thought he was the villain of the piece. Villains are brutes and madmen, are they not?"

"Never mind." She cut off a section of the salve-soaked cloth and pressed it gently to his bruised cheek. "Hold this while I prepare another bandage for your ribs."

Absently he held the cloth in place. "Where are Emma and Milly?"

"At the theater. Mrs. Plummer is here but she is asleep upstairs." She soaked another section of cloth in the tonic. "This is for your ribs. Stand still while I remove your shirt."

He sucked in his breath when she gently tugged off his shirt, but he said nothing.

It was only the second time she had seen him without a shirt. The sight of his bare chest lightly covered in crisp, curling hair momentarily diverted her

285

attention. He was her lover, she thought. She had a right to see him like this.

Pulling her scattered senses together with an effort of will, she wrapped the long strip of damp cloth around his ribs. Adam winced and swallowed the rest of the sherry.

"Did I hurt you?" she asked anxiously.

"No. The salve is cold, that's all."

"That is part of the benefit." She tied the ends of the strip very carefully. "Cold helps restrain the bruising."

He looked down, watching her hands as she worked. "I trust that your aunt does not use arnica in her salve?"

"No. She says that although it is very good for bruising, it is simply too dangerous to use. If it enters the body through a cut or an open wound, the effect is quite poisonous. Adam, these men who attacked you — do you think by any chance they were involved in the murders?"

"I'm almost certain they were not. They claimed that they were hired by our old acquaintance, the man of business who sports too many whiskers and walks with a limp."

"But what if —"

Without warning, he tossed aside the cloth he had been holding to his cheek, bent his head and kissed her with a fierceness that shook her to her toes.

When he eventually raised his head, she had to clutch his sleek shoulders in order to steady herself.

"Adam?"

"I shouldn't have come here tonight. I should have gone straight home."

"No, it is all right." She cleared her throat. "We have embarked on an affair. You have every right to be here."

"Do I?" He captured her face between his hands. "Do I really have every right to be here with you alone like this? Tell me the truth, Caroline."

"Y-yes." She swallowed, unsure of his mood. "We are lovers now."

"Lovers." He repeated the word as though he was not certain of its meaning. "Yes, I am most certainly your *lover*."

He kissed her again. This time when he raised his head, she could scarcely catch her breath.

"Adam, you really should not exert yourself in this manner," she managed. "Not after the ordeal you went through this evening."

"I want you."

She stopped breathing altogether.

"Here?" she finally got out. "Now?"

"Here. Now."

She moistened her lips. "Oh."

"You say that we are lovers." He eased aside the collar of her dressing gown and kissed the curve of her shoulder. "That is what lovers do. They make love."

She stared at the bookshelves on the wall behind his head. "In . . . in a study?"

"Anywhere that is convenient." He unfastened the first button of the dressing gown. "Lovers must take advantage of every opportunity."

"Yes, I suppose that is true, isn't it?" she said, struck by that observation. "But what if someone were to walk in on us?"

"We will worry about that if the problem arises. Kiss me, Caroline."

She put her arms tentatively around his neck, fearful of hurting him.

"I said, kiss me," he whispered roughly against her mouth.

The raw, masculine scent of his recent battle was still on him. She could feel the unnatural energy riding him.

She kissed him gently, seeking to replace the lingering aura of violence with love.

He opened the front of her robe with quick, ruthless movements. The next thing she knew, his hands were around her waist, lifting her.

She expected him to lower her onto the carpet. It seemed the only suitable location in the room. Instead, she found herself seated on the edge of the desk.

When he parted her knees and moved between her thighs, she was too startled to protest. The next thing she knew, his hands were on her, probing, stroking, making her wet and desperate.

There was a strange, fierce tension in him tonight but there was also control. She would always be safe with him, no matter how wild the passion that flowed between them.

It was a heady, glorious feeling.

He freed himself from his trousers. She encircled the length of him with her hands, familiarizing herself with the intriguing size and shape of him.

"You astonish me," she whispered, dazed.

His laughter was low and exciting. Then he did things to her with his fingers, truly astonishing things.

288

Everything within her tightened to an unbearable degree; tightened until she could not stand it any longer. Her fingers sank into his shoulders.

"*Adam.*"

Without warning the compelling tension within her dissolved in a series of powerful, rippling pulsations that filled her with a near-violent pleasure.

Before she could even begin to recover, Adam curved his hands around her buttocks and thrust heavily into her.

His own release crashed through him. She heard him choke back an exultant groan and knew another kind of delight in the realization that he had found such satisfaction in her arms. It was no doubt quite petty of her but she hoped with all her heart that he would never be able to entirely duplicate the experience with any other woman.

She clung to him, her thighs clamped snugly around him until the world returned to normal.

An eternity later, Adam roused himself with obvious reluctance and went about the business of putting his clothing to rights.

"I must be off," he said, glancing at the clock. "Your aunts will be home soon and I am in no condition to greet them."

"Promise me that you will summon a cab. I do not want you walking all the way back to your house."

He grinned, put his hands around her waist, lifted her off the desk and set her on her feet.

"I assure you, after that delightful tonic, I am feeling quite invigorated."

"But what if those two men try to attack you again?"

"I do not think I will see them any time soon." He kissed her lightly on the tip of her nose and reached for his shirt. "Good night, my sweet. I will call upon you tomorrow."

She was startled by the change in his mood. It was indeed as if he had taken some potent tonic or elixir. Was it possible that making love could have such a therapeutic effect on a man?

Adam was already striding toward the door. She hurried after him.

"You will be careful," she pleaded.

"Certainly," he said.

He spoke much too casually for her taste. But there was little she could do. She trailed after him and saw him out onto the street.

When he was gone she closed the door and leaned back against it, clutching the knob in both hands.

Men, she reflected, were an odd lot.

After a while she went back into the study and sat down at the desk. She reviewed what she had written prior to Adam's arrival and was more unsatisfied with the lines than ever. Somehow, she simply could not allow Edmund Drake to lose control over his passions to the extent that he would harm Miss Lydia; not even if he believed that she had betrayed him.

Only a brute or a madman is allowed that excuse.

Then she recalled what he had said when she had bound his ribs with Emma's salve.

I trust that your aunt does not use arnica in her salve?

And her own response: *No. If it enters the body . . . the effect is quite poisonous.*

Poison.

If Edmund Drake had been poisoned, he might well act out of character.

She picked up her pen, crossed out several paragraphs and wrote new ones.

"Edmund, you must listen to me," Lydia pleaded. "You are not yourself, sir. I believe you may have been poisoned."

Edmund went still, sanity and intelligence returning slowly to his fevered gaze. "Poisoned? But how is that possible?"

"The cakes," she said, glancing at the tea tray on the table. "This dark mood came upon you after you ate one of them a short while ago."

"Devil take it, you are right." Edmund shook his head, as though ridding himself of some mist clouding his brain. "Something is wrong. I do not feel at all well." He got to his feet and looked down at her with mounting horror. "What have I done? Forgive me, Miss Lydia. I would never harm you."

"I know." She sat up, hastily adjusting her skirts. "There has been a great misunderstanding. I can explain everything."

Much better, Caroline thought.

But she could no longer deny the obvious. Edmund Drake was rapidly becoming hero material. That left her with a serious problem. She had to find another villain and quickly. There were only a few chapters left to write before the story ended.

CHAPTER
THIRTY-TWO

Shortly after eleven o'clock the following evening, Adam slipped out of the noisy, crowded ballroom. He went quickly along a servants' hall, taking a short cut through the big house to his library.

The music and the dull roar of voices faded slowly behind him. Julia had another resounding success on her hands, he thought. The fountains all worked, there had been no leaks and the ruins were extraordinarily realistic in their final form. The Roman villa theme would no doubt be imitated by every aspiring hostess in town.

But the most satisfactory aspect of the evening as far as he was concerned was Caroline. She glowed in an elegantly draped garnet red gown. Tiny gold flowers glittered in her upswept hair.

It amused him that she had been an immediate success, not because of her connection to his powerful family but because of her status as the author of *The Mysterious Gentleman*. A crowd had gathered around her the moment she entered the ballroom. It seemed that nearly everyone present wanted to know what dire fate she had in store for Edmund Drake.

He opened the door of the library and walked into the room.

"I got your message, Harold."

Harold Filby stopped his nervous pacing and spun around. Behind the lenses of his spectacles his eyes were uncharacteristically troubled.

"I am sorry to interrupt your evening, sir, but I got back to London a short time ago and came here immediately. I thought you should hear my news at once."

"Do not concern yourself with the interruption." Adam closed the library door and crossed the carpet. "I assure you, no one will miss me. Mrs. Fordyce is the main attraction in the ballroom tonight."

"I say." Harold peered at him more closely. "What happened to your eye, sir? Were you in an accident?"

"It is a complicated tale. I will give it to you later."

Harold cleared his throat. "Yes, well, I'm afraid the information I have for you concerns Mrs. Fordyce. After I received your telegram, I set off for the village of Chillingham. It was not easy but I finally managed to discover the details of the scandal in which she was involved."

"Do you know, what with all that has been going on, I almost forgot that I had sent you off to investigate." Adam leaned back against the edge of his desk and crossed his arms. "Well? What did you learn?"

"I regret to say that the events in question were not of an innocuous nature. We are talking about attempted murder, a madwoman, suicide, implications of an illicit love affair and a lady's reputation."

294

A chill tightened Adam's insides. "Trust Mrs. Fordyce not to do anything by half measures."

"There are a number of alarming facts but the most important one at the moment is that there was a gentleman involved."

"I assumed as much, given the general nature of scandals."

"No doubt. The rather disturbing bit is that the gentleman's name is Ivybridge."

Adam went still. "I am acquainted with the man."

"Indeed, sir. But the more pressing matter is that he and his wife are in town at the moment. They are well-connected socially. Need I remind you that everyone who is anyone in Society is on Lady Southwood's guest list this evening?"

"Damn." Adam straightened and made for the door. "Ivybridge may be out there in the ballroom at this very moment. I've got to find Caroline before he does."

Do not panic, Caroline thought. *He didn't see you.*

She hurried through a pair of French doors at the far end of the ballroom and escaped onto a small stone terrace. There was no one around. In the shadows at the far end she saw some artistically arrayed chunks of false stone veiled by a swath of blue velvet. The faint sound of gurgling water could be heard coming from behind a curtain tied back with a golden sash.

The drapery marked one of several such private retreats that Julia had provided for her guests. They were scattered about the lantern-lit gardens and tucked away on side terraces such as this one. The secluded spaces had been designed for the use of couples or small groups desiring to escape the noise and activity of the brilliantly lit ballroom.

As Caroline had hoped, this particular bower had gone unnoticed here on this remote little terrace.

She ducked behind the swath of blue velvet drapery and found herself in a miniature replica of a Roman garden. A carved wooden bench and a small fountain decorated the setting.

She collapsed onto the bench and allowed herself to breathe again. She was safe for the moment. Luckily she had spotted Ivybridge just as he walked into the ballroom with his wife. He had no reason to search for her in the crowd, she reminded herself. Even if he heard people discussing the fact that Mrs. Fordyce, the author, was present tonight, he could not possibly connect the name to her. She had invented her pen name after the events in Chillingham.

Emma and Milly had vanished into the card room an hour ago. She would have to find a way to alert them to Ivybridge's presence so that they could all slip away from the ball before he accidentally happened across any of them.

As an afterthought, she untied the gold sash to release the blue velvet curtain. The drapery closed, concealing her completely. If anyone chanced to discover this little retreat, they would assume that it was occupied and go elsewhere.

She forced herself to concentrate. What she needed now was a plan. She must send a message to Emma and Milly via one of the footmen, instructing them to sneak out through a side door. Then she would have to get word to Adam informing him that she had been forced to leave the ball early. She would explain everything to him tomorrow.

Footsteps rang softly on the terrace, interrupting her thoughts. Alarmed, she tried not to move or breathe. Had Ivybridge noticed her and followed her?

"I trust you are not so worn out from dancing that you are unable to waltz with me, Mrs. Fordyce." Adam pulled aside the blue velvet drapery. He was smiling slightly but his eyes were unreadable in the dim light. "I realize that you are much in demand this evening, but we are very good friends, after all."

"*Adam.*" Relief mingled with the anxiety that was making her pulse race. She leaped to her feet. "Thank goodness you are here. There is a disastrous scandal brewing."

"Another one? They are mounting up so rapidly, I confess I am in danger of losing track of all of them."

"This one will cause all of the others to pale into insignificance. You must trust me when I tell you that it is imperative that I find Emma and Milly at once. The three of us must arrange to leave this house as secretly as possible."

"It sounds as though another startling incident has occurred." He shook his head a little, bemused. "I vow, my life has become a sensation novel since meeting you."

"This is no occasion for humor, sir, I assure you." She realized that in her agitation, she was waving her folded fan in a haphazard manner. Embarrassed, she forced herself to still her movements. "I should have told you the entire story before now but we have been so occupied with murder and mediums and such that I never got around to the details of the disaster in Chillingham."

"No, I don't believe you did."

"It was quite dreadful, Adam. Truly. And a certain person who was the cause of it all is here in this very house. I just saw him. If he happens to see me or my aunts, the scandal in which we are presently involved will become a thousand times worse."

"We are discussing Ivybridge, I assume?"

She froze. "You know about Ivybridge?"

"I am not in possession of the full particulars of the situation, but I am aware that he was the gentleman who ruined your reputation when you were known as Miss Connor."

"Good heavens. This is amazing. How on earth did you learn that?"

"It wasn't easy, especially given the fact that you deliberately misled me with the mention of Bath."

Guilt assailed her. "Oh, yes, I forgot about that part. I beg your pardon, but at the time I did not want to risk providing you with too many clues in the event that you were not entirely, uh —"

"Not entirely to be trusted?"

She flushed. "I did not know you very well a few days ago, and I had to be cautious."

"I understand." He inclined his head. "One cannot be too careful when one is attempting to conceal the past. I have had some experience with that sort of thing myself, if you will recall."

"Yes, of course. I was just concocting a scheme that would allow my aunts and me to sneak out of the house. Given your own expertise in such matters, you could be of great assistance."

"What did you have in mind?"

"I was thinking in terms of departing through the servants' hall."

"How odd. I was thinking in terms of a waltz."

She glared. "Have you been drinking heavily tonight, Adam?"

"Not yet. But given the manner in which events are progressing, I would not be surprised to find myself resorting to some restoratives before the night is over."

"I fail to comprehend why you insist upon making light of this extremely serious situation. I promise you, if Emma, Milly and I do not manage to escape without being seen by Ivybridge, you and your family will be embroiled in a scandal far worse than anything that you can imagine."

He unfolded his arms and touched his fingertips to her lips, silencing her.

"First, we waltz," he said.

He took her arm and drew her out of the imitation Roman garden.

"Adam, wait, you do not seem to comprehend —"

"If you continue to glare at me like that, everyone will believe that we are quarreling," he said, guiding her back into the ballroom. "Think of the gossip *that* would cause."

Mesmerized with dread, she offered no further resistance. She had done what she could, she told herself. She had tried to warn him. His fate was now in his own hands.

When they reached the dance floor, she felt Adam's arm, strong and sure, go around her waist. The next thing she knew she was gliding across the room in time to the intoxicating strains of a waltz.

It should have been a dream, she thought. The setting was so very romantic. Adam was disturbingly sensual and dangerously intriguing in his formal black-and-white evening wear. He radiated an aura of masculine power and control that made her intensely conscious of her own femininity.

But in reality it was all a nightmare. Heads were turning everywhere in the room. People had noticed that the mysterious Mr. Hardesty had taken the floor with his very good friend, the author. It was only a matter of time before Ivybridge spotted her.

When the confrontation occurred, it happened so swiftly and with such military precision that Caroline knew Adam had planned it right down to the last detail.

He swept her to a halt directly in front of a startled Ivybridge. The latter stared openmouthed at Caroline as though a spirit had materialized before him.

"Ivybridge," Adam said with deceptive ease. "Thought I saw you earlier."

Ivybridge swallowed hard and tore his shocked gaze away from Caroline. "Hardesty." He appeared momentarily distracted by Adam's face. "I say, did you walk into a door, sir?"

300

"Nothing quite that simple." Adam's smile could have frozen the fires of hell. He glanced at Caroline. "My dear, allow me to present Mr. Ivybridge. The family has some property in a little village called Chillingham, I believe. You may have heard of it. Quite near Bath. Ivybridge, this is my very good friend, Mrs. Fordyce. She is an author who crafts the most astonishing sensation novels. You have no doubt heard of her."

Caroline watched Ivybridge's eyes tighten at the corners.

"Mr. Ivybridge," she said, trying for the same cold, aloof tone that Adam had used.

It was obvious that Ivybridge had been blindsided by the introduction. Uncertain how to respond, he took the safe way out and acknowledged Caroline with a curt inclination of his head.

"Mrs. Fordyce," he mumbled.

"Come, my dear, we must be off." Adam tightened his grip on her arm. "I believe I see my sister at the door of the buffet room. She seems to be signaling us."

He whisked her away through the crowd so quickly that neither she nor Ivybridge was obliged to make their farewells.

"What on earth did you hope to accomplish with that maneuver?" she whispered to Adam.

"When I engage the enemy, I prefer to do so on grounds of my own choosing, not his."

"Another one of your rules?"

"Yes."

"Adam, I don't know what you're planning but I am very worried," she said, her anxiety growing with every passing second. "You do not know the enormity of the scandal that hangs over my head."

"I'm sure I shall find out soon enough. Events always happen quite rapidly in a sensation novel, I have discovered. One never gets bored."

He brought her to a stop in front of Julia, who stood with a small group of guests.

"There you are, Adam." Julia beamed at Caroline. "The two of you made such an attractive couple on the dance floor."

"I am going to leave Caroline with you for a while, if you don't mind," Adam said. "I have some business to attend to in the library."

"Business? Tonight?" Julia gave him a reproachful look. "Really, Adam, surely you could put it off until tomorrow."

"I'm afraid this is an extremely pressing matter." He raised Caroline's hand to his mouth and kissed it lightly. "See to it that Wilson dances with my very good friend, will you?"

Julia seemed to comprehend immediately that something was amiss. She did not question him further.

"I'm sure Uncle Wilson will be delighted to dance with her."

Caroline cleared her throat. "I appreciate your consideration, but I am not actually in a mood to dance at the moment."

"Pity." Wilson materialized at her side. "I was so looking forward to a waltz. I hope you will relent."

"But —"

It was too late. He had already taken her arm and was guiding her back through the crowd to the dance floor.

"I do not know what the three of you think that you are doing," she said in low tones as Wilson put his arm very formally around her waist. "But I can promise you that you are only making matters worse."

"I admit I have no notion of what is going on and I can see that Julia does not, either," Wilson said, unperturbed. "But Adam is obviously in command of the situation."

"He certainly appears to think he is. The problem is that he doesn't know what is going on, either, at least not all of it." She realized that she was becoming breathless trying to keep up with Wilson's surprisingly energetic dancing. "I assure you, there is another great scandal brewing."

"Indeed? It will be interesting to see if it can top the current one."

"But Adam told me that he has a rule against becoming involved in public sensations."

"Adam has a long list of rules," Wilson said. "But evidently he has not told you about the most important one of all."

"What is that?"

"Why, that there is an exception to every rule."

CHAPTER
THIRTY-THREE

"Regret to be the messenger who brings the bad news, old chap," Ivybridge said. He settled comfortably into one of the leather-upholstered wingback chairs and gave Adam a man-to-man look. "But we are members of the same club and all that sort of thing. It would be remiss of me not to pass along a word or two of advice concerning your association with the woman who calls herself Mrs. Fordyce."

Adam leaned back in his chair and contemplated his visitor. When he had returned to the library, he had sent Filby away to another room along with a bottle of claret and some sandwiches ordered up from the buffet. Then he had sat down to wait for Ivybridge. His intuition had told him he would not be obliged to wait long. He had been right.

"You know the traditional fate of the messenger," Adam said without inflection.

Ivybridge blinked, frowning a little at that. Then he relaxed into a chuckle. "You'll thank me for this news, Hardesty."

"Will I?"

"Indeed. No man likes to be cast in the role of fool."

"I can see you are very eager to impart your gossip."

"It's not gossip, sir. What I am about to tell you are facts. For starters, the lady's name isn't Mrs. Fordyce." Ivybridge glanced expectantly at the brandy decanter. "Caroline Connor is her real name. I suspect she invented the alias of Mrs. Fordyce to conceal her past."

Adam ignored the unsubtle hint concerning the brandy. He had no intention of serving his excellent spirits to the likes of Ivybridge.

"I assume you are going to tell me why she would wish to hide certain facts," he said.

"I will not bore you with all of the details but I can assure you that Miss Connor was involved in a great scandal that left her reputation entirely in ruins."

"I see."

"I must say, I am astonished to learn that she somehow managed to resurrect herself under a new name. But then she did strike me as a rather clever woman."

Adam steepled his fingers. "I have found her to be very intelligent and resourceful."

"Well, those are necessary qualities in a successful adventuress, are they not?" Ivybridge laughed. "I admit that she is an interesting creature, assuming one is in the mood for a taste of something out of the ordinary. But hardly a model of proper female behavior, eh?"

Adam pondered the various methods he could employ to dispatch Ivybridge. Unfortunately, most of them involved creating a considerable mess on the carpet.

"Not your sort?" he said instead.

"Alas, I fear that given the unfortunate circumstances in Chillingham, she has become a woman whose reputation is such that no gentleman would even think of introducing her to his family." Ivybridge winked knowingly. "I'm sure you take my meaning."

"I do, indeed," Adam said. He allowed himself to contemplate briefly the temptations offered by the extremely sharp point of the silver letter opener. "I suggest we return to the subject of dead messengers."

Ivybridge scowled in confusion. "Beg your pardon?"

The door crashed open without warning and with such force that it banged against the wall. Caroline swept into the room, jewel-red skirts flaring out behind her. Wilson followed in her wake. He appeared highly amused.

"My dear." Adam got to his feet. "What an unexpected pleasure."

She ignored him. "There you are, Ivybridge." She came to a halt in the center of the carpet. "I saw you leave the ballroom and I knew exactly what you intended. You could not wait to give Mr. Hardesty your version of the events in Chillingham, could you?"

Ivybridge surveyed her with a derisive glance, not bothering to rise. Then he looked at Adam. "As I was saying, hardly a model of womanly behavior."

Adam paid no attention to the remark. "Please be seated, my dear."

Either she did not hear him or else she was not of a mind to sit down. She continued to fix Ivybridge with a glare that was a mix of fury and disdain.

Adam looked at Wilson.

"Sorry," Wilson said cheerfully, not looking the least bit regretful. "Couldn't stop her. Once she realized that Ivybridge had left the ballroom, she was off like a hound after a fox."

He should have known better, Adam thought. Wilson was enjoying himself enormously. So much for maintaining control over the situation.

He walked deliberately around to the front of the desk and propped himself against it. Bracing his hands on either side of his thighs, he studied his small audience.

"I will admit that I am quite curious about the events that took place in Chillingham," he said mildly.

"They caused a great deal of nasty gossip, I can tell you that," Ivybridge said darkly.

Caroline whirled to face Adam. "I will tell you exactly what happened."

The door opened again before she could continue. Julia and Richard walked into the room.

"Lady Southwood." Ivybridge sprang to his feet with a great show of deference and bowed deeply to Julia. "Madam, might I suggest that you take your leave? I'm sure you will not want to listen to this extremely unpleasant conversation. Your delicate female nerves —"

"Do not concern yourself with my nerves, Mr. Ivybridge," Julia said coldly.

"I assure you, my wife has very steady nerves, Ivybridge." Richard raised a brow at Adam. "What the devil is going on here?"

"Caroline was just about to tell us the details of a great scandal in which she was involved three years ago," Adam said.

"How thrilling." Julia took a seat and assumed an attentive expression.

"Nothing like a good scandal," Richard agreed. He took up a position near the mantel.

The door was flung open yet again. This time Emma and Milly stormed into the library. Their expressions changed from anxious alarm to outrage when they caught sight of Ivybridge.

"What is that bastard doing here?" Milly asked.

"Such language." Ivybridge looked deeply pained. "I did try to warn you, Hardesty." He settled himself back into his chair. "The entire family lacks any sense of propriety."

Emma looked at him with utter loathing. "You have come here to try to ruin Caroline again, haven't you?"

"Mrs. Fordyce was just about to tell us the entire tale." Richard gave Caroline an inviting look. "Please continue."

Ivybridge's mouth thinned with annoyance. "I do not know what you hope to gain by embarrassing yourself in this extraordinary fashion, Miss Connor. You will only make things worse."

Julia was immediately intrigued. "Is that your real name? Connor?"

"Yes," Caroline said.

"Go on," Adam said to Caroline.

"I shall try to keep my version of events as brief as possible," she said. "Mr. Ivybridge has a large estate

308

outside the village. His family has held land in the neighborhood for some time."

"Six generations, to be exact," Ivybridge said with the arrogance of a man who knows that he occupies one of the higher rungs of the social ladder.

"Three years ago Ivybridge decided to marry," Caroline continued. "It was no secret in the village that his goal was to find a wife who could bring him some additional property in the vicinity of Chillingham. So he hunted for a wife among the local gentry. For a brief time, he paid court to Miss Aurora Kent, the daughter of another well-established family in the area. But for reasons of his own, he chose not to make an offer."

Ivybridge tut-tutted. "Family finances proved not to be as represented," he explained in a confidential tone to Wilson and Adam.

"In other words, the lady's inheritance was not rich enough to suit you," Caroline said icily. "You withdrew from that quarter and fixed your interests in a different direction."

"My lovely Helen," Ivybridge agreed, his satisfaction plain. "It proved to be an excellent match."

"She was not only quite pretty, she came with a handsome property that bordered the Ivybridge estate," Caroline said. "But there was a small problem with Miss Aurora Kent, who did not take kindly to being cast aside."

Ivybridge grimaced. "My change of plans evidently affected the lady's nerves in a rather peculiar fashion. She began acting decidedly odd. Actually showed up at my house on two occasions, unescorted during both instances, I might add. Demanded to know whom I had chosen to take her place. There was a dreadful scene in the course of the second visit. Threats were made."

Adam's stomach clenched. "Aurora Kent was mentally unbalanced?"

"Afraid so." Ivybridge shuddered. "I had a very close call, I can tell you. When I think of how close I came to marrying that woman, well, it still sends shivers through me."

"Ivybridge perceived, quite rightly, that Aurora Kent was not entirely sane," Caroline said. "When he withdrew his offer, she became a woman obsessed. He concluded that it would be most unwise to give her the name of his real intended."

"I feared she might do some harm to Helen," Ivybridge said, once again looking to the men in the room for understanding and approval. "Obviously I had a duty to protect my future wife from a madwoman."

"So he gave Aurora Kent my name instead." Caroline's gloved hands tightened into small fists at her side. "He told that poor, demented woman that he intended to marry *me*. And he never even had the courtesy to let me know what he had done."

Ivybridge's face pinched in rage. "How dare you accuse me of putting you in harm's way?"

"That is precisely what you did," Caroline said. "You wanted revenge."

"Nonsense," Ivybridge said swiftly. "You are inventing more fiction here."

Caroline's gaze was unwavering. "You were infuriated because I had repulsed your lecherous advances.

310

When you saw an opportunity to punish me for turning down your despicable offer to make me your mistress, you seized upon it."

"How dare you accuse me of making unwanted advances?" Ivybridge glanced nervously at Adam and then just as quickly looked away. "You invited my attentions with your unconventional behavior. Always wandering about the countryside on your own without a respectable chaperone — what did you expect a gentleman to think?"

All of the oxygen seemed to have been sucked out of Adam's lungs. He dared not move. He knew that if he did not control himself utterly at this moment, he would surely kill Ivybridge.

"It is true that I was in the habit of going off on long walks to think through my plots and ideas," Caroline said. Her mouth tightened. "Things are different in the country. Manners are more relaxed. No one in the village took any notice of me except you. And you were furious that day when I refused your advances. Later, when Aurora Kent showed signs of becoming quite dangerous, you pointed her in my direction."

"What happened?" Julia asked.

"Aurora followed me one afternoon," Caroline said. "I swear, she stalked me as if she was a hunter and I was the quarry."

"Dear heaven," Julia whispered.

Ivybridge rolled his eyes. "Such a melodramatic imagination. No wonder Miss Connor became a sensation novelist."

Caroline looked at Adam. "Aurora came upon me while I was sitting beneath a tree, making some notes. I saw at once that something was terribly wrong. She was dressed in only a nightgown and a pair of shoes. I spoke to her, asking her if she was ill. She did not seem to hear my question. She just kept repeating the same words over and over again."

Adam could not abide the cloudy veil of old terror gathering in her eyes. He straightened and crossed to where she stood in the center of the room. He put his hands gently on her bare shoulders.

No one moved or spoke. Even Ivybridge seemed suddenly bespelled.

"What did she say?" Adam asked Caroline, speaking to her as if they were alone.

"She said, 'You have to go away. Don't you see? He will come back to me if you go away.'"

When she repeated Aurora's words, her voice changed subtly, sliding into an eerie sing-song. She was falling back into the memory, he realized, reliving a nightmare. Beneath his hands, her skin had gone cold. He could feel the shivers arcing through her. Very carefully, he tightened his fingers, forcing her to take notice of him.

"What happened next?" he asked into the crystalline silence.

Caroline watched him as if she were trapped in a whirlpool and he held the rope that she could use to pull herself to safety. "She had been clutching a carving knife behind her back. She brought it out, raised it high and rushed at me. She tried to kill me, Adam."

He pulled her close against him, wrapped his arms around her and tried to warm her with the heat of his own body.

"You lived," he said into her ear, rocking her gently. "You lived. You are all right, Caroline. It is over."

"I turned to run," she whispered into his coat. "But my skirts got tangled around my ankles, tripping me. I fell. She was right there, almost on top of me. She went for my throat with the blade of the knife. I managed to roll to the side and scramble to my feet. I ran."

"Caroline." Emma started forward, one arm outstretched.

Out of the corner of his eye, Adam saw Milly wrap her hand around Emma's shoulders, silently halting her.

Ivybridge gave another disgusted snort. "For the information of everyone present, no knife was ever found. I fear it was but another figment of Miss Connor's overheated imagination."

"I picked up my skirts and fled toward the river," Caroline said numbly. "She was right behind me every step of the way. So close. I knew that I could not outpace her for long in my heavy dress. I reached the river and started across the footbridge. But she was almost upon me."

Caroline was as tense as though she were still in the act of fleeing for her life, Adam thought.

"What in God's name did you do?" he asked tightly.

"I finally remembered my parasol. It was attached to my waist by the new chatelaine that Aunt Emma and Aunt Milly had given me for my birthday. I unsnapped

313

it and stopped on the bridge. I used the parasol as though it were a long sword, stabbing toward Aurora's face. She fell back, instinctively trying to protect her eyes, I suppose. But she was off balance. The back of her knee struck the low railing of the footbridge. She went over the edge and into the river. The water was very deep. She could not swim."

"She drowned?" Adam asked.

Ivybridge snorted. "Nothing so neat and tidy. It happens that, among her other unladylike accomplishments, Miss Connor is an excellent swimmer. She stripped down to her chemise without a thought to propriety, went into the water and dragged the wretched Miss Kent to safety. Both women were discovered, soaking wet and dressed in their lingerie, by one of the tenants on my estate. A shocking sight, I assure you. The gossip did not die down for months."

"What happened to Aurora Kent?" Richard asked. "I trust she was sent to an asylum?"

Caroline raised her head from Adam's shoulder. "She took her own life later that same afternoon."

"Used her father's pistol to accomplish what the river had failed to do," Ivybridge said offhandedly. "Rendering Miss Connor's ridiculous rescue entirely moot."

"What happened to the knife?" Adam asked.

"Aurora Kent had it in her hand when she fell into the river," Caroline whispered. "She dropped it in the deep water beneath the footbridge. I suppose it is still there in the mud on the bottom."

314

"It was all a great uproar, I assure you," Ivybridge said. "Just to top it off, there were rumors to the effect that Miss Connor and I had been involved in an illicit affair. What with one thing and another, Miss Connor's reputation was in tatters."

Richard took his hand off the mantel and bowed respectfully to Caroline. "I stand in awe of your heroic nature, Miss Connor."

Julia got to her feet. "As do I, Caroline. Indeed, I am greatly moved by this sad tale. In my opinion, Ivybridge's actions lack any semblance of honor or nobility."

Ivybridge was thunderstruck. "I beg your pardon, madam. I am a gentleman."

"I agree entirely with my wife," Richard said. He looked at Ivybridge. "You, sir, are no gentleman."

"I never did like you, Ivybridge," Wilson said. "Please find your wife in the ballroom and leave immediately. You are no longer welcome as a guest in this household."

Ivybridge's face scrunched up first in disbelief and then in growing alarm. Adam could see that it had finally dawned on him that his role in the episode in Chillingham was not viewed with approval by anyone present.

"Now, see here." Ivybridge lurched to his feet. "I was attempting to do you a favor, Hardesty. If you wish to offend Society by forming a very public liaison with a woman who was involved in a great scandal, that is your affair."

"You're right." Adam released Caroline and started across the room toward Ivybridge. "It is my affair. And there is another aspect of this situation that you would do well to bear in mind."

Ivybridge gripped the back of the chair. "What do you mean?"

"Miss Connor is not only a very close friend, but I am hoping that in due time she will consider accepting a proposal of marriage from me."

Ivybridge's heavy jaw dropped. Adam heard Caroline utter a tiny squeak of astonishment. It amused him that no one else in the room seemed the least bit amazed by his announcement.

He halted in front of Ivybridge. "I'm sure you can guess how extremely annoyed I would be if Miss Connor were to be embarrassed in any way by gossip concerning the events in Chillingham."

"How dare you threaten me, sir?" Ivybridge blurted.

"I would be so annoyed, in fact, that I would not hesitate to disclose your investment in a certain establishment in Marbury Street to every intrepid newspaper correspondent in town."

Shock glazed Ivybridge's face. "I have no notion of what you are talking about."

"It is one thing for a gentleman to purchase some discreet entertainment at a brothel, but it is another thing altogether for him to invest in one, isn't it? Imagine how that will appear to your friends when they read it in the press."

"See here, I don't know what you are implying but I can assure you that you cannot prove anything."

Adam spread his hands. "That is the amazing thing about a newspaper sensation, isn't it? Great damage can be done to a gentleman's reputation and his standing in Society without going to the bother of supplying hard facts or proof of any kind." He paused. "But if it eases your mind, rest assured, I shall be able to provide the correspondents with a quantity of evidence."

"I have no intention of discussing Miss Connor's past," Ivybridge said, clearly shaken. "But what about my wife? She will surely recognize her."

"I strongly suggest that she does not recognize her," Adam said. "If any rumors, even the merest hint of Mrs. Fordyce's connection to the events in Chillingham of three years ago, happen to reach my ears, I will assume that they originated with you, Ivybridge, and respond accordingly."

"You can hardly blame me if someone else recognizes Miss Connor and relates the gossip."

"On the contrary, I won't hesitate to blame you. Not for a moment. I'm sure you can persuade your wife of the wisdom of not spreading gossip over tea." Adam glanced at the tall clock. "You have five minutes to collect her and depart this house."

Dazed, Ivybridge staggered to the door, jerked it open and rushed out into the hall.

A short silence fell upon the small group left in the library.

Milly shattered it by whipping open her fan. She gave Adam an approving smile.

"That was the most entertaining sight that I have seen in ages, sir," she said. "Thank you for rounding off a most enjoyable evening with such a pleasant farce."

Emma took a step forward and halted. "Do you really have damaging information concerning Ivybridge's investment in a brothel?"

It was Wilson who answered. He chuckled. "You may depend upon it, madam. Adam knows everyone's secrets in Society."

"I certainly don't regret cutting him off our guest list," Richard said. He took Julia's arm and went toward the door. "He was on it only because his father and mine were old acquaintances. But as it happens, both of those gentlemen are dead. I see no need to pursue the connection, do you, my dear?"

"Not at all," Julia said.

"Come, we must return to our guests." Richard paused at the door and grinned at Adam. "By the way, allow me to wish you good luck with your wedding plans, Hardesty. About time you tied the knot. You're not getting any younger, you know."

Adam inclined his head. "Thank you for pointing out my advancing years, Southwood."

"Think nothing of it. Felt it was my responsibility as your brother-in-law." He whisked a laughing Julia out the door.

"Let me echo Southwood's sentiments on the subject of your marriage plans, Adam." Wilson gave Caroline a gratified smile. "Excellent choice of bride, I might add. She'll fit right into the family."

Milly fanned herself happily. "This is so romantic."

318

Emma's brows came together in a severe line. "Are you serious in your intentions toward my niece, Mr. Hardesty? Or was the subject of marriage mentioned solely to intimidate Ivybridge?"

"Of course he is serious." Wilson took Emma's arm in one hand, grasped Milly's in the other and headed toward the door. "Adam has rules when it comes to dealing with a lady. Trust me, he would not have mentioned the subject of marriage unless he was very serious indeed."

The threesome disappeared through the doorway.

Adam found himself alone with Caroline.

"Adam."

She ran to him and threw herself into his arms, holding him so tightly that he hoped she would never let go. He put his arms around her, savoring the vibrant, feminine warmth and feel of her.

"I cannot believe what you and your family just did," she whispered.

He smiled into her hair. She did not know the half of it, he thought. The mild threats that had sent Ivybridge running from the room were the least of it. Over the course of the next few months the real justice would be delivered. Ivybridge would slowly but surely discover that he was no longer on the guest lists of some of Society's most important hostesses. He would be left out of certain private investment consortiums. He would no longer be welcome in certain clubs. In the end he would pay, and pay dearly, for what he had done to Caroline. But there was no need to burden her with the details.

"It was little enough, given what he put you through," he said aloud.

"I appreciate your feelings." She raised her head and stepped back reluctantly. "Unfortunately, in your desire to quell Ivybridge, I fear that you took matters a step too far."

"Damn. I find it so annoying when that happens."

CHAPTER
THIRTY-FOUR

He was obviously not giving the situation the serious attention it required. Perhaps he had not yet thought through the implications.

"This is not amusing, Adam," she said reproachfully. "Your family knows how you are about your rules."

He inclined his head. "True."

"After what you just said to Ivybridge, they will no doubt expect us to become engaged. Really, sir, what were you thinking?"

"Apparently I was thinking of marriage." He crossed the room to the brandy table and picked up the decanter. Light sparkled on the cut crystal facets when he tipped the bottle over a glass. "Everyone else, with the glaring exception of Ivybridge, seems to feel that we would make an excellent match." He paused, holding the glittering decanter aloft. "Would you care for a brandy?"

"No, thank you. One of us must remain clear-headed here."

"Better you than me." He drank a large measure of the brandy.

She whirled and began to pace the long room, struggling to pull her chaotic emotions into some sort of order.

"Please do not misunderstand me," she said quickly. "I am deeply indebted to you for the manner in which you dealt with Ivybridge. Indeed, I do not know how I shall ever be able to repay you."

For the first time since Ivybridge had departed the library, Adam appeared displeased. "There is no need to repay me," he said, a chill in his words. "You owe me nothing. I am the one who is indebted to you for providing me with an alibi for the murder of Irene Toller."

"Nonsense. I merely told the truth."

He shrugged. "I did the same just now."

"But you told Ivybridge that you planned to offer marriage."

"Yes, I did, didn't I?"

She sighed. "I realize that it was all part of your brilliant plan to intimidate him. And I do not doubt that he will certainly think twice before spreading gossip about the mysterious Mr. Hardesty's intended bride. But you did not have to go that far. Surely you can see that. He was already trembling in his shoes after you brought up his connection to that brothel."

Adam swallowed more brandy, looking pensive. "Thank you. The subject of his connection to that establishment was rather effective, wasn't it?"

"It was a very clever piece of strategy." She stopped at the far end of the room and gestured wildly with her folded fan. "But then everything you do is generally clever and well-planned. So why on earth did you feel compelled to say that you intended to ask me to marry you?"

He angled himself onto the corner of the desk and drank some more brandy while he considered the question.

"Probably because that is precisely what I intend to do," he said.

She felt as though she had been glued to the floor. She could not have moved if someone had yelled "Fire."

"I don't understand," she said, suddenly light-headed. "I thought our affair was going rather well."

"A matter of opinion, I'm afraid."

Her spirits plummeted. "Oh. I see. I didn't realize that you were not . . . That is to say, I . . . Well, I suppose my lack of prior experience has turned out to be something of a disappointment to you. But I assure you, I am a fast learner."

He gave her his most enigmatic look. "Tell me the truth, Caroline. Are you merely using me as your writer's muse?"

She was horrified. "No, no, of course not."

"You're certain?"

"Absolutely."

"I am not just a plaything for you, then?"

She felt herself turn very hot. Her face was probably as red as her gown. "How can you even suggest such a thing?"

"If I am more to you than just a toy or a useful muse, why are you so reluctant to speak of marriage?"

Because you do not seem to be able to tell me that you are madly, wildly, passionately in love with me, she thought. But she could hardly say that out loud.

"Well . . ." She broke off, trying to come up with a reason that would appeal to the logical side of his nature. "Time is a factor, sir. I'm sure you will agree that it is much too soon to discuss the subject. After all, we have been acquainted for only a matter of a few days."

"But we do appear to be well suited. Everyone else certainly seems to believe that to be the case."

Well suited. Hardly a declaration of undying love.

She cleared her throat, steadying her nerves. "Exactly how are we well suited?"

He gave her a slow, sensual smile. "You know my secrets and I know yours."

That stopped her for a few heartbeats but she managed to cling to a few wispy tendrils of logic.

"Yes, well, that may be true," she allowed. "But do you think that constitutes sufficient grounds for marriage?"

"In this particular instance it does, at least as far as I am concerned." He put down the brandy glass and came up off the desk. "But rest assured there are other ways in which we are well suited."

Her brain went utterly blank. "Such as?"

He walked toward her, looking dangerous indeed, with his darkly bruised eye and grimly determined expression.

"This way, for example," he whispered.

324

He put his powerful hands very gently around her bare throat and tilted her head slightly for his kiss.

A shiver of excitement coursed through her. This was no doubt the path to disaster, she reminded herself. If she wanted to retain any degree of common sense she would turn away from him right now, this very minute, before his mouth touched hers.

But she could not seem to get unstuck from the floor. And then it was much too late because he was kissing her in a slow, searing way that melted everything inside her and set fire to her blood.

She did not want to think about his business-like suggestion of marriage. Instead, she wanted to concentrate on the way she felt when he took her in his arms.

His tongue slid along the edge of her mouth and ever so slightly between her lips. She leaned heavily against him, wrapping her arms around his neck. The thrilling heat and strength of his body enveloped her.

He deepened the kiss, drawing it out until she was clinging to him.

The knowledge that he wanted her so intensely gave her courage and hope. She understood his wariness. He had taught himself to survive first on the streets and then in a glittering, superficial world where love was treated, at best, with amused disdain. He had learned his lessons well and established his own rules. It was only to be expected that he would be deeply cautious.

She was taking a risk, she thought. But Adam was worth it.

A discreet knock sounded on the door.

Adam raised his head, frowning slightly. "It must be Morton, and that means that it will be important. Excuse me, my dear."

He crossed to the door and opened it. Caroline saw the formidable butler in the corridor. Morton was very careful not to look at her. She heard him speak to Adam in low, serious-sounding tones. Adam gave some crisp directions in response.

When he turned back to her and closed the door, she knew at once that something had happened. All the sensual satisfaction had vanished from his expression. It had been replaced by the concentrated attention of the hunter.

"What is it?" she asked.

"Morton brought me a message from an old friend of mine named Florence Stotley. Thanks to her I now have an address for Irene Toller's missing assistant, Bess Whaley. I must leave at once."

"You are going to see Bess tonight?"

"Yes." He shrugged out of his jacket. "I do not want to take the risk of losing her again. Morton is bringing me another jacket and a pair of boots."

"I think I should go with you to speak with the assistant."

"There is no need for that. The address I was given is not in the best part of town."

"Bess obviously fled for a reason. She will likely panic when she finds you at her door at this hour. Perhaps my presence will reassure her."

He hesitated and then nodded abruptly. "Very well. I will send for your wrap."

326

CHAPTER
THIRTY-FIVE

The neighborhood where Bess Whaley had sought to hide was not in the stews, but neither was it a comfortable place at this hour of the night. Adam instructed Ned to halt the carriage in the street some distance from the address he sought. He did not want to risk waking Whaley prematurely with the rattle of wheels and hooves.

"You understand what I want you to do?" he said to Ned, assisting Caroline down from the carriage.

"Aye, sir."

Adam looked at Caroline. "Are you sure you want to come with me?"

"We have been through this often enough, Adam. I am coming with you." She bent down to make certain the long skirts of her gown were hooked up and securely fastened.

He smiled slightly, admiration welling up inside him. Caroline's spirit drew him the way expensive perfume might draw another man. Which was not to say that she did not also possess a most unique and delightful fragrance, he thought, amused by his own bemusement.

Following the plan that he had hurriedly concocted enroute to Bess Whaley's lodgings, he guided Caroline down a narrow walk into the alley that ran behind the building. He counted off the small gardens until they came to the one that guarded the rear door of Whaley's new address.

It was no trick at all to get inside the gate. He and Caroline went to stand in the deep shadows near the back door and waited.

A short time later the carriage clattered loudly in the street in front of the address. Ned had followed orders to the letter. A moment later Adam heard the distant thud that meant that Ned had knocked on the front door.

There was a long pause. Adam wondered if he had miscalculated.

Hurried footsteps sounded in the back hall. The kitchen door opened abruptly. There was enough moonlight to make out the figure of a woman garbed in a robe and slippers rushing out of the house into the garden.

"Bess Whaley, I presume?" Adam said, moving into her path.

Bess stifled a small screech and floundered to a halt. "Get away from me." Raw fear laced her words. "Get away, I say. Please don't hurt me. I'll never say a word."

"Calm yourself, Bess," Caroline said gently. "I am Mrs. Fordyce. You remember me, don't you?"

Bess swung around. "Mrs. Fordyce? Is it really you, ma'am?"

"Yes. And this is my assistant, Mr. Grove. You remember him from the séance, don't you?"

"What are you two doing here?"

"We want to help you," Caroline said soothingly.

"I don't understand." Bess peered more closely at Adam. "When I heard the carriage in the street, I was sure it was either him or the police, and I didn't know which was worse, to tell you the truth. I've been so afraid that one or the other would find me."

Caroline took her hand and led her back toward the door. "We must talk. Let us go inside out of the cold."

Adam sat at the small, scarred kitchen table with a shaken Bess Whaley. Caroline had lit a lamp and immediately become very busy with the kettle and some mugs. He wondered if she realized what a rare sight she made, bustling around these humble surroundings in her elegant ball gown and dainty shoes. If so, she gave no sign. Rather, she seemed to have made herself right at home, as though offering a comforting cup of tea to the former housekeeper and assistant of a fraudulent medium was not the least out of the ordinary.

"You say you're trying to find the person who killed Mrs. Delmont and Mrs. Toller?" Bess's heavy features skewed into an expression of uneasy confusion.

"He is a very dangerous person, Bess," Adam said. "It will be better for everyone involved if he is found as soon as possible."

"But you don't understand," Bess said again for what must have been the fifth or sixth time. The words were fast becoming a litany.

"Then you must explain everything to us, Bess." Caroline put tea leaves into the pot. "It is important that you tell us what you know of this matter."

"You can start by telling us why you ran away after Mrs. Toller was murdered," Adam said. "Did you see the killer? Are you afraid that he saw you?"

"No." Bess hesitated. "I didn't see him. Not exactly. I found Mrs. Toller's body very early the next morning when I arrived to start my chores. The séance room was in a shambles, but I knew straight off it was no housebreaker or thief who had killed her, because none of the valuables had gone missing."

"A very clever observation," Adam said.

"Yes, sir. Thank you, sir." Bess clutched the lapels of her wrapper. "When I found her, Mrs. Toller was still wearing the gown she'd worn to conduct the séance. The front door was unlocked."

"Was it, indeed?" Adam asked softly.

Bess looked at him with anguished eyes. "She'd been expecting him, you see."

At the stove, Caroline went very still. "Who was she expecting, Bess?"

"Her lover, of course." Bess shrugged. "She always sent me away on the nights when he was to come to her. He hadn't been around much in the past few weeks but she was expecting him that night, I'm sure of it."

"Who is he, Bess?" Adam asked. The warning look he got from Caroline told him that he had spoken too roughly.

Bess's eyes widened in renewed alarm. "I told you, I don't know, sir. I swear I don't. I never saw him. Not once. They were very secretive. She said he insisted on it."

"Here's your tea, Bess," Caroline glided over to the table, silk skirts swaying gently, and set the full mug in front of Bess. "I put some sugar and milk in it for you."

Distracted, Bess stopped clutching her wrapper and gripped the mug in both hands instead. She stared at the tea as though she had never seen anything like it before in her life.

"Thank you, ma'am," Bess whispered.

Caroline put a mug in front of Adam and then sat down across from Bess. "Take your time, Bess. There is no need to rush. You say you don't know the identity of Mrs. Toller's lover?"

"No, ma'am." Bess took a tentative sip of tea. It seemed to steady her. "He insisted that she be alone when he came to call. He was very strict about it."

"How did Mrs. Toller know what nights he would call on her?" he asked Bess.

Bess appeared baffled. "I don't know, sir. She just knew."

"He didn't send a message to the house alerting her?" Caroline asked.

Bess pressed her lips together very tightly and shook her head. "None that I ever saw."

"But you believe that he was there the night she died and that he was the one who murdered her?" Adam asked.

"All I know for certain is that he was supposed to visit that evening." Bess swallowed more tea. "She was angry with him. I expect they quarreled and he killed her."

Adam leaned forward slightly, watching Bess's face in the flaring lamplight. "How do you know that Mrs. Toller was angry with him?"

"I've worked for her for years. I got to know her ways quite well. Started out as her housekeeper and eventually took on the duties of her assistant. She felt she could trust me, you see."

"You helped her stage the tricks that made her séances look real," Adam stated.

Bess heaved a sigh. "It was a good position. I'm going to miss it. Not likely I'll find another that pays as well, and that's a fact."

Caroline eased her mug aside. "Do you know why Mrs. Toller was angry with her lover?"

Bess snorted. "For the oldest reason in the world."

Caroline's brows rose. "She discovered that he was cheating on her?"

"Yes, ma'am." Bess drank more tea. "And with her competition, at that."

Adam set his mug down hard. "Elizabeth Delmont."

"Yes, sir." Bess shook her head sadly. "Made Mrs. Toller cry for days, it did. Then she went all cold and fierce-like. I knew she was planning something, but I reckoned she intended to confront her lover and tell him she wouldn't put up with his cheating. I swear it never occurred to me that she meant to do what she did."

Another link in the chain snapped into place. Adam watched Bess's face closely.

332

"Irene Toller murdered Elizabeth Delmont, didn't she?" he said.

"Yes, sir," Bess said. Her voice was barely above a whisper. She contemplated her unfinished tea. "I never let on that I knew. I didn't dare. I kept my mouth shut and did my work like nothing had ever happened."

"How did you reason it out?" Caroline asked.

"Mrs. Toller sent me away that night, too. At first I assumed that her lover would be paying her a visit. But when I arrived at the house the next morning, I realized that he hadn't been there."

"How did you know that?" Adam asked.

Bess raised one shoulder in a matter-of-fact manner. "A housekeeper sees things that others don't notice. Mrs. Toller and her friend had been getting together on special evenings for a few months. They had their habits."

"Such as?" Caroline asked.

"Little things. She kept a bottle of his favorite brandy on hand. It was their custom to drink some before they got down to their more personal business. The glasses they used were always left out on the table in the parlor. But there were no glasses the morning after Mrs. Delmont was murdered."

"What else was different?" Adam asked.

"Mrs. Toller was in her dressing gown when I arrived that day but she was acting very strange. I thought perhaps she was suffering from an attack of nerves or the like. And her bed was made up. She never would have made her own bed. I don't think she slept at all that night. But the thing that chilled me to my bones was what I found in her wardrobe."

"What was it?" Caroline asked.

"It wasn't what was there, it was what was missing." Bess looked knowing. "Her new gown was gone. It was her favorite. Very expensive it was, too. He had paid for it. A dress like that just doesn't up and vanish."

Caroline tensed. "What happened to it?"

"I asked her that very question." Bess folded her hands on the table and bowed her head. "Mrs. Toller told me that it had been ruined the previous day when a passing carriage had splashed mud all over it. She told me that she had sent it off to a charity house. But I knew that wasn't the truth. She had never given so much as a penny to any charity as long as I had known her. She said they were all frauds."

"What do you think happened to the dress?" Caroline asked.

"She hid it in one of the secret compartments in the séance room," Bess said tightly. "I found it quite by accident when I was straightening up the chamber for the séance that you two attended. I couldn't understand what it was doing in the secret cupboard. Then I saw all the dried blood on the skirts. I knew right off what Mrs. Toller had done. I was scared to death, I can tell you."

"I don't blame you." Caroline shuddered.

"Yes, ma'am." Bess sighed. "Knew I'd likely have to look for another position."

"What did you do with the dress?" Adam asked.

334

"Put it straight back into the cupboard and pretended I never saw a thing." Bess shrugged. "Doubt if she had a chance to get rid of it before she was killed. It's probably still there unless the police found it."

They sat for a while, drinking the tea and watching one another in the light of the flaring lamp.

He studied the frightened woman. "You told us that you ran away the morning you found Mrs. Toller's body because you feared both the killer and the police."

"Yes, sir," she said glumly. "I was terrified that the police would think I'd killed Mrs. Toller because we'd argued about my wages. The neighbors heard us. But I was also afraid that her lover might decide that I knew too much about their business and come after me."

Adam gripped the mug more tightly. "Business? Do you refer to the fraudulent investment schemes Mrs. Toller operated?"

"You know about those, do you?" Bess looked more miserable than ever. "Right you are, sir. That's why Mrs. Toller and I quarreled, you see. I figured out that something quite profitable was going on and that she was sharing the income with him. I told her that since I was assisting her, I deserved a portion of the profits. She warned me to keep silent. Threatened to let me go without a reference. I told her that if she did, I'd expose her tricks. It was a very heated argument and I expect some of the neighbors heard the shouting."

"I have a few more questions for you, Bess," Adam said. "And then I am going to give you enough money to take the train to wherever you wish and stay there

335

until we have found Mrs. Toller's killer and turned him over to the police."

For the first time Bess looked cautiously hopeful. "That's very kind of you, sir. What more do you want to know?"

"Do you have any notion of why Mrs. Toller's lover murdered her?"

Bess hesitated. "I've been thinking about that. I expect it was because he knew that she had murdered Mrs. Delmont and was afraid of what she might do next in her great rage. Perhaps he feared she might expose him and the investment scheme. Like I told you, whoever he is, he's a very secretive sort."

"Would you please tell me exactly what you saw when you found Mrs. Toller's body?" Adam asked.

Bess gave that some close consideration. "There was a lot of blood. He'd bashed in her skull, you see. She was lying on her back. There was a pocket watch on the floor beside her. The room was in a shambles. I remember thinking that it was just like the way Mrs. Delmont's death had been described in the papers. That seemed odd because I knew that Mrs. Toller, not her lover, had killed Mrs. Delmont. Couldn't understand why he went to all that trouble to make it look the same."

"Was there anything else on or near the body that seemed unusual?" Adam asked. "Some type of mourning jewelry or a veil, for instance?"

Bess's brow furrowed. "No, sir. I didn't see anything like that."

"One last question, Bess," Adam said. "Were you the one who sent the messages summoning Mrs. Fordyce and me to Mrs. Toller's house the morning after the murder?"

Bess looked quite blank. "No, sir. I didn't send any messages. I was too busy packing my things and trying to find a place to hide."

Caroline got into the carriage and sat down across from Adam. She was feeling decidedly odd, an unsettling mix of excitement and exhaustion, she concluded. She tried to pull her scattered thoughts into some semblance of order.

"If Bess is correct, then it would seem that Mrs. Toller did indeed kill Elizabeth Delmont in a jealous rage," she said. "But it was not professional jealousy that drove her; rather, it was the more traditional, personal sort. She had discovered that her lover had betrayed her with another woman."

"Yes." Adam lounged moodily in the shadows. "Toller must have been the one who left the wedding veil, the smashed watch and the mourning brooch at the scene of Delmont's death. The question is why?"

"Perhaps those items had some symbolic meaning for her. But in that case, who removed them?"

Adam looked at her from the shadows. "The lover who was also the business partner? He may well have planned a tryst with Delmont that same night. If so, he would have found the veil and the brooch with the body, just as I did. Perhaps he feared that if the police discovered them, they would raise questions that he did not want answered."

"Because those answers might have implicated him in some fashion?"

"It is the only possibility that seems logical, at least at this moment."

Caroline couldn't help herself. She patted a small yawn. "What do you intend to do now?"

"I am going to take you home and then I am going to get some sleep. It has been a very long night."

CHAPTER
THIRTY-SIX

He got the message from Bassingthorpe late the following afternoon. The old forger received him in a comfortable house tucked away in an unmarked lane.

Bassingthorpe squinted at Adam through a pair of spectacles and heaved a weary sigh. "Eyes aren't what they used to be. Leave most of the fine work to my grandson these days. He's got talent, right enough."

"But you still look after the business, I assume?" Adam said.

"Certainly." Bassingthorpe snorted. "Can't be too careful in this profession. Teaching my granddaughter that side of the trade. She's no artist but she has a head for numbers and she's got the sort of common sense it takes to avoid trouble."

"Your grandson produced the stock certificates, then?" Adam asked.

"Yes, indeed," Bassingthorpe stated proudly. "Rather a nice job, if I do say so myself. He's as good as I was at his age."

"It is the client who interests me," Adam said. "In the past, you were always very cautious in your business dealings."

Bassingthorpe raised one finger in an admonishing manner. "First rule of success in the profession is Know thy client. It is those who get greedy and take on any commission that comes along just for the sake of the money who land in prison."

"I have reason to believe that the person who commissioned the stock certificates from you may have murdered a woman. Irene Toller, the medium, to be specific."

Bassingthorpe frowned. "I say, are you certain of that?"

"Not entirely. I am still in the process of making inquiries."

"Huh." Bassingthorpe put his fingertips together and looked wise. "I've had a great deal of experience with clients, as you well know. Wouldn't have said this one was the murderous sort. More of a man of business."

"You may be correct. But either way, he is a link in the chain that I am following. I am very eager to locate him."

"You know I'll be glad to help you. I owe you one or two favors from the old days. Always pay my debts."

"I am very grateful, sir." Adam rested his arms on the sides of his chair. "The description I have been given is that of a heavily whiskered man who walks with a severe limp."

Bassingthorpe chuckled. "He affected that appearance when he met with me, also. But I took my usual precautions. Made certain that we met on neutral ground so that he did not have my address, and I set one of the lads who works in the shop to follow him after we came to an agreement."

Anticipation flashed through Adam. "The boy was successful?"

"Certainly. Young Harry comes from the same sort of neighborhood that you came from, Adam. No one knows more about following a man through the streets than a lad who was raised on them, eh?"

"What did young Harry discover?"

"Among other things, your man is a rather accomplished actor. He maintained his disguise right up until the moment when he entered the back door of his lodgings. But then such talents are no doubt a requirement in his trade."

"And just what is his line?" Adam asked.

"Why, he's in the psychical research business. Gaining quite a reputation, too. I understand he gave a most astonishing performance for the police the other afternoon. Claimed he could help them identify the villain who murdered the mediums."

"Please come in, Mrs. Fordyce." Durward Reed ushered her into his cluttered office and motioned her to a chair. "I cannot tell you how much I appreciate your time today. I understand that you are an extremely busy person, what with your writing and your, uh, other affairs." He broke off, reddening. "I refer to the social demands that are made upon you due to your connection to Mr. Hardesty, of course."

"Of course." Caroline sat down and adjusted the heavy folds of her green gown. She pretended not to

341

notice Reed's moment of awkwardness. A woman who was engaged in an affair with a notoriously mysterious and powerful gentleman had to become accustomed to the occasional social lapse on the part of others. "I was delighted to receive your message. I appreciate your interest in my novels."

"Yes, indeed, I am a great admirer of your work, both as a publisher and as a reader." He motioned toward a tea tray. "May I pour you a cup?"

"Thank you."

While he busied himself with the pot and two cups, she took advantage of the opportunity to look around the office. It was not unlike Spraggett's domain, littered with papers, books and files. One entire shelf was crammed with old copies of *New Dawn*.

A photograph of the queen occupied a place of pride on one wall.

"My wife, Sarah, was very fond of novels. I'm sure she would have enjoyed your stories." Reed set a cup of tea on the table beside Caroline. "She was a medium of great power. Sadly, I lost her several years ago. Some monstrous villain attacked her the morning after our wedding night while she was walking in the park across the street."

"I am sorry for your loss, Mr. Reed."

"Thank you. It is my most fervent desire to contact her on the Other Side. Indeed, I have dedicated my life to that project."

A chill slithered through Caroline. "I see."

He moved one hand to indicate the office and the huge, dark mansion that seemed to press down upon

342

them. "She was the last of her family. This house was part of her inheritance. I stayed on here after her death because I felt certain that it would be easier for her spirit to return to the place that had been her home in her earthly life."

"I understand."

"As the years passed and no contact was made, I devoted myself to the study of psychical research. I established the Society and I try to encourage mediums and others who are interested in such matters. It is my hope that someone more gifted than I will help me find the answers I seek."

"You have contributed greatly to the field of psychical research, Mr. Reed." Out of politeness she tried another sip of the strong tea. The milk and sugar made it palatable, but just barely.

Reed folded his broad hands on his desk. Caroline noticed that he wore mourning cuff links fashioned of jet and silver.

"Everything I have done since Sarah's death has been guided by my hope of contacting her," he said. "But thus far, it has all been to no avail."

"It may be that such things are not meant to be," she suggested as kindly as possible.

He frowned. "If that were so, mediums such as my Sarah would not exist. She really did possess the most amazing gifts, Mrs. Fordyce. There is no doubt in my mind. Knowing that is what gives me the resolve to press on with all forms of psychical research. Sooner or later, I will find a medium who will be able to contact her. When that happens, I will not only be able to communicate with Sarah, I will prove to the world that psychical investigation is a legitimate field of science."

"I know that you are not alone in your convictions, sir." She paused delicately. "And I wish you well in your explorations. But I believe that you asked me to come here today to discuss more mundane business?"

"Not mundane at all, madam. I have been searching for ways to expand the readership of *New Dawn* and also membership in the Society. It is my firm belief that the more people who study psychical matters, the more likely we are to make a breakthrough."

"That sounds reasonable."

He leaned forward earnestly. "It occurred to me that if *New Dawn* were to publish one of your stories in a serialized fashion, I could attract a very large number of new readers and possibly discover new, talented mediums."

She swallowed, aware that her throat seemed to have gone quite dry and raspy. She hoped she was not coming down with a cold.

"I am flattered, Mr. Reed, but do you think my type of novels are suited to your publication?"

"You have told me that you are researching a new novel that will feature a powerful medium and several startling incidents involving the Other Side. I would very much like to offer you a contract to publish that story in *New Dawn*."

She took another sip of tea to moisten her unnaturally dry mouth and tongue. "It is an intriguing proposition, sir."

344

"I am well aware that your current publisher will no doubt make you an excellent offer for your next novel. All I ask is that you give me an opportunity to counter his offer with a better one. I confess I do not know how much one pays an author but I am not without resources. I trust we will be able to come to an agreement."

A discreet knock sounded on the office door.

Reed broke off, irritated. "Yes, Miller, what is it?"

The door opened. A diffident-looking young man nodded apologetically at Caroline and then cleared his throat.

"I am sorry to interrupt you, sir, but you did ask to be notified when Mr. Elsworth arrived."

"Elsworth?" Reed was clearly annoyed. "He's here?"

"Yes, sir. He says he wishes to discuss the arrangements for this evening's reception and demonstration. Evidently there are some changes he wants to make."

"This is most awkward." Reed got to his feet. "It is just after three. My appointment with Elsworth was for four o'clock."

"Shall I ask him to come back?"

"No, no, you must not do anything that will cause him to take offense. This institution needs his illustrious presence. He has brought us a great deal of attention and credibility." Reed hurried around the desk. "You know how temperamental he is."

"Yes, sir." Miller waited for instructions.

345

Reed paused by Caroline's chair. "Mrs. Fordyce, will you excuse me for a few minutes? Elsworth can be quite difficult.

"I understand." A small, unpleasant wave of nausea roiled her stomach. Her skin went suddenly cold. "Perhaps I should return at some other time."

"No, please, wait here. I will be only a moment."

Reed vanished, ushering Miller ahead of him, before she could think of an excuse to leave. The door closed solidly.

Caroline sat very still for a moment, breathing deeply and hoping that her stomach would settle. She looked at the half-empty cup of cloyingly sweet, milky tea. The lines she had written the other evening after Adam had left her study came back to her. *You are not yourself . . . I believe you may have been poisoned . . .*

Impossible, she thought. *Do not let your writer's imagination run wild. Reed has no reason on earth to harm you.*

Nevertheless, she was *not* herself. She wanted nothing more than to go home, crawl into her own bed, pull up the covers and sleep.

It took all of her strength to get out of the chair. For a few disorienting seconds she stood in the center of the room, trying to maintain her balance, trying not to be ill.

She closed her eyes against another churning twist of nausea. When the nasty sensation passed, she took a deep breath, opened her eyes and turned toward the door.

She found herself looking at a photograph. Not the one of the queen; rather another one that hung on the wall beside the door. She had been sitting with her back to it and had not noticed it until now.

It was a picture of a young woman dressed in an elegant dress and a long white veil. Her beautiful face was set in unhappy lines, as though she was resigned to some unpleasant fate.

"Sarah Reed, I presume?" she whispered. "Were you a real medium? Did you actually reach through the veil to communicate with the Other Side?"

The veil.

There was something about the portrait . . .

The bride's pale hair was bound up in a style that had been fashionable a decade earlier.

Sarah Reed had evidently been blond, Caroline thought. Why was that important?

She moved closer to the photograph as though compelled. It required a great effort to concentrate on the details. Sarah Reed's gown and veil were both white. That was not unusual. After the queen had chosen to wear white for her marriage to her beloved Albert, the color had become somewhat fashionable with brides. Many still preferred other colors, of course, but white was not uncommon.

She looked closer and noticed that Sarah Reed wore a brooch pinned to the bodice of her gown. It appeared to be covered in black enamel.

Dread whispered through Caroline. Her thoughts were starting to blur but somewhere in the haze she managed to summon up some of the elements that

Adam had mentioned when he had described the brooch that he had found on Elizabeth Delmont's bodice. It had been enameled in black — she was quite certain of that. He had said that there was a photograph of a woman dressed in white and wearing a veil inside ... A twist of blond hair had been set beneath the beveled crystal.

Dear heaven. Terror turned her blood to ice. She had to get out of here immediately.

The door of the office opened before she could take a single step.

"Mrs. Fordyce." Reed walked into the room, frowning in concern. "Are you all right?"

"No, I am ill. Please excuse me." She started forward, fighting to keep her balance. "I must go home at once."

"Allow me to assist you."

Reed closed the door and came toward her, arms outstretched.

"Don't touch me," she rasped, trying to evade his grasp.

"But you are ill, Mrs. Fordyce. You need help."

"No. I must leave."

But the room was spinning more violently now. A thick, murky darkness was closing in around her, leaving no solid shapes that she could use to orient herself. She tried to grab the back of a chair, missed and crumpled to her knees.

"Don't worry, Mrs. Fordyce. I will take care of you."

348

Reed reached down and picked her up in his arms. There was more strength in his square, stocky, broad-shouldered body than she would have imagined.

She opened her mouth to scream for help but the strange fog enveloped her completely. She found herself suddenly cast adrift in a vast, uncharted sea of nothingness, neither fully asleep nor entirely awake. A dreamworld.

She wondered if this was the Other Side.

CHAPTER
THIRTY-SEVEN

Adam waited for his prey in the stillness and shadows of the well-furnished lodgings. He heard the key in the lock shortly before six o'clock that evening.

The door opened. Elsworth let himself into the room and made to turn up the nearest lamp.

Adam moved out of the shadows, caught him by the back of his coat and hurled him against the wall.

Elsworth grunted heavily, bounced off the paneling and landed hard on his side. He scrambled frantically to right himself.

"If you move so much as a finger, I will break it," Adam said.

Elsworth froze half-sitting, half-sprawled on the floor. "Hardesty? What the deuce is this about?"

Adam lit the lamp. "It is about two murders and a missing diary."

"Have you gone mad, sir? How dare you invade my residence like this and imply that I am in any way connected to murder?"

"I want answers, Elsworth, and I want them quickly. Tell me everything you know about the deaths of Elizabeth Delmont and Irene Toller."

"I was barely acquainted with those two frauds. I had nothing to do with their deaths and you cannot prove otherwise. Now, I advise you to leave at once or I shall summon a constable. I have an important reception and a demonstration at Wintersett House to prepare for this evening."

"If you don't tell me what I want to know, you are not only going to miss this evening's performance, I will also make certain that your career as London's most fashionable medium comes to an end tonight."

Elsworth stared. "Are you threatening my life, sir?"

"At the moment, merely your livelihood. But that could certainly change."

"Bah." Elsworth relaxed visibly. "Do you really think that anything you say can persuade people not to believe in my powers? If so, you are a fool. People believe what they wish to believe and at the moment, most of London is pleased to believe that I am the most powerful practitioner of psychical powers who has ever lived."

"You misunderstand me, Elsworth. I do not intend to expose you as a fraudulent practitioner, but rather as a financial fraud." Adam picked up the envelope he had placed on a table a short time before. He opened it, turned it upside down and let the Drexford & Co. stock certificates fall to the carpet.

Elsworth glanced uneasily at the documents. "Where did you get those?"

"Out of the bottom drawer of your desk."

"See here, I don't know what makes you think that I know anything about those certificates."

351

"The printer who arranged to produce those for you is an old and trusted acquaintance of mine," Adam said. "He is also the cautious sort. He had you followed after the two of you did business together. He likes to know as much as possible about his clients, you see. It provides him with a measure of security."

Elsworth grimaced. "That old villain. Should have known he would pull a trick like that. Well, it won't do you any good. He is hardly likely to testify against me. He's got too many secrets of his own to hide."

"I don't need his testimony to destroy your career. You do not appear to be aware of the fact that I have some powers of my own."

Elsworth eyed him warily. "What are you talking about?"

"One word from me concerning the true nature of your business operations, Elsworth, and every newspaper in the city will take great delight in exposing the financial scandal you perpetrated with the help of two murdered mediums."

"You have no proof," Elsworth said weakly.

"You know as well as I do that evidence and proof are unimportant trifles when it comes to a press sensation. But, to be frank, exposure in the papers should be the least of your concerns."

"What do you mean?"

"I would remind you of my position in the Polite World," Adam said gently. "I not only control a fortune, I am Wilson Grendon's heir and I have a very close connection to the Earl of Southwood. I promise you that before I am finished, all the important doors in

Society that are presently open to you will close so suddenly and with such force that you will be able to hear the echoes all the way across England."

Elsworth gave that statement about two seconds' thought.

"What, precisely, do you want to know?" he asked wearily.

Adam picked up the diary that he had found hidden beneath the bed. "As a matter of curiosity, where did you find this? I searched Elizabeth Delmont's house very carefully that night."

"I was more closely acquainted with her than you were, sir. Delmont actually considered herself a professional colleague of mine. When I expressed some passing interest in her tricks and devices, she very proudly gave me a tour of her secrets." Elsworth gave a gentlemanly snort. "She wanted to impress me, and I will admit she was somewhat more clever than many of her competitors. She had installed a number of concealed cupboards and cabinets. One of them was behind the wall sconce in the séance room. I found the diary in it."

"Unfortunately, I missed that particular cupboard." Adam put the journal down. "If I had located the diary that night, I could have saved myself a good deal of trouble." He watched Elsworth closely. "How did you know to search for it?"

"Delmont had told me that she had recently come into possession of a private journal that had great potential for blackmail. She actually bragged about it. As I told you, she wanted to make me see her as an

353

equal, not as a lowly assistant. After I found her body, I decided it might be worthwhile to make a quick search to see if I could locate the diary. I admit, she had made me curious about the possibility of an easy profit."

"You found the journal."

"Yes, but once I read the damned thing, I decided it would be best not to use it."

"What made you come to that conclusion?"

"I make my living by my wits," Elsworth said dryly. "I'm not a fool. I did not want to take the risk of blackmailing a man as powerful and as dangerous as you are, Hardesty. But you forced my hand when you continued to investigate the murders. I knew that sooner or later you would uncover my very profitable little investment scheme."

"You sent those two men to warn me off, didn't you?"

Elsworth shrugged. "I was getting desperate. The diary was all I had to use against you."

"I understand why you took the diary. But why did you take the mourning brooch and the veil?"

Elsworth scowled, genuinely confused. "What brooch? What veil?"

"The veil was soaked with Mrs. Delmont's blood. The brooch was decorated with black enamel. It contained a photograph of a young woman in a white gown and veil. It also held a lock of blond hair."

Elsworth went very still. "Are you certain?"

"Yes. The veil and the brooch were both on Delmont's body when I found her. I'm certain Toller placed them there deliberately. But I don't know why or where she got them."

Elsworth's voice grew tense. "I have met with Durward Reed in his office at Wintersett House several times. There is a certain photograph on the wall next to the door."

"What are you saying?"

"I fear that the situation may be far worse than you know."

A short time later, Adam banged the knocker on the door at Number 22 Corley Lane. Mrs. Plummer answered. She looked confused when he asked to see Caroline.

"She left this afternoon, sir. Got a note from Mr. Reed at the Society for Psychical Investigations saying he wanted to talk about a contract for one of her sensation novels. I expected her home before now, but she hasn't returned. She must have been delayed."

He told himself to stay calm.

"Are either of her aunts home?"

"No, sir. They've gone off to dine with friends and play some cards. They won't be back until quite late. Is something wrong, Mr. Hardesty?"

"I'm sure all is well, Mrs. Plummer."

But he knew that he was lying to both of them.

CHAPTER
THIRTY-EIGHT

Caroline drifted back to full awareness a long time later.

She opened her eyes and stared at the night-shadowed ceiling while she mentally assessed her physical condition.

The nausea had disappeared, she noted.

She sat up cautiously and abruptly recalled that Reed had placed her on a bed. A fresh wave of fear choked her so that she could not breathe. What had happened to her while she had been sailing in that gray fog?

Frantic, she scrambled to her feet beside the large bed. An overwhelming sense of relief descended when she felt the familiar weight of her skirts and petticoats fall into place around her legs. She was still fully dressed. Her stockings were neatly gartered and her drawers were fastened, just as they had been when she had left home. That was reassuring.

She forced herself to give the matter close thought, summoning up memories from the eerie twilight world in which she had been drifting. She would know if Reed had assaulted her, she thought. She had not been rendered completely unconscious by the drugged tea, most likely because she had consumed only a few sips.

Indeed, she had a hazy recollection of the oddly decorous manner in which Reed had placed her on the bed. He had even taken time to arrange her skirts modestly around her ankles before he had left her in this room.

She turned on her heel, examining the shadowy chamber. She had to get out of here before Reed returned.

She crossed first to the door and tried it in the vain hope that it was not locked. But of course it was.

Faint, muffled sounds of activity came from somewhere far below. Music played in the distance. The reception for Julian Elsworth had begun.

She hurried to the window and saw at once that it had been nailed shut. Through the tiny panes of leaded glass she could see the vast expanse of the empty gardens at the back of the big house. Moonlight reflected off the light fog.

It was a long way down, she noticed, dismayed. The room in which she was trapped was evidently on the top floor of the old mansion.

Shouting for help would be useless. Given the thick walls and the commotion on the ground floor, no one would be able to hear her.

She turned slowly back around to examine the room in detail. There was enough light coming from the moonlit fog to reveal the bed, a wardrobe and a chair. There were no lamps or candles visible in the chamber.

She crossed to the wardrobe and opened it, expecting to find it empty. Shock reverberated through her when she caught sight of the unmistakable sheen of white satin.

She pulled the old-fashioned gown out of the wardrobe and held it up to get a better look at the bodice. Recognition jolted through her.

Sarah Reed's wedding dress.

The long, lacy veil was neatly folded on one of the wardrobe shelves. It was matted with dried blood. She found the black enameled mourning brooch in a drawer together with a pair of white gloves.

Sooner or later Reed would return. She had to come up with a plan. The word that Adam had used once or twice to describe the various twists and turns in his investigation came back to her. He had said something about it being the oldest and most reliable trick in the world.

Distraction.

CHAPTER
THIRTY-NINE

Adam looked at Elsworth, who sat on the opposite side of the carriage, dressed in formal evening attire.

"I require a distraction," Adam said. "You will provide it. I doubt that anyone is more skilled in such matters."

"I shall take that as a compliment." Elsworth adjusted his white bow tie. "But bear in mind that even the most accomplished practitioner can succeed only if the audience is a willing participant in the game. I cannot be responsible for what might happen if Reed walks out of my performance and discovers you searching his mansion."

"You attend to your role." Adam patted his jacket, feeling for the familiar shape of the knife sheath. "I shall take care of mine."

"Very well." Elsworth smoothed his gloves, collected his overcoat and got out of the hansom. He hesitated. "Believe it or not, I wish you luck, Hardesty. I must admit I have grown rather fond of Mrs. Fordyce's work. I would hate to miss the ending of *The Mysterious Gentleman*."

"In that case, make certain that you give the most compelling performance of your career this evening, Elsworth."

Elsworth inclined his head, turned and walked away toward the lights of the big mansion.

If Reed had Caroline, which now seemed the most likely possibility, he would have hidden her somewhere in that old mausoleum of a house, Adam thought.

There was another possibility, of course, but he would not allow himself to consider it. For the past hour he had been assuring himself that Reed would not kill Caroline, at least not before he had used her for whatever strange purpose he intended. With all of the excitement related to the reception tonight and Elsworth's latest demonstration of psychic powers, presumably Reed had not had time to carry out his plans.

Adam waited until he saw the medium go up the steps and disappear into the brightly lit front hall of the Society's headquarters. Then he got out of the cab, tipped the driver and moved into the shadows of a nearby alley.

From that position he took another look at Wintersett House. The contrast between the well-illuminated windows of the ground floor and the ominous darkness that oozed from the upper floors chilled his soul.

Caroline was up there somewhere. He could feel it.

He went swiftly down the dank alley.

When he emerged at the far end, the high stone barrier that enclosed the mansion's gardens loomed directly ahead in the foggy darkness.

360

It had been a few years since he had last climbed a garden wall. He was relieved to discover that he had not lost the knack.

Without a stiff crinoline to shape the gown into the wide bell that had been fashionable ten years earlier, the skirts of Sarah Reed's wedding dress hung limp and overlong around Caroline's feet.

But a crinoline cage would not only have been dangerously unwieldy, it would have taken up far too much space and given away her hiding place, she thought. She would never have been able to conceal herself inside the wardrobe.

She had left the doors of the large wardrobe slightly ajar. Through the crack, she had a clear view of the bedchamber door and a portion of the four-poster bed. When Reed returned she would have to time her escape with exquisite care if she was to have any chance at all.

It seemed to her that she had been trapped in the wardrobe for aeons but she knew that, in reality, she had been there for only an hour at most. She dared not move. There was simply no way to know when Reed would return.

Standing in the close confines of the wardrobe was taking a toll on both her nerves and her stamina. She had recovered from the worst effects of the drug, but her senses had not entirely returned to normal. It seemed to her that the distant sounds of the crowded reception going on below ebbed and flowed like an eerie, invisible tide. A sense of morbid unreality had settled upon her. She wondered if it was the result of wearing the dead woman's wedding dress.

The rasp of iron on iron jolted her out of her strange daze. Her pulse leaped and her skin went cold and prickly.

Stay calm, she thought. *Make sure you hold up your skirts so that you can run. You must not trip as you did three years ago. There will be no second chance.*

Through the slender crack in the wardrobe panels, she watched the bedchamber door open. Lamplight spilled across the floor.

"Have you awakened yet, my dear Mrs. Fordyce? The reception is at its height downstairs. Elsworth is the center of attention, so I was able to slip away to see how you are faring. That drug I was forced to use can be extremely unpleasant, I'm told."

Reed walked into the room, leaving the door ajar behind him. He carried a lamp in one hand. In the other he held a pistol.

"Still asleep, I see." He moved closer to the bed, holding the lamp aloft. "Or perhaps you are merely pretending, eh? Either way, it does not matter. This unfortunate business will soon be finished."

He had almost reached the bed. For some reason he paused. Caroline held her breath, watching as the lamplight illuminated the folds of her green gown. She had done her best to pad the bodice and skirts with the wadded-up sheet and some pillows. But she knew that the ruse would not hold up long under close scrutiny.

"What a pity that you allowed yourself to be seduced by Hardesty to the extent that you would be drawn into a great scandal," Reed said, moving forward again. "Have you no care at all for your reputation? You succumbed to your weak, feminine nature, just as Sarah did, I suppose. I cannot begin to describe to you my anguish and my rage when I discovered on our wedding night that Sarah was not pure. Her lover had died, you see. She never told me about him. But on our wedding day she wore a mourning brooch devoted to him on her beautiful white gown."

He reached the bed and halted.

"When I realized how she had deceived me, I went mad. I am certain that some dark spirit from the Other Side took possession of me, forcing me to wrap the scarf around her beautiful throat, forcing me to tighten it until she —"

He broke off suddenly and appeared to collect himself.

"Later I was grief-stricken, horrified by what I had done. I knew I had to get rid of the body so that no one would know what had happened. Shortly before dawn, I dressed her in her best walking gown and carried her across the street into the park. I took the brooch, and later I replaced her lover's photo and hair with her own. But by then it was too late. She had already begun to haunt me."

Caroline saw him reach toward the pillow she had propped over the space where her head would have been if she had still been inside the gown.

"But you are the one I have been waiting for, the one who can contact my Sarah on the Other Side. I know that now. When you reach through the veil, I will

363

explain to her that I was not myself on our wedding night, but rather a man possessed. She will forgive me and leave me in peace."

He pulled aside the pillow.

"What's this?" Reed stared at the empty dress. He appeared frozen in disbelief.

She would never get a better opportunity, Caroline thought. Clutching the white satin skirts, she pushed open the wardrobe door, jumped down and ran for the door.

Reed turned slowly, as though confused.

"Sarah? It cannot be. *Sarah*."

Caroline dashed through the door and found herself in a shadowy hallway. A weak wall sconce cast just enough light to allow her to see a row of closed doors on either side of the corridor.

Frantically she looked in both directions, searching for the main staircase. But all she saw was the endless series of doors.

Footsteps sounded behind her. Reed had snapped out of his momentary shock and disorientation. He was giving chase.

"Come back, Sarah."

She had to choose a direction.

Instinctively she turned to the right and fled down the hall toward the dimly illuminated window at the far end. If she did not come across the main staircase, perhaps she would at least find a flight of servants' stairs.

"Sarah, stop. You must let me explain. I was not the one who killed you. I was possessed."

364

Caroline glanced over her shoulder and saw Reed in the shadows behind her.

"Tell me what I must do to be free of your spirit," he raged. "You are driving me mad."

The gun thundered in the hallway. Caroline heard wood paneling splinter somewhere nearby. She had almost reached the end of the corridor and still saw no sign of a staircase. Maybe she ought to try one of the doors she was passing. If she could get inside and find a way to secure it, she could buy a little more time.

She would also be trapped again.

"Sarah."

Reed's gun roared. The glass window in front of her exploded.

A door slammed open in the middle of the hall behind Caroline.

"Reed," Adam shouted. "Halt or you're a dead man."

"Hardesty." Reed stopped, whirled and raised the gun, aiming at Adam, who was no more than a few steps away.

"No," Caroline screamed. At that distance, Reed could not possibly miss.

She saw Adam's arm move in a swift, tight motion, as though he were throwing an object.

Steel gleamed in the lantern light for an instant.

Reed jerked violently. The gun in his hand fired one more time but the shot must have gone wide of its mark because Adam did not falter.

Reed crumpled face down onto the floor and lay very still.

Adam kicked the gun aside and looked at Caroline.

"Are you hurt?" he asked in a voice that seemed to emanate from the coldest rings of hell.

"No." Clutching the bridal skirts, she drifted slowly back along the hallway. "No, I am all right, Adam. He did not touch me."

He held out one arm. She ran to him in a swirl of ghostly white satin. When she reached his side, he pinned her tightly to him.

He held her fiercely for a long moment. Then he released her to crouch beside Reed.

Caroline had been certain that Reed was dead. But he groaned when Adam turned him face up. For the first time, Caroline saw the hilt of the knife that was buried in Reed's chest.

Reed opened his eyes and stared up at Caroline.

"Sarah. You have haunted me all these years. Now, at last, I will join you on the Other Side."

Reed closed his eyes. He did not open them again.

CHAPTER
FORTY

The following afternoon they sat together in the library at Laxton Square. Adam poured brandy for Wilson, Richard, Elsworth and himself. Caroline, Julia, Emma and Milly contented themselves with tea.

He examined Caroline's face covertly while he replaced the decanter. Her eyes were shadowed, and the strain of last night's harrowing events etched her face but he could see that her strong, resilient spirit still burned with a bright flame. She was recovering nicely.

He was not nearly so certain of his own progress in that regard. He suspected that he would have nightmares of those last few moments in the corridor of Wintersett House for years to come.

If he had arrived only a few minutes later or if he had not eventually stumbled onto that flight of servants' stairs . . .

Don't think about it. You'll go mad.

He swallowed some of the potent brandy and sat down behind his desk.

"It was the fact that Toller and Delmont were each involved with both Reed and Elsworth that complicated the situation," he said to the others. "It seems that Elsworth here had established a relatively straightforward

367

business connection with a number of mediums, including Toller and Delmont."

"But that was all there was to the arrangements." Elsworth took a sip of brandy and lowered the glass. "I make it a practice never to become romantically involved with my business associates. In my experience such liaisons always lead to financial disaster."

Caroline looked at him. "Did you know that Mr. Reed had established a more intimate sort of connection with both Delmont and Toller?"

"I had my suspicions," Elsworth admitted. "It seemed to me that Reed was a little too generous in allowing Toller to advertise her rather amateurish services with those ridiculous demonstrations of the planchette at the Society's headquarters. But I also suspected that the arrangement was rapidly coming to an end. Reed was paying more and more attention to Delmont."

"Did he ever approach you to request a séance in hopes of contacting his dead wife?" Julia asked.

"No." Elsworth swirled the brandy in his glass. "I made it clear from the outset that I do not claim to be able to contact the dead. My powers are of another sort altogether."

Richard eyed him skeptically. "As a matter of sheer curiosity, how many other mediums in London do you use to carry out your investment schemes?"

Elsworth contrived to appear both innocent and affronted. "You cannot expect me to reveal a professional secret, sir."

368

Adam looked at him. "Elsworth has, however, agreed to repay those clients of Delmont's and Toller's who gave him money to invest. Isn't that right, sir?"

Elsworth sighed. "Indeed."

Wilson drummed his fingers on the leather arm of his chair. "If Toller and Delmont were inept mediums, why did Reed favor them?"

Elsworth wrinkled his elegant nose in disgust. "Reed was remarkably obtuse in such matters. The fool did not know a fraud when he saw one. After all, he married a medium, if you will recall. He may have done so to secure her fortune, but he genuinely believed that she had powers."

Adam hefted the large volume on his desk. "This is Reed's private journal. I found it in his study this morning when I met there with the police. It appears that Reed had little interest in male mediums. He had concluded that a female would be more likely to be able to contact the spirit of his dead wife."

Elsworth shrugged. "Most people in the field of psychical research are convinced the women are, generally speaking, more adept at communicating with the Other Side."

Adam turned a couple of pages, noting names and dates. "Reed appears to have systematically worked his way through any number of attractive female mediums in recent years. He makes no secret of the fact that he established an intimate liaison with each one because he believed that such a connection enhanced the medium's powers."

Caroline shuddered. "It is a common assumption in certain quarters."

Adam turned another page. "After a suitable period of seduction and testing, as it were, he gave his favored medium the final test in Sarah's old bedchamber. He was convinced that his dead wife haunted that room. If the medium failed the last test, he moved on to another candidate."

"He murdered Sarah in that bedchamber on their wedding night," Caroline whispered.

Adam nodded. "According to the journal, he dressed the body and carried it into the park to be found the following day. None of the servants reported her missing the next morning because they all believed that, like any proper bride, she was so strongly affected by the traumatic events of her wedding night, she had slept late to recover. Later it was assumed that she had left the house unnoticed to take a walk."

Julia tilted her head slightly to one side. "Reed was certainly not the most handsome or charming of men. I wonder why Toller and Delmont and the other mediums he employed were so eager to accept his advances?"

"There were certain decided advantages for any medium who formed a relationship with Durward Reed," Elsworth said, very matter-of-fact. "While each was in favor, she reaped the benefits of the Society's sponsorship, which, in turn, enhanced her own reputation and resulting income."

"Yes, of course," Milly murmured. "One can understand the motivation, I suppose."

"It is a very competitive business," Elsworth allowed. "Especially at the lower end."

"But Irene Toller made the fatal mistake of falling in love with Reed," Caroline said quietly. "When she discovered that he was preparing to leave her and move on to Elizabeth Delmont, she became distraught and enraged."

"I expect the situation was especially painful to her because she had long viewed Delmont as a serious professional rival," Emma observed. "Toller saw herself as a woman scorned."

"She knew Wintersett House well, especially Sarah Reed's bedchamber, having conducted her own final test séance there for Reed," Adam continued. "She must have made her way upstairs one day without Reed's knowledge and stolen the brooch and the wedding veil from the wardrobe."

Caroline nodded. "She took them with her the night she murdered Elizabeth Delmont and left them at the scene. They obviously had significance to her because they had belonged to the dead woman with whom Reed was obsessed."

"What about the pocket watch that was also found with Delmont's body?" Julia asked. "The one that was reported in the papers?"

"It belonged to Elizabeth Delmont," Adam said. "It had been a gift to her from Reed. Irene Toller must have known that and deliberately smashed it in her rage. I was the first one to arrive at Delmont's house that night after the killer had left. When I found her, the veil, brooch and watch were all still there."

"Reed was the second one to arrive," Wilson said. "He was no doubt horrified to find his dead wife's brooch and veil at the scene. He must have guessed immediately who had stolen them and murdered Delmont. He took the brooch and veil but he left the watch. It meant nothing to him."

"I was the last to arrive," Elsworth continued. "I called after returning from a long evening on the town. It was almost dawn."

Milly looked curious. "Why on earth did you go to her house at such a late hour?"

"I had concluded that Delmont, having learned a few tricks from me, was preparing to set up her own financial scheme without my assistance. I wanted to make her think twice about such a move. My intention was to threaten to expose her if she tried to go into business on her own. When I got there, the door was open. I went inside and found the body."

"And Maud's diary," Adam added.

Elsworth moved one hand in a what-do-you-expect? fashion. "I am not one to overlook an opportunity. But as I told you, when I read it I decided it was not the sort of project I wanted to pursue. Much too reckless."

"By then it was too late, though, wasn't it?" Milly said cheerfully. "You knew that Adam was already on your tail."

Elsworth grimaced. "When I saw him together with Mrs. Fordyce after Irene Toller's demonstration, I knew I confronted a disastrous situation. I did my best to redirect everyone's attention and generally muddy the waters by giving the psychical consultation to the police. I was certain that the papers would make a great sensation of it. When I saw you in the audience that day, Mrs. Fordyce, I tried to warn you that there was danger afoot. I thought that might distract you and Hardesty both. When all failed to have an effect, I resorted to stronger tactics."

"You paid two villains to attack Adam," Caroline said with an accusing look.

"Yes, well, what can I say, madam? I was desperate."

"Reed was even more desperate," Adam said. "According to his journal, he had great hopes that Elizabeth Delmont would prove to be the medium who could make contact with his dead wife's spirit. But before he could hold his final test séance with her in Sarah's bedchamber, Toller murdered her. Then Toller sent him a message ordering him to come see her. He suspected that she intended to blackmail him by threatening to take the story of his bedchamber séances to the press."

"So he killed her," Julia concluded. "And made the murder scene appear just as it had been described in the newspapers, knowing that the press would seize on the similarities."

Adam nodded. "After Delmont was killed, Reed concluded that Caroline's recent association with Wintersett House was no mere coincidence. He believed that psychical forces had directed her to him so that he could use her to reach Sarah. Yesterday he lured Caroline into his trap."

Emma frowned. "I don't understand. Did he really expect to get away with kidnapping Caroline and using her in some dreadful séance? He must have known that you would investigate her disappearance, Adam."

"When he was finished with Caroline, he intended to kill her in a manner similar to the other two murders," Wilson said, his mouth tightening with quiet anger. "He planned to leave her body and another broken pocket watch in her own house with more evidence pointing to Adam."

Julia shuddered. "The press would certainly have seized upon a story that involved a sensation novelist being murdered by her lover."

Milly was aghast. "He actually expected such a scheme to work?"

Elsworth shook his head. "You do not understand how it is with those who are willing to suspend all logic and common sense in their desire to believe in the possibility of communicating with the Other Side. Trust me when I tell you that Reed was one of the most gullible people I have ever met."

Caroline looked at him. "Were you the one who sent the messages to Adam and me summoning us to Toller's house on the morning after she was murdered?"

"No." Ellsworth raised both hands, palms out. "I plead innocent to that charge."

"Reed sent them." Adam closed the journal. "He also sent an anonymous message to the police and several members of the press. He wanted to create a sensation."

"He no doubt hoped that you would be arrested," Wilson said. "At the very least, you would be placed under a heavy cloud of suspicion and scandal. His primary goal was to drive a wedge between you and Caroline. He assumed she would be shocked and horrified when she discovered that you were linked to a murder. He thought she would turn her back on you to protect her own reputation."

Adam smiled slowly and looked at Caroline. "Reed obviously had no psychical talent of his own. He failed to foresee that you would supply me with an alibi even though it meant that you would become more deeply entangled in a great scandal."

Laughter lit her eyes for the first time since her ordeal at Wintersett House. "He obviously knew nothing about sensation novelists. We thrive on that sort of thing."

CHAPTER
FORTY-ONE

One month later . . .

"I say." Wilson's loud exclamation reverberated off the walls of the breakfast room. He slapped the copy of the *Flying Intelligencer* down onto the table. "This is indeed a very surprising turn of events."

Adam scooped jam out of a pot. "It is too early in the day to be shouting. What is it that has alarmed you? Bad financial news?"

"Hang the financial news. This is a far more earthshaking matter." Wilson stabbed at the newspaper with a forefinger. "This is the last chapter of *The Mysterious Gentleman*. You will not credit it, but Edmund Drake has emerged as the hero."

Adam felt something inside him go very still. Hope flared. He lowered the knife that he had been about to use to spread the jam on a slice of toast.

"I thought Drake was the villain of the piece," he said carefully.

"So did I and everyone else who is following the story, I'll wager." Wilson reached for the coffee. "But there you have it. I just finished the last chapter in which Drake rescues Miss Lydia and unmasks that priggish Jonathan St. Claire."

"The character everyone assumed was the hero?"

"Yes. Never did like him. Too well-mannered and so excruciatingly proper. Quite a boring chap, really. I should have realized that Caroline would never allow him to marry Miss Lydia. Drake was the right man all along."

"Edmund Drake marries Miss Lydia?"

"Yes, indeed." Wilson grunted. "All very exciting stuff. Can't wait to hear what Julia has to say about it. I'm sure that all over London this morning readers are astonished and amazed. Once again the clever Mrs. Fordyce has thrilled us with a final, unexpected startling incident. The woman is brilliant, I tell you."

Adam whipped his napkin off his lap and tossed it onto the table. "You must excuse me, sir."

He got to his feet and headed toward the door.

"What's this? Where the deuce are you going, Adam? You haven't finished your breakfast."

"My apologies, sir, but I must be off immediately. There is a matter of vital importance that cannot wait any longer."

Wilson blinked owlishly and then the bewilderment cleared from his expression. Satisfaction replaced it.

He picked up the newspaper again. "Give my regards to Caroline."

She was in her study, enjoying the warm sunlight that poured through the window and idly making some notes for her next story, when Adam walked into the room. She looked up, anticipation sleeting through her. Then she got a closer look at his expression. The smoldering heat in his eyes made her catch her breath.

"Adam? Is something wrong? You look a bit feverish."

He came toward her with long, purposeful strides.

"You made Edmund Drake the hero of your story," he said.

"Well, yes, I did. What of it?"

He halted in front of her desk, flattened his powerful hands on the surface and leaned forward. "Why did you do that?"

"I thought it made a rather exciting twist," she said cautiously. "I must say, I'm surprised you know how *The Mysterious Gentleman* ended. I thought you stopped after reading that one chapter."

"Wilson told me about your last startling incident."

"I see. May I ask why the matter is of such concern to you? Given that you do not read that sort of novel, I mean?"

He straightened and moved around the desk before she realized his intent. Leaning down, he seized her shoulders, hauled her out of the chair and set her on her feet.

"Because it gives me hope that you might love me as much as I love you," he said.

Wonder and joy flashed through her. "You love me?"

"Since the first moment I saw you here in this very room."

"Oh, Adam, I do love you with all my heart." She flung her arms around his neck.

378

"Now will you put me out of my misery and marry me?"

"Yes, of course. I have been hesitating only because I was afraid that it was your rules that obliged you to make the offer. I am well aware that your noble nature imposes a heavy sense of responsibility on you."

"Caroline," he said very evenly and with great force. "I love you more than words can say and I will love you for the rest of my life and beyond. Knowing that I have your love makes me the happiest man on earth. But I must tell you that there is nothing noble about my desire for you. I want you desperately. I would lie, cheat, steal or worse to get you."

She laughed. "What is the matter, sir? Does it unnerve you to know that you are fashioned of heroic material?"

"Heroes are for novels." He stroked her lower lip with the edge of his thumb. "I am a man. All I care about is that you love me the way a woman loves a man."

"For the rest of my life and beyond," she vowed.

He kissed her there in the golden sunlight, holding her so close and so tight that she forgot about all else.

It was the sound of familiar voices that brought her back to reality.

"Good day to you, Mr. Hardesty," Emma said from the doorway. "It is rather early for this sort of thing, is it not?"

Adam raised his head. "Good day to you, madam. In answer to your question, no, it is not too early for this sort of thing. As it happens, I intend to marry Caroline and make it a regular practice to begin every day in a similar manner."

"How romantic." Milly hurried into the room with a tray and set it on a table. She picked up the pot and looked around expectantly. "Tea, anyone?"

"I think we could all use a cup," Caroline said from the circle of Adam's arms. "Adam was just attempting to convince me that he is not the heroic sort."

"Nonsense." Milly sat down and poured tea into four cups. "It is obvious that he is every inch the hero."

"That was certainly my impression," Emma said, taking a chair.

Adam assumed a deeply pained expression. "If we could change the subject, I would be extremely grateful."

"As you wish," Caroline said. "Actually, there was another topic that is of considerable interest to me. In fact, I was just making some notes for the first chapter of my new novel."

"The one that involves psychical research?" Emma asked.

"Yes." Caroline stepped back and moved to her desk. "I believe Adam will once again be my inspiration."

Adam groaned. "Please, my dear —"

"Calm yourself, sir. It is not your heroic qualities that I intend to make use of this time."

He looked wary. "My financial skills, perhaps?"

She sat down, picked up her pen and tapped the tip lightly against the blotter. "No. I was thinking of your psychical talents."

He straightened abruptly. "My *what?*"

"I believe they are obvious."

"Obvious to whom? What are you talking about?"

"Only consider the facts, sir." She smiled reassuringly, pleased with her own logic. "At certain critical junctures in this affair, you acted on your intuition in ways that could very well be considered psychical."

"Of all the nonsensical —"

Emma raised a finger. "I believe Caroline has a point, sir."

"Indeed," Milly agreed, nodding sagely.

"I defy you to name one example of my psychical abilities," he growled.

"There was the manner in which you concluded that I was involved in this affair right at the start," Caroline said. "Had you not reached that conclusion and come to see me the morning after Elizabeth Delmont's murder, there is no telling what might have happened to me. As we now know, Reed had already begun to view me as a possible successor to Delmont."

"Hold on, I had a perfectly logical reason for coming here that day," Adam said. "Your name was on Delmont's list of sitters."

"And then there is the matter of that evening we spent together in that room in Stone Street," she continued. "Had you not chosen that night to seduce me —"

"Damnation, Caroline."

He gave Emma and Milly quick, appalled looks. They smiled back. Fiery heat burned on his high cheekbones.

"There are a few other things that strike me as excellent examples of your talents, sir, but the one that stands out the most is something you said the night you came here after your encounter with the ruffians Elsworth sent to attack you."

He scowled. "I don't recall saying anything that night that was of a psychical nature."

"You read some lines that I had just written," she said softly. "It was the scene in which Edmund Drake was about to ravish Miss Lydia. I told you that, in his great rage, Drake had lost control of his passions. You said that only a brute or a madman would use such an excuse to assault a woman."

"What of it?"

"I had written myself into a corner with that scene and I knew it. After you left, I rewrote it. I could not change it entirely because the previous chapter had already gone off to Mr. Spraggett." She paused for emphasis. "So I was obliged to come up with another reason for Drake's behavior."

Adam looked at her, uncomprehending.

"The poison," Emma exclaimed.

"Yes, of course." Milly was delighted. "I should have thought of that myself."

"Thought of what?" Adam demanded.

She chuckled. "Because of your editorial comments, Mr. Hardesty, Caroline was obliged to come up with another explanation for Drake's unchivalrous actions. Namely, poisoned cakes."

"What in blazes does that have to do with any of this?" he asked blankly.

"That day when I found myself drinking the tea Reed had prepared for me, I sensed that something was wrong," Caroline said quietly. "Because of that scene, it occurred to me that Reed had poisoned me. I stopped after only a couple of sips. That was enough to make me feel very odd for some time but at least I did not succumb entirely to the drug. I was able to run for my life when the opportunity arose."

"Thus providing you, Mr. Hardesty, with the chance to kill Reed," Emma concluded. "Who knows how it all would have ended if he had been able to take Caroline hostage?"

He folded his arms. "And because of that small coincidence, you decided that I might have some psychical abilities?"

"Psychical research is still in its earliest stages," Caroline reminded him very seriously. "We know so little yet. Who is to say what will be discovered in the field?"

"That is the most illogical, most fantastical piece of reasoning I have ever heard in my life." He smiled his slow, rare, startling smile. "But in light of the fact that I intend to marry an author of sensation novels, I suppose I had better become accustomed to that sort of thing."

She was aware of the familiar thrilling frissons of certainty sparkling through all her senses.

"Yes, indeed," she said. "But never fear, I am a great believer in happy endings."

Epilogue

Epilogue

Noted Author Weds Mr. Hardesty

By
Gilbert Otford
Correspondent
The Flying Intelligencer

The well-known author Caroline Fordyce and Mr. Adam Hardesty were recently wed in a fashionable ceremony that was attended by many of the most prominent members of Society.

Faithful readers will recall that the newlyweds were recently involved in a great sensation involving a number of violent deaths that some attributed to supernatural causes. Indeed, for a time it appeared that the dark clouds of scandal and murder would doom forever the prospect of future happiness for the two.

This correspondent is pleased to report, however, that on the day of the wedding the sun shone brightly, as if to underscore the fact that the ominous threats of the past had been overcome and successfully banished.

All who were present agreed that the radiant bride and the proud, distinguished groom were enveloped in an unmistakable aura of sincere, abiding love. It was clear that a lifetime of marital bliss awaits the couple.

"Astonishing. Talk about your startling incidents." Adam tossed the copy of the *Flying Intelligencer* onto the nightstand, climbed into the big, shadowed bed and gathered a laughing Caroline into his arms. "For once the newspapers got it right."